boYs

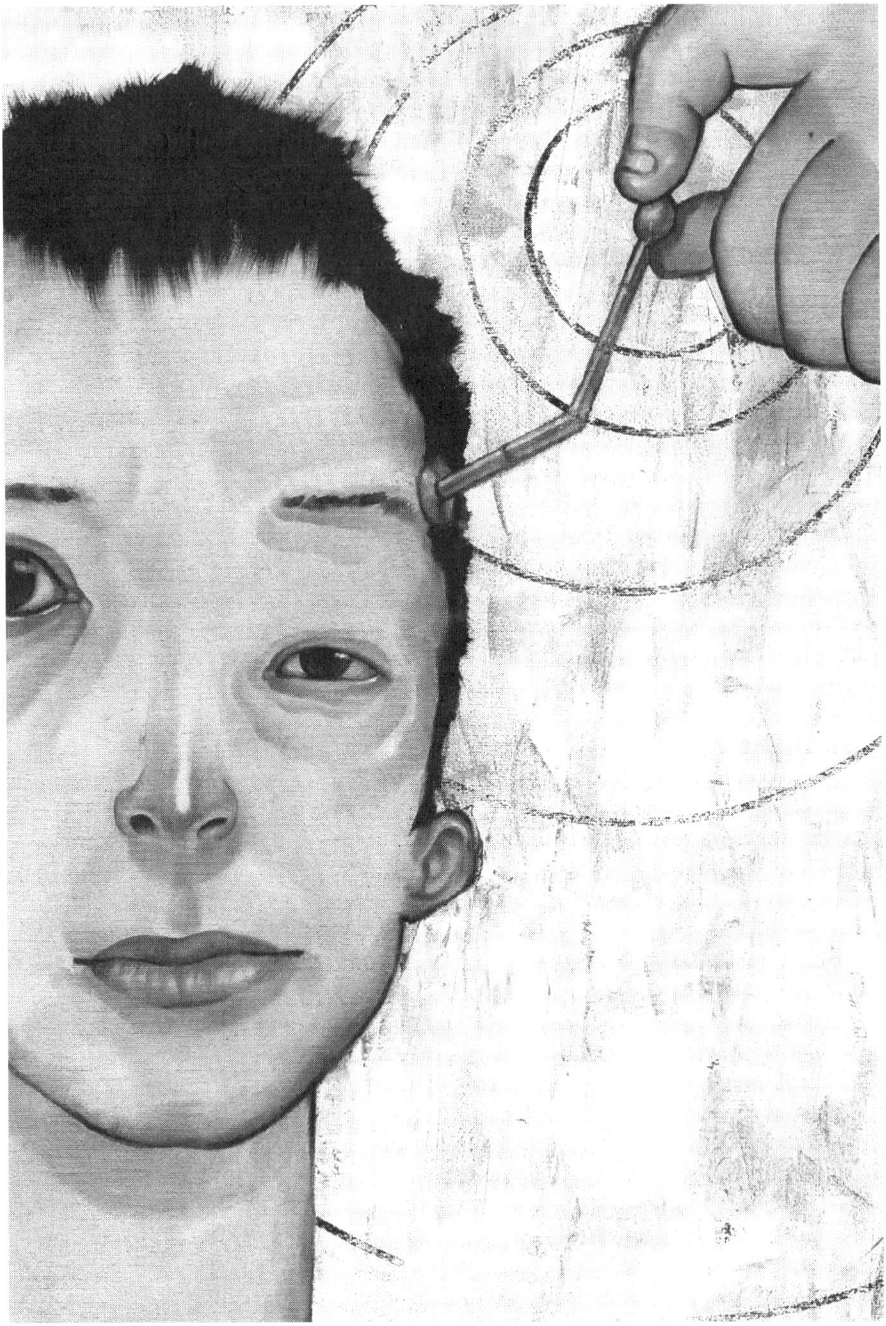

bOYs

(stories)

Kathleen Winter

BIBLIOASIS

Copyright © 2007 Kathleen Winter

All rights reserved. No part of this publication may be reproduced or transmitted in any form or by any means, electronic or mechanical, including photocopying, recording, or any information storage and retrieval system, without permission in writing from the publisher.

FIRST EDITION

Library and Archives Canada Cataloguing in Publication

Winter, Kathleen
    Boys / Kathleen Winter.

ISBN 978-1-897231-35-7

    I. Title.
PS8595.I618B69 2007   C813'.54   C2007-904544-8

Cover: Detail from "Radiohead" by Martin Wittfooth

Canada Council for the Arts   Conseil des Arts du Canada

ONTARIO ARTS COUNCIL
CONSEIL DES ARTS DE L'ONTARIO

We gratefully acknowledge the support of the Canada Council for the Arts and the Ontario Arts Council for our publishing program.

PRINTED AND BOUND IN CANADA

Dedication:
Annie and Walter, Kitty and Tom

STORIES

You Can Keep One Thing / 9
Jolly Trolley / 23
My Heart Used to Dance / 27
Where the Nightingales are Singing / 41
French Doors / 55
The Tree / 63
The Incinerator Times / 69
boYs / 77
Town with Moses / 83
Burt's Shawarma / 89
A True Conductor / 95
Eating the Bones / 101
Jerome Hepditch / 107
Rock Talking to Bone about Light / 113
Cremona Has a Secret / 119
Black Petunia / 127
Nothing but Bethlehem / 131
Room Full of Blood / 137
Violin Woods / 143
Old Games / 149
The History of Zero / 157
Binocular / 169
Malcolm in Blue / 177
Everything in the Bag Changed / 183

You Can Keep One Thing

*H*ere *comes the bride bride bride briide.*" I hate that bird. He never finishes the bride song. He promises you the song but it doesn't happen, just like what happened to me with the Lillys.

I'm busting sap bubbles. You use your thumbnail. I like the smell but the sap gets in your clothes. There's a dried glob on my uniform. Sister Annunciata doesn't care 'cause mine's not real Newfoundland tartan. Mam says it's almost the same, and real Newfoundland tartan is highway robbery. It's Mom here, not Mam. Desks are destes. Ghosts are ghostes. Chimneys are chimleys. I put my hand up and said, "Can I go to the toilet, please," and they gave me talking lessons at recess.

"You have to call it the bathroom."

I told Dad and he said, "That's silly, there's no bath in it." He had just got the kaleidoscope back that he entered in the Light and Colour craft show. It lay beside his plate. He made it out of birch and mirrors and shiny twists of Quality Street toffee papers. He was looking at the letter the judges had wrapped it in. "Your entry is whimsical," it said, "but we are returning it as it doesn't really fit our theme."

"Those aren't fish fingers either," I told him. "You have to call those fish sticks."

"I'll call them whatever I want," he said. Dad eats with his mouth open and I can see silver slaver stretch between his teeth. He tilts his plate and scrapes the last peas into his mouth with his knife.

"Fish don't have fingers," I said.

"Do you want this?" he asked me, and he gave me his kaleidoscope.

The kids at school only gave me talking lessons twice then got sick of me, specially when I got Bev Ducey's lice. I'd give anything to sit behind Eugenia Lilly, but that will never happen. Bev Ducey and I both keep touching our necks to feel our bristles. When she looks at the board I can see the tape on her glasses. I thought Dad would have to get her new ones.

I can see lots of chimleys from this tree. Our house is stuck to the Carrolls' and the Flemings' and our row is all green. The next row is yellow and the next one's blue. Grandma wrote, "*I'd love to live there with all them different coloured houses,*" after Dad sent her photos. "*Your Mam's the one who won't let me come. Don't tell.*" Grandma scrawls big and the paper is blue airmail tissue. "*Mrs. Melia had the twins I told her about in the tea leaves.*"

IN HER PANTRY IN HEBBURN, Grandma had candle stubs shaped like people. One was Mrs. Melia and one was Grandma's step-sister who wouldn't give Grandma her share of the money their father left, and I don't know who the others were. Grandma stuck eight pins in Mrs. Melia because she was trying to get the council to throw Grandma and Grandad out of their flat so her cousin could move in. The step-sister had so many pins I couldn't count them. The candles were white but their heads had turned black when Grandma melted them into people. After her dinner Grandma read her own tea leaves.

"Two pieces of money are coming from far away." She rattled through her chronic bronchitis. She wore scarlet lipstick and a black wig, and ate lemon bon bons, for her diabetes, out of a paper bag, and she let me have as many as I wanted. "Someone is going to get a ring." She took out the cards and read those. "Beware a dark man. That must be the rent man. If he comes we won't open the door."

Mam said, "I do not believe in divination." She had sent us to Grandma's before she went to hospital to have Daniel. Mam did not like Grandma's secrets, or how, when Percy and I stayed there, and even when Grandma came to look after us at our house, there were accidents. The kettle scalded him. I woke in pools of vomit after her dinners.

"Please don't let Maggy and Percy sit on your knee like that, they'll fall and split their heads open," Mam said on her way out the door to be baptized in Newcastle at the church none of us knew anything about. "And please don't let Cassius in. I don't want mud and dog smell all over the carpet."

"But it's raining," Grandma stuck her head out the window and shouted after my mother, "and I can hear that poor dog crying from in here." When she brought her head back in she said, "Your mother didn't answer me. She pretended she never heard."

"Mam doesn't answer anybody who shouts out of a window."

"Don't tell your mam we let Cassius in." Mud was everywhere. "Don't tell her you like my dinners better than hers."

"Especially the gravy," I said.

"Don't tell her that. Don't tell her I made Mrs. Melia fall down the stairs by sticking pins in the Mrs. Melia doll, and that she broke both her ankles. And don't tell her your father always liked any girl who happened to have ginger hair, not just her." Percy and I sat on her knee again and while my mother was getting baptized we fell and cracked our heads on the hearth.

WHILE WE WAITED at her house for Daniel to be born, Grandad and Percy slept in the bedroom and Grandma and I shared the couch covered in her crocheted blankets, and we sucked the powder off her bon bons.

"Tell me about before you were married."

"The world was even more full of ships than it is now, and sailors came from all over the place on colliers that tied up in Bill Quay waiting for coal."

"Tell me who you fell in love with."

"I fell in love with a Danish one called Dirk. He was lovely."

"What was lovely about him?"

"He had curly hair and he had a real ruby in his pocket that hadn't been cut. It was like a knob of Turkish delight, and he could dance, and he sneaked me on the boat and gave me a very crisp bacon sandwich from his own breakfast and promised me he would come back."

"Where is Dirk now and why did you marry Grandad and not him?"

She and Grandad fought about what they had just eaten and what they were about to eat, and what she had done with his cigarettes, and why she couldn't remember she had put her glasses on her head where she always put them. They fought about things that happened years ago, such as why he had to go and get his teeth out when there was nothing wrong with them just because she got hers done. Part of the reason they both yelled all the time was that she had to shout for him to hear anything. By the time he heard it she was shouting so loud anyone would think she was about to murder him, and he shouted right back, then he put his hanky over his whole head. I didn't mind the shouting. It wasn't like when it's your own parents and you hear every snarl and whimper and you think the world is going to end.

If the minstrels weren't on television Grandad kept lying in his chair with his hanky covering his head like a dead man.

"Your grandad used to be a limelight lad," Grandma said. "He used to stop the buses with his nose."

"Maybe you and Dirk wouldn't have shouted."

"When you get married," she said, " make sure he loves you a little bit more than you love him. And don't tweeze your eyebrows. And don't cut your hair short, it's your crowning glory."

"Tell about the clogs you wore in the brickyard. Tell about the horrible dinners your stepmother gave you, and the lovely ones she gave her real daughters."

WHEN I GOT THE LICE Mam tried a small tooth comb but she could only drag it through my hair an inch at a time, crying and saying, "The filth, the filth." Mam says Mrs. Melia's ankles have nothing to do with Grandma's dolls.

I can't see the Lillys' house from here. I never knew it was there until the day I saw Eugenia slide down the stones making dust. There's dust here wherever there's no bog or woods. The only other place there isn't dust is the riverbank, and that's cracked mud. Before I met Eugenia I used to go there and make bricks like Grandma, and bake mud cakes on boulders with hard berries off those bushes that creep for raisins, and crackerberries for cherries. Crackerberries are all over the place. They don't have a taste but when you eat them they crack loud. They're orange and come in fours, fours, fours. Even their flowers have four petals.

The ground under this tree is covered in crackerberries. The ground says, "Four, four, four," wherever I go. "Four, four, four," pointy and uncomfortable. Everything here is like that, a big unfriendly surprise. In winter it gets so cold Mam and Dad bought me a coat with fluff on it like bright green dog fur and I was still cold. Snow comes up to our upstairs windows. I saw three snowflakes the other day and I'll be glad when more come even though there's too much, 'cause then we won't have to pick berries. Dad makes us go to the bog. The car bumps and dust crunches in our teeth then we get out and have to pick until we fill a five gallon bucket each.

Dad says, "That's what everyone does here," but I never see anyone except us. Those are big buckets. The berries roll around with a hollow noise for a long time before the bottom gets filled. The bog sucks my sneakers and sparkles around my ankles. The last thing Grandma said was, "Don't go in any bright green grass in Canada 'cause you'll sink." I have big fly bites all over me. Behind my ears is one big pink itchy bleeding fly bite lump. We eat Klik sandwiches with slimy lettuce in them. I don't pull the lettuce out and throw it away with the wet part of the bread like I do at school, 'cause Mam'll see.

One kind of plant puts a hospital smell all over the bog. The leaves have orange fur underneath. I want to shout to Mam and Dad, "You're not supposed to let me sink!"

You Can Keep One Thing

IN BILL QUAY I ROLLERSKATED down the cobblestones until my legs turned into cushions. In the waste ground between the pub and the cranes I nipped holes in the stems of the pinkest-edged daisies and I wound the daisy chains around my shoulders until I heard the ice cream man's bell. He poured raspberry sauce on my cone and when he was gone the rag man pulled his cart down our lane, shouting, "Any rags or bones," and if me or Rhona brought him rags he gave us a balloon each. Dad said when he was little he got goldfish from the rag man, and a day-old chick.

"I raised it to henhood," he told me. "We got eggs for two years and then we ate the hen." I went to Sharpe's butcher with Mam at eleven o'clock every morning. The shop smelled of sawdust and suet and new lamb, and Mam bought a quarter of a pound of mince. Dad wants roast potatoes and other food that has to be watched, and that my mother never had to make before in her life. Mam doesn't like cooking. She would rather eat at Nana's, or at the big house of her two aunts who had the basket of poodles and the nursery with the rocking horse in it, where the curtains are lace and you can sit in the window sills. It was a relief for Mam on Saturdays when we went to Newcastle and stopped at dinner time in a pork shop to buy pork pies and ate them on the street. She laughed then, dropping crumbs on the pavement, crinkling the wrappers, her toes peeping out of her shiny black high heels. It was a relief for her on Sundays as well when Dad took me down the tracks to the allotment a quarter of a mile away. A lot of things, like meat and miles, were measured by quarters, instead of by the hundreds like they are here. There is no relief for Mam here, and she bangs the walls with her Hoover.

After dinner Jacqueline knocked on our courtyard door and we sailed our boats in the gutter, or Rhona came and we climbed the park pipes and watched the man who wipes the bottom of his white dog, and before we got in trouble we used to run to the streets on the other side of the park and into Rhona's aunt's shop and eat mint chews. Mam said it was stealing, but I don't think it's stealing when it's your aunt's shop. It might not be polite but it isn't stealing. I don't think Rhona should have to pay for chews like she would in an ordinary shop, but I did not answer my mother back.

Percy and I did not stay with Mam's parents overnight. When we visited them nobody cooked. Her father, Maurice, walked up Roman Road in his cravat and bowler hat and bought fish and chips, and when we had eaten those my nana brought out a bakery box tied with string, full of cream cakes. The box was white with perfect corners and there was one kind of cake that made me wonder why any other sort needed to exist. Cream with chocolate around it and no cake part at all. There were two in the box and I always got one. The romance of cream cakes in the house in a white box will not leave me. I will never understand why anyone would make cakes when there are French bakeries.

DAD BLEW TINY BUBBLES that floated all over our house, and told me about when he was in school. He blew the bubbles only when Mam was not in the room. If she caught him she said, "You're doing it now and you don't even know you're doing it."

I tried and I tried and I couldn't do it.

"How do you do it Dad?"

"You find the bubbles somewhere behind your teeth. Jim Millan taught me it when I was twelve and I've done it ever since. In the air force. In the shipyard. In the van. In this chair. Until your mother forbade it. Jim Millan had our whole class doing it, but he was nothing compared to Archie Carmichael."

"What did Archie Carmichael do?"

"Archie Carmichael used to put a piece of blotting paper up his nose and snort back on it until it came out of his mouth. Nobody else could do that. We used to mark Xs on it to make sure it was the same piece. It took him a good half hour, always in history class, the most boring class of them all."

Dad took me to see if Tommy Thurgood had any crabs – we went through our back fence over the tracks and down the riverbank, and Dad showed me how to tell the difference between a dandelion and a coltsfoot.

"The coltsfoot has a leaf, see here, shaped like a horseshoe. A dandelion doesn't have that."

I pictured colts, and their feet, and Tommy Thurgood gave us a box of crabs and we sat by the coal fire and sucked the meat out of their sweet legs and my father decided to tell me the difference between something that is absurd and something that is not.

"It's absurd," he said, "that on the news tonight they said a hundred people dying in that train crash was a bigger tragedy than the one person who died when he was crushed by a crane. No matter how many people die, the amount of tragedy is the same. Now I'll sing an absurd song."

I sat on his knee and he sang "There's a Hole in my Bucket," then he read me *Uncle Tom's Cabin*, which was not a very good book to read me when I wasn't even eight, but Dad's name is Tom like his dad's, and he wanted a cabin, and he still wants one, and he will build one soon here in the woods of

Newfoundland, and my brothers and I will help him skin every strip of bark from the spruce logs with two-handled blades until only the blond wood shows, wet with sap. He read *Uncle Tom's Cabin* until I got so tired he had to carry me up the stairs. I watched the ships' lights fizz on the Tyne from my bed, and I loved how they rippled and blurred, and how there were millions. In the morning we went down to the river again and Tommy Thurgood gave us a few racks of honeycomb, and we ate those in front of the fire. Dad's friends were always giving us honey and rabbits and licorice root and Welsh onions.

"They are," Dad told me, "the only truly perennial onion in existence, and no one except Tommy Thurgood knows where to get them."

"What's a limelight lad, Dad?"

"Your grandad was one of those when he was young."

"I know but what is it?"

"He ran the lights in the music hall in Jarrow. He could do all sorts of things when he was young you know."

"He let me and Percy race him down Mayfair Court in his wheel chair."

"He was a boxer in the Depression. That's how his nose got squashed. When he was half-cut he could tap dance and swing a cane and recite *Christmas Eve in the Workhouse* and a lot of other very long poems. And his father, my grandfather, he was a real show-off. He used to take his belt off, hook it on a crane hook, bite it and be lifted fifty feet in the air onto the deck of whatever ship he was working on."

DAD WAS A VEGETABLE MAN. The pigeon fanciers were down at the bottom allotments, where his best pal Les Lakey had pigeons and hens and rabbits. Dad's only animal, before we moved to our second house and we got Cassius and our own rabbits, was his greenhouse toad, which I never saw.

"That," said my father, "is an ingenious toad. No one will ever see it."

"What does it drink?"

"It manages."

I searched for the toad while Dad topped up the soil around his leeks. I imagined it with beautiful spots, flatter than other toads, unique and alone.

My mother hardly ever came to the allotment. "Your father announced," she told me, "on the third day we were married, that he was going out to apply for that allotment. He never had one before. He never mentioned wanting one. I think it was so he wouldn't have to be in the house with me on Sundays."

I ate blackberries behind the allotment fence while Dad checked his cold frames and measured his leeks with a ruler he designed that measures the bulb underground. He was getting second place in the leek shows and he wanted to move up to first, and he and Les Lakey took turns watching that nobody sneaked into the allotment at night and overwatered his specimens so they would burst. We went to Les's allotment and measured the length of his giant white Californian rabbits, then we went to find out how the pigeon races were going, and there was a lot of intrigue around that, with baskets and flags and rushing on trains to Morpeth and Gateshead, and the allotments were a mysterious place. Anything was mysterious where Dad was the creative head. There was always something out of the ordinary with him, like the windy time we took Cassius to the vet and I realized at the bus stop that if I didn't hold my skirt down three scarved women and a man in a black hat would see my bottom as somehow my underpants had been left on the ironing board, or the time Brownies had a Hallowe'en costume contest and Dad made me a helmet, trident and shield that transformed me into Britannia.

"Who's that?" I asked him, not really caring as everything about her shone and was glorious.

"She's the personification of Britain," he said. "She's on the money."

I knew nobody else at Brownies would be Britannia, and as we danced around the toadstool and ducked for apples I surveyed the scene and saw my costume was three hundred times better than anyone else's. When the time came to announce the winner I knew it would be me but it wasn't. The winner was a witch with a long black dress and black pointy hat. This was the first time I wondered if the world had whole rooms of people in it who did not know anything.

"Who are you?" Brownie parents and even leaders asked me between egg-and-tomato sandwiches.

"I'm Britannia."

"Who?"

"I am the personification of Britain."

"What's that?"

"She's on the money."

"Oh."

Dad bought an old van and started taking us all over the place in it.

"They call it Volkswagen," he told me, "because they wanted ordinary people to be able to travel. Volks is German for folks, and it means ordinary people who might not otherwise have enough money to see the world."

You Can Keep One Thing

We drove to Land's End. I lay in my hammock and smelled the lovely gas stove. It hissed and the cups clinked and my parents murmured and did not fight. Sausages sizzled and I smelled them and my mouth watered. I was supposed to be asleep. My father handed me a sausage on a fork and I will never forget that sausage.

THE DAY EUGENIA LILLY brought me home, her mom and dad and eight brothers and two sisters said grace holding hands round the table like Jesus and the disciples. There was a plate of potatoes with steam coming off it, and peas in a bowl and meat on a plate that was oval, not round. They gave me a chair and everyone took up their own food. They waited for each other and ate slowly and nobody took too much food and there was lots left.

"Do you want more, Maggy?" Eugenia's mom said, and when she said my name it felt like she touched me.

"Yes, please."

"Give her lots of meat, Caroline," Eugenia's dad said, and her mom gave me the kind of slices Dad usually gets. The potatoes were whole, not cut up like at home.

I was polite with the Lillys and that's my real self. At school they can't tell the difference between me and Bev Ducey. At first they could 'cause I got a hundred when Sister tested us on how many syllables were in a bunch of words. I didn't know what a syllable was. Sister read out the words and I figured in *house* there must only be enough room for one syllable, whatever a syllable is, and in *automobile* there must be enough room for about four.

Last time we had a spelling bee we got to ask the words and nobody could spell my word. Quay. It sounds like key. Nobody here ever heard of Bill Quay. After nearly the whole class had to sit down I changed my word to Mississippi. Sister Annunciata asked me why I did it and I didn't say anything. The reason I got zero on our test today is that music was coming through the wall and I forgot about Sister reading the words out. The music is a nun playing "Daisy, Daisy," "Sidewalks of New York," and one other one, I don't know the name but I know the tune by heart because she plays it every morning. I sing it in bed till Mam comes in and tells me to stop. I wish I was in that room and I could play the piano. I told Mam I wished we had a piano and she found me one made of paper. It's flat, and it has the black and white keys drawn on it, and I practice it in my bedroom and try not to hear the vacuum cleaner.

Mam's vacuum cleaner knocks the walls outside my bedroom every day. It wants to crash through my door. Then it knocks the walls down the hall and in the living room and dining room. It knocks and crashes and wants to come through the walls and flatten me. That Hoover roars louder than Dad shouting at Mam. I think the Hoover is Mam shouting when he's gone. That Hoover roaring is my mother's real voice.

Sometimes Mam's beautiful like when she was eating pork pies. She wore her white sleeveless shirt with white sequins all over it at her party. It was the only time we ever had a party at our house, and Dad got drunk. He had to hang on the banister to get downstairs, and Mam took him up and put him to bed when the party wasn't even over. Her lipstick was the same colour as crackerberries.

WHEN IT WAS DECIDED we were moving to Canada Mam said, "Maggy, Percy, Daniel, we have to have a jumble sale."

"What do you mean?"

"We can't take all your toys with us. We can hardly take anything. And we thought instead of throwing your toys away and wasting them, you could sell them in the front garden and keep the money and buy new toys when we get to Canada."

"You mean my crown?"

Dad had finally made me a crown I had asked him for over and over again, for months and even years.

"Yes."

"And my trumpet?"

"We don't really have room for your trumpet."

"But I got it this Christmas."

"You can keep one thing."

"Well I'll keep my crown."

"Not the crown because it's too pointy. You can keep Hilda Boswell's *Treasury of Nursery Rhymes*."

"But I hate the goblins with bluebells on their heads. They're on every page."

Percy had to sell his tri-coloured torch. It had a disc that changed the lens to red, blue or green. We stood at a desk in front of our marigolds, and the Cullens and the McGuckens and Alison Taite and the people who owned the Alsation at the end of Marian Drive, the one I had gone for a ride on around the whole block one day and no one knew, all came to look, amazed that we would let them have our toys, and that each of them could afford two, three and even four things with their pocket money, as Dad told us to charge no more than threepence for anything. Catherine Cullen bought my crown and trumpet immediately, and her brother bought Percy's torch, and I knew neither of them properly understood the majesty they were inheriting. The Cullens lived next door and they had a paddling pool and were allowed to colour the illustrations in their books and walk on the wall.

Dad came here before us, and he wrote my mother a letter.

"What does it say?" I asked. Normally my mother would not tell me what was in a letter addressed to her, but she had no one else to tell.

"It says Dear Eleanor, I'm going to tell you the truth. It's horrible. The other fellows in the new jobs at the shipyard are writing to their wives and lying to them but I'm telling you the truth. The roads are dust and stones. The blackberries are sour and dry and small, and I wish with my whole heart that I had not sold our cherry wood bedroom set as there is not one piece of nice furniture in this whole place. Nobody has gardens of any kind. You will absolutely hate the house. I will come home the minute you ask and never mention log cabins or Canada again."

"What are we going to do?"

"I'm going to tell him he's there now and we're coming."

On the plane my plate had a black thing on it. I asked Mam what it was. She was sitting three seats behind me and Percy, on the other side of the plane with Daniel on her lap, and my question vexed her. All she said was, "It's a gherkin," as if that answered everything. Dad met us and we stayed in St. John's buying leather chairs and a mustard coloured carpet. "Whoever is responsible for designing these chairs," he said, "wants to be shot." When we got to Marystown there was a letter for me from Grandma. *"I saw your plane take off,"* it said, *"and the airport was playing Engelbert Humperdinck singing there goes my everything, and I cried so much I had to sit on one of the chairs and I missed my bus. A man came up and gave me an orange with no seeds and a Cadbury flake. I got a taxi home and it cost eighty pounds. Don't tell."*

AT FIRST EUGENIA took me on trail rides with her father. No one else here has a ranch but the Lillys are American. They gave me a red horse to ride on called Demerara. I never dreamed I could gallop but I can, and it felt like flying. I was surprised it was easy. Galloping on a ranch seems like something you have to be born into, or train for over a long time.

It took Eugenia a few extra days to get to school in September because the Lillys had to go to the States to bring back two more horses. When she came her uniform was different too. Hers was real Newfoundland tartan but it was long. It was almost down to her ankles. I was afraid they would pick on her but they didn't. At recess they crowded around her.

"Your skirt's nice."

"Old-fashioned like a girl on a farm in the old days."

They all wanted one like it. They found out she had horses. Some had already heard of the horses, and everyone wanted to be her friend. There were so many girls crowded around her that even if she'd wanted to talk to me she couldn't have. Even if she'd wanted to look at me it would have been hard, 'cause they all would have wondered, "What's Eugenia Lilly looking at Maggy Carter for?"

Sister Annunciata let everyone eat their Scotties Chips and drink their Pepsi beside Eugenia's desk. I went out in the schoolyard and so did Bev Ducey, and Bev pushed me in the chin a few times and scuffed my socks and kicked my ankles and said she'd beat me up the next day after school 'cause it would be Friday and the principal would never find out.

"Bev Ducey was picking on me again," I told Dad.

"Finish her off," he said. "Punch her hard in the nose." So I did the next day at recess. She wasn't expecting it. I just walked up and did it, and she started crying and I kept punching her in the nose another few times and her glasses fell in the gravel and broke. I was surprised how easy it was, like when I galloped at the Lillys'. After recess Sister Annunciata stood in front of the class holding Bev's glasses and said, "Maggy Carter did this," and everybody stared at me like I was a piece of slime.

I cried in bed. Dad heard me and he came in.

One other time he'd heard me cry in bed it was because I was reading Dear Doctor Thosteson in the paper and I thought I had all the things those people had. I thought I had a brain tumour and cancer of the blood, and that I might have to get a colostomy. I'd already asked Mam, "What's a colostomy?"

"They cut some of your intestines out and your poo has to come out of a tube in your side and it hangs in a plastic bag under your skirt."

So I was crying, but I never told Dad why that time. That time I told him I was worried about the toad, all by itself in the greenhouse.

"Maggy," he said, "That toad died long before we came here."

"It died?"

"I put a chemical bomb in the greenhouse to kill the greenfly and I forgot about the toad."

"But the toad ate greenflies. That was why you had it. You said it was a good toad."

"It was. It was a very good working toad." He started to laugh. "It was completely unobtrusive."

"But it was a lovely toad, you said. You shouldn't laugh."

"I'm not laughing because it died. I'm laughing at what a good toad it was."

"You shouldn't laugh." I was crying for the toad now, on top of colostomies and all the other sad things.

My father kept laughing. "It was ingenious really, how that toad hid. In a way it was too ingenious for its own good. It hid so well I forgot it was there, and I annihilated it."

But this time I was not crying about his toad. "Everyone," I said, "has got a real Newfoundland tartan uniform except me."

"I never knew that," he said. "I thought you had a uniform the same as everybody else."

I thought, maybe he's going to make sure I get a real one now, but he didn't. He said, "Your grandma used to have a nice kilt," then went out for his pork and stuffing sandwich.

I sang the songs from through the wall in school and put my flashlight on and read Grandma's last letter. *"When I get my pension that means I can go on all the buses free. I'm going to Morpeth. Don't tell your dad. I'm buying a pork roast. You only live once."* I'd never thought of my uniform as a kilt before. I shone the flashlight into my kaleidoscope and saw palaces and forest paths hung with golden pears, like in *The Twelve Dancing Sisters*.

THE WORST PART OF WEARING my wrong uniform was when we all sang "Ode to Newfoundland" on stage at our assembly. Mam didn't go because the cadets were there with their guns. If she'd gone, she could have seen how wrong my uniform looked next to all the others. She would have seen how anything would be better than that uniform. If I was my mother and I didn't feel like paying for Newfoundland tartan, I would buy something as far away from Newfoundland tartan as possible. Even something that's Dad's favourite colour, which is sky-blue pink. Not something with almost the same colours as Newfoundland tartan only in the wrong order, which makes me feel like every part of me is in the wrong order, even my face and head and toes.

Here is what I told Grandma in my last letter, on a secret page: *"Here is a piece of tartan I cut out of my hem, and here is a picture of some Newfoundland tartan that I cut out of the school magazine, which shows what our uniform is supposed to be like. You can see how different they are. Mine has no red stripe at all,* and the green is the wrong green. Mam will not buy me the right kind, and Dad does not really understand. What would you do?"

Grandma wrote back. Her letter came in a pillowcase with stamps on it, and she had put a crocheted vest inside made of blue and purple and turquoise and yellow and orange squares with brown shoulders and buttons, and her letter said, *"Dear Maggy, don't put all your stock in having that uniform because number one, you aren't going to get it. If your mother doesn't like something that's it. She put salt in my tea not once but twice. I never said anything to your father because he's stuck with her now but that's the way your mother is. Number two, your tartan might not be like the other girls' tartan but with tartan you are never the only one wearing it. There is always a clan you belong to. If you keep your eyes peeled you will see the rest of your clan. You will know each other even without the tartan. Keep looking all your life. Don't tell about the salt whatever you do."*

I told about the salt. Mam kept rolling pastry and she said, "I never did that."

"Maybe you did it accidentally and Grandma thought it was on purpose."

"No. I did not do it accidentally because I did not do it at all. That is not something I would ever do." Mam looked like a person who has decided not to tell even half of what she knows. She was not going to say one more word about it. That information was locked away where no one in the history of the world was ever going to find it. She did not thump her rolling pin on the pastry too hard, but it was not too soft either. It was exactly the right amount of thump for pastry and nothing else, and every time the rolling pin went down it made the same sound. I wanted to know more about the salt but I knew I was not allowed to ask. I went in my room and played my paper piano. It might be only paper but it has the black and white notes in the right places, and I lie it on my desk and sit at it and play it even though it makes no sound. I practice on it for fifteen minutes every day, and when I hear the lovely songs through the wall at school I promise myself I am going to keep practicing in case I ever have a chance to play a piano everyone can hear.

I've just busted another sap bubble and got more sap on my uniform. Dad hasn't come home yet from fibreglassing at the shipyard, and Mam is out trying to get her driver's license. I'm going in the house and I'm going to put different clothes on and I'm going to roll this uniform up and take it to the riverbank and bury it in the clay under a rock where no one will ever find it again. When Mam asks where it is I'm just going to tell her it must be in the house somewhere. I'm going to make her think she's the one who has lost it. I'm going to act like she acted about the salt in Grandma's tea, and she won't be able to tell from my face one single thing about what really happened.

Jolly Trolley

Marianne could see Mrs. McGettigan getting out of the truck that brought her home from the fish plant. Mrs. McGettigan wore her blue uniform over a couple of sweaters. It was a cold summer. Mrs. McGettigan had on her fish plant headpiece; a white plastic scalloped tiara and hairnet, and she carried two plastic bags. Fish and her leftover lunch. She watched through her window as Mrs. McGettigan went up her driveway. She watched her rattle her screen door and peer in the dark window and realized she was locked out. She watched her try to rattle the window open then look up at Marianne's house. Marianne went to the door and called out, "Come up."

"I'm off early. He's not home," the tiara bobbed up the hill. The wind lost her voice in the grass. Mrs. McGettigan was meek and a bit lonely. Nobody seemed to like her husband Leonard and their family had a faint outcast quality. They burned electric heat instead of wood, and Leonard built houses in subdivisions instead of being a fisherman. They were sixty.

Mrs. McGettigan laid her bags by the daybed and sat down. She kept her headpiece on and did not loosen her uniform buttons. She sat with her hands clasped and knees together. Marianne could see the print of long johns under her navy stretch pants. The fish plant was cold and the floor was always wet. Marianne made two slices of buttered toast and peeled a banana and put it all on a plate and gave it to Mrs. McGettigan with hot tea.

"Leonard wouldn't like it if he knew I tried to go in through the window." Mrs. McGettigan did not move her lips much when she spoke. Her bottom lip was going numb and lately so was her right hand. She was going to the doctor about it tomorrow. Her voice was high with a sad tone in it.

"Does he expect you to sit and wait for him in the driveway?" Marianne shouted because Mrs. McGettigan was deaf in the left ear. Her husband told everyone it came from always rooting around in it with a hairpin even in the night in bed. Marianne's cat rubbed Mrs. McGettigan's ankles. Mrs. McGettigan had six cats. She bent and stroked Marianne's with big strong strokes. She picked it up and hugged it, rocked it and kissed its head, puckering her lips generously as if they had not a bit of numbness in them.

"No but he wouldn't like it. I'd rather he didn't know." They talked about cats, the cold summer, the coming garden parties. "Nothing like they once were. There's nothing there for children now. When we were young there were pony rides and games. Now you're up to your knees in scratch-and-win. I'll make lemon squares for the tea." Her house was always full of iced cakes and puddings. Marianne worried about the toast and banana but Mrs. McGettigan said, "The bread's nice, it's the brown bread isn't it?"

"It didn't rise very much."

"They had maggots in the machine and they had to clean it out. That's why I'm off early. I wasn't supposed to get off till six and it's only three. I don't know when Stuart will get home." Stuart was her daughter's husband. "He went for a blood test. He had his heart operated on last year. I don't know what time they went."

"I saw them go a couple of hours ago. Laura was all dressed up." Marianne remembered Laura getting in the car with an unlit cigarette in her mouth and a blouse covered in flowers. Their little girl had on black patent leather shoes and a red baseball cap. "How's your cup?" Marianne filled it. Past the McGettigans' house the fences and islands were unlit. "It's hard to get a second fine day." Thomas Silver had said that to Marianne the other day from his turnip garden.

"It is so." Mrs. McGettigan smiled. Timidly she said, "I've been thinking of going south again."

"South?"

"Down to Florida. I was there seven times."

"Seven?"

"Yes. The first time, I went by myself."

"You went to Florida alone?"

"The first time yes, and then I went again with some other girls from the shore. But I haven't been these four years now. I'd love to go down again."

"I can't believe you went to Florida alone." It was obvious Mrs. McGettigan didn't mind her surprise. Her eyes were wearing little proud hoods.

"Oh yes, I loved every minute of it. It was easy. I asked them at the travel agent's here before I went what to do and they said go around the corner when you leave the airport and told me what bus to take to Pasadena where the hotel was."

"And what did you do then?"

"I got settled away and I was downstairs asking directions and out on the street in no time."

"What did you do?"

"I went shopping. Shopping at the malls. Window shopping. They told me where to get the bus. I just had to go across the street and wait, and the bus would come and take me to the Tyrone Square Mall, and I'd ask the driver at the other end how to get back, and I'd do that every single day." She looked as happy as Marianne had ever seen her. "I'd even go to the bingo, two nights a week, down there." She went to bingo two nights a week up here. If she couldn't get her husband to take her she scandalized the cove by hitch-hiking.

"The Tyrone Square Mall has a hundred and forty-four stores. I'd go to K-Mart because I'm used to K-Mart here. They had a JCPenney. There was a good bargain basement there. They had beautiful blouses. That was the first time I went now. The other times five of us went shopping together. One of the girls who works at the Arcade here says the same blouse that was five dollars in Florida would be seventeen fifty or twenty-five dollars at the Arcade." Her body lost its stiffness. She sat back among the cushions and dreamed. She picked the banana up, tore a piece off and ate it. "We went to Indian Shores first. We didn't like it. All you could see was a bridge and a few hotels, and I saw a few pelicans out on the water. So we moved to Clearwater where they have the Jolly Trolley that takes you to the Sunshine Mall where all the clothes is cheap." She finished her banana. "I love bananas."

Marianne felt surprised she said this so fervently in the middle of Florida. "Did you enjoy Florida more by yourself or with the others?"

"With the others. They would go down on the beach and I'd not be one for the beach. I'd cook supper, set the table and everything. One time we bought a big round roast for seven dollars and they said how will you ever cook that, we've got no oven. In Clearwater they only had four burners and the fridge underneath. It was cute. Anyway I made a pot roast out of the roast. It fit right in the pot and I fried out a bit of pork, no, shortening, and then kept adding a bit of water and onions until it was cooked, and made mashed potatoes with it and with a small bag of flour – you could get different sizes of everything – I thickened the gravy. So we had a good meal out of it. They couldn't believe it. And the roast was so big we had meals out of it for days after. We'd make roast beef sandwiches."

She stroked the cat. "At the Sunshine Mall they had balloons with a number inside each one. You'd prick the balloon and I got a banana split every single day for seven days for one cent except the eighth day I had to pay forty-nine cents. That was my last day there."

"Were the banana splits good?"

"Good, yes they were good."

"Were they big?"

"Big, yes they were really big. The other four would be jealous of me because they'd have to pay full price, sixty-nine cents."

The door opened and Mrs. McGettigan's granddaughter came in eating Glossettes. She scrambled on the daybed and looked at her nanny. "We thought you weren't home." She tried feeding a Glossette to the cat. Mrs. McGettigan did not seem to be in any hurry to go home.

"Is the fare expensive?"

"It's four hundred dollars return, plus eighteen dollars a night if you share four to a room." She said the woman who works at the Arcade phoned yesterday thinking maybe they'd go back down in September.

"And are you going?"

Mrs. McGettigan got up then. She should be home making supper instead of sitting down eating banana and toast and talking about Florida with Marianne. "I must go now." She picked her bags up and said come on to her little granddaughter. She didn't answer Marianne.

"Do you think you'll be going?" Marianne shouted.

As she was going out the door Mrs. McGettigan spoke in an automatic voice. "If I win the seven digit number tonight maybe I'll go down." Marianne asked her how much the prize was. It was five hundred. But Mrs. McGettigan had to get supper. She should never have tried to get in the house through the kitchen window. She should never have forgotten her keys. She had not known there would be maggots in the machine. All the same Leonard would be mad if he found out. Marianne watched them bob down the bank, the white plastic tiara and little red hat. Murres and puffins screamed around the island. From the wind over Thomas Silver's turnip garden she caught scents of peas pudding and wild roses.

My Heart Used to Dance

In the back garden full of bare trees the birds were singing and singing, coaxing the furled nubbins of leaf out of their twigs. All day long they had been singing. It was the eighteenth of April. Marianne went in Sandy Milandy's bedroom to tell him about the birds, how they'd been singing all day. She opened his curtains.

"Have they?" His hands appeared over the edge of his sheet. He opened his eyes. They were a thick, milky blue because he had cataracts. He was wearing his glasses in bed, and he still had his hat on. It was a little black hat that fit like a boat upside down over his head and folded into a flat rectangle when he took it off. It had tight black curls all over it, like a lamb. His hair was white under the hat, and thick, and spiky. It sprang off his head like sun-rays when he took the hat off. When he asked about the birds his voice was soft and hopeful, although he could not see the birds or the sunlight, and he could not hear the birds either, because he was a bit deaf.

Marianne had been looking after Sandy Milandy all winter, four days a week, twelve hours a day. She had been looking after his wife, Julia, as well, until a week and a half ago, when Julia had died of pneumonia in the hospital. Julia had gone to hospital to get her cast off. She had had it on her arm since she'd fallen in the kitchen two months before. Now Sandy was sleeping through the days. He was sad. But the little hopeful voice came out again. It was different from the voice he had owned before Julia died.

"Concerned for wife," read the card the home care company had given Marianne when she'd started. "Can become agitated when things don't go right. Help to get Mrs. Milandy dressed, washed if necessary, and meals."

"He used to be chairman of the Tobacco Import Federation," Mrs. Shiering told Marianne when she gave her the card at Harper's Home Care. "He's used to bossing a lot of people around. He's like a general. Just ignore him and look after her."

The Milandys were private clients. That meant they were paying Harper's Home Care out of their own money, and not through Social Services. Sandy Milandy was continuing to pay for a homemaker even though Julia was dead.

The sun lit Jesus' face in the sepia-coloured portrait over his head. Marianne sat in the chair at the foot of the bed. "All the little birds are singing because it's spring," he said. "Do you know the song the young fellow was singing to the little bird?

"You know the little bird doesn't want a cage. They want freedom. In the air. To perch on trees. And the young fellow was singing . . .

> *Little bird little bird*
> *come to me*
> *I have a clean cage*
> *all ready for thee*
> *and many bright flowers*
> *all decked with dew . . .*

"The little bird don't want no part of it. He wants to be in the wide open country. Among all the trees. . . . Is my supper ready yet? I'll have a ham sandwich and half an orange, and I'll have a cup of tea." He had the same thing every day. "What time is it?"

"Quarter to four."

"And I'll have my orange the way I like it, cut around with the special knife so I can eat it with a spoon. What do you call that?"

"Circulated?"

"Circularized! And then cut in . . . what are they? Strips? Stripped?"

"Wedged."

"Wedged! That's it. Circularized and wedged. That's a good one. We'll put that one in the paper. Where's my slippers? Will you put my slippers on for me? Will you guide me along the hall? How am I going to get to the kitchen? Will you help me, Darlene? Josephine? Marianne! Marianne Evans from Poplar Dam. Will you guide me to the kitchen, Marianne?"

"Yes."

"Because I can't see, you know. I'm blind. I can't find my way to the kitchen by myself. You'll have to help me. That's what they're paying you for at Harper's Home Help. And I'm paying them. So you will guide me to the kitchen, won't you? And then I can have my supper. Darlene. Marianne. Yes I'm paying them. A thousand dollars a week. Did you know that? They're not paying you that much, are they?"

"No."

"No, I know they're not. Now I'll go to the bathroom and you'll wait for me and then we'll go out and I'll have my supper and you'll have your supper too. Have you got any supper?"

"I'll have a cup of tea with you."

"A cup of tea? That's not very much. Will you have a bun? Did Mrs. Monahan bring any buns? She used to bring buns all the time for Julia."

"I'll make some buns."

"Julia's dead now. . . . It's Easter Sunday tomorrow isn't it?"

"Yes."

"Maybe Mrs. Monahan will bring some hot cross buns tomorrow. She didn't bring any yet did she?"

"No."

"No. Well I'll go to the bathroom now."

As he climbed out of bed Marianne could see his testicles falling out through his long johns flap like a bundle of spiny, exotic cactus.

"Do you want your trousers on?"

"No. Do you think anyone will come?"

"What about Mrs. Monahan with the hot cross buns?"

"Call her. Call Mrs. Monahan. Tell her to bring Sandy over some of her delicious buns. And I'll put my pants on. Here," he sat on the bed and offered her his feet. She slipped the pants over them.

"Now where is everything?" He was tucking his napkin at his throat, gazing at Marianne across the little table that folded out of the kitchen wall. "Is this my orange?" He touched a novel that the night shift homemaker had left on the table. It was a Silhouette Desire novel called *Star Light Star Bright.*

"No, that's a book. Here's your orange."

"A book?" Alarm. The general. "What kind of book? Is it my pocketbook with all my private financial records in it? Give me that!"

"No, it's just a love story. One of the other homemakers must have left it."

"A love story." He let go of the book. His voice had gone small and wondering. "Is it any good?"

Marianne laughed. "I don't know."

"Is this my ham sandwich?" His voice broke, in an incredulous whimper. He was patting the bread softly with his fingertips, and staring at Marianne through the cataracts. His top teeth were sliding down very slowly as he waited with his mouth open for her to answer.

"Yes." She said it before the teeth could come crashing down. Just in time. When he chewed his sandwich she could see how the teeth were not part of him and had no sensitivity. It was as if he were transforming his food into swallowable pieces with a pair of plastic scissors. Scraps and corners of the sandwich dropped to the table and floor. Every second day he had a chicken leg at noon. He loved chicken legs. Baked. He wrapped the knob at the small end in a paper napkin. The false teeth made a plasticy clack-clack noise against the pink bone. Meals on Wheels came the other days. Planks of grey beef with translucent blue veins of gristle through them, lying in thick gravy; mashed potato shot with a trigger out of an ice-cream scoop; alphabet soup; sponge flan soaked in red sauce that tasted like bandages; all in semi-transparent white plastic tubs arranged in an insulated styrofoam spaceship to keep them lukewarm. Sandy's fridge was full of the tubs. The spaceships you had to give back to Meals on Wheels.

The fridge still contained leftovers from the funeral supper. The relatives had been very surprised to hear he was having a tea for everyone after the funeral. They hadn't wanted to think of what he might have had in his mind. Whenever he invited one of them, they had said, "Really? That's a lovely thought," and had for a minute dropped the false tone they used whenever they spoke to him. He wasn't going to let anyone down. They'd never have dreamed he was capable.

"What do you think we should do?" he had asked Marianne. "Will I take them all out for their supper to a restaurant?" Marianne thought of the tea her mother had had for everyone after the funeral of Marianne's grandfather. She suggested he invite all the people home, and the homemaker would fix a nice table. In the end Marianne had come to help, with two other homemakers. Relatives had come from everywhere, and the supper had looked beautiful.

The party had gone on while Sandy lay in bed, the curtains drawn, under the face of Jesus. Every fifteen minutes Marianne had gone in to sit with him. He was too weak to see anyone.

"He's lying down," she told them one by one. "He's exhausted after the funeral." They always believed what she told them. So did Sandy. They trusted her. "Everyone is having a good time," she had told him. "The supper is beautiful. They're drinking coffee and talking to each other. Some of them haven't seen each other in years. They're doing fine."

In the church they had all had to sit farther back than they would have liked. Sandy had drawn up a plan to which they'd had to submit. They were all Julia's relatives; nieces and cousins. She and Sandy had had no children. At the front Sandy had reserved places for his own party, which consisted of a nephew and niece from his side of the family, one friend in his nineties, and Marianne and Camellia, his two favourite homemakers. In the middle of the service Marianne had had to go to the vestibule and get a styrofoam cup of water for him. Then he had started whimpering. Marianne and Camellia had brought him home in the limousine and put him to bed while everyone else was at the graveyard. Marianne was glad Harper's Home Care had provided its homemakers with pale green smocks and nametags. It meant the relatives could tell themselves she was Sandy's nurse, and it meant they could remain innocent of the fact that Sandy trusted her and loved her. For they all knew he did not trust them, and they knew he did not love them.

They belonged to the world of sensible people, thought Marianne. People who were neither too old nor too young. Rational and consecutive. Sometimes they came to visit at difficult times, like the time Sandy's nephew had come and found Sandy sitting on a box of Moirs *Pot of Gold* chocolates on the coffee table with his long johns and his hat on, waiting for Marianne to come out of the bathroom, where she was helping Julia, and lead him to the kitchen. They had smart clothes, and faces that were tired from all the responsibility life had piled on them while they hadn't been looking. If Marianne felt sorry for Sandy because he was helpless, she felt sorry for these people because they were expected to cope, and because most of them were lonely.

They came once a week to visit Sandy, but what they really did was sit on the couch that had come from Boston when Sandy and Julia were young, and drink cups of tea made by Marianne, and eat slices of cake, or now the dainty things left over from the funeral. They sat holding their teacups and told Marianne not to wake Sandy; that it was okay, they didn't want to disturb him, they just wanted to know how he was. Then they told Marianne things about their own lives, and all of them had pure loneliness pouring out of them in a cold current.

"You know, I always feel tense right here," Darlene, Julia's red-haired niece said, and she pointed to her heart. "Always. The tension never leaves me. I know I should be doing my breathing exercises, but I never do them." Darlene had three sons at home. She brought refrigerator cookies in Tupperware containers. When she came to visit Sandy, Marianne got the impression she had left her kitchen light on and a casserole in the oven, and she had to get home before everyone ate everything that was supposed to be for their lunches tomorrow, and her husband was in the shower, and she should be back by the time he was dry.

Madeline was Julia's second niece. She was a widow. Her daughters were unselfish and worked in administrative jobs and had all gone away. She lived in a basement apartment and worked part time as a clerk in the lab and X-ray section of St. Hilda's Hospital. The job was too much for her. She had disc problems in her back. Both nieces did.

When they came together to deal with anything connected with their aunt Julia, who was the only reason they ever came together, there was this undercurrent; "She should have had her own daughter." They would do things for their Aunt Jewel, don't worry, but if anything went wrong . . . Madeline had locked the keys in her car one day while they were visiting their aunt in the hospital. They had to get a taxi and pay for a new key. Who would pay? Which niece? The one who locked the keys in?

"She's my aunt as well as yours . . ." Darlene had said. Marianne had been surprised by the revelation that the accused, ultimately, was Aunt Julia Milandy, who, unaware of keys, cars, taxis or even impending visitors, had lain hooked up to her intravenous antibiotics, with fluid around her heart and lungs, with congestive heart failure, without her prayer beads or her teeth, glasses, or even a bit of raisin bun. And they wouldn't take the cast off her arm, and two big fat nurses were bawling at her to keep still and not try to sit up. She couldn't sleep lying down, but nobody understood that.

Sandy had a niece and a nephew; Maura and Edgar Milandy. He had banished them from his home most of his married life, as he had done with Julia's nieces and friends. But he had to let them in now. Maura came twice a week to take a shopping list compiled by Marianne: chicken legs, sliced ham, half a dozen large oranges . . . She would bring back the food and she might have a cup of tea if Marianne was especially warm with her. You had to be especially warm with Maura, Marianne had decided, because she was especially hurt and lonely. Maura had a lovely slim body with nice curves, and she wore forest-green silk dresses and powder-blue pleated dresses and dresses with soft peaches and peach blossoms on the sleeves. Her hair was always blushing with a sheen of warm, tea-coloured dye, and she wore expensive shoes that Marianne would have enjoyed looking at for hours. The pair of shoes Marianne loved most was a pair made of green alligator skin that glistened. Maura didn't look anywhere near sixty, but she was sixty. She lived in a high-rise apartment that cost over one thousand five hundred a month, Sandy told Marianne. He told her that Maura had had a lover but that the lover hadn't married her, and that meant she was impure.

"You know what I mean don't you, Norma? Marianne! That's it, Marianne Evans from Poplar Dam. Are you pure, Marianne? Now you don't have to answer that. I shouldn't have asked. I know you are respectable. And trustworthy."

Edgar Milandy came every Sunday after Mass. Marianne found out he had read the library books she took out of her purse to show him. Gandhi, Malcolm Muggeridge, Rabindranath Tagore.

"Did you see the books Sandy has in his bookshelves?" he asked Marianne. She had assumed they were trash. They had come from a mail order company and all had maroon plastic upholstered binding with black labels and gilt lettering. She hadn't even bothered to read the titles.

"No."

"You should take a look. He's got all the classics." And so he had.

Edgar was especially eager not to waken Sandy. He always polished off whatever Marianne fed him. He liked brie cheese and lemon pound cake. He seemed used to it. He was ruddy and stolid. He lived all alone in the big house he had built, Sandy told her. His wife had died five years ago. Before he'd retired he had worked in the federal government.

"His house is bigger than my house," Sandy said, "but he has terribly low ceilings. He's not as well-off as I am. But he's nearly as well-off as me. And I'm very well-off."

"Is there any cake?" He had finished his sandwich. There was always cake. When Julia had been alive, the mahogany table in the dining room had always carried upon its lace tablecloth some large box that contained a ludicrous cake with froth and beads and icing dolloped over it. In February it had been a Valentine cake, and during the two weeks it had taken to consume it, Sandy had announced his desire for it by asking, "Is there any Hallowe'en cake left?"

"And where's my juice? Give me a glass of juice, will you please, Darlene? Marianne?" He kept a perpetual glass of juice going. It was not really juice, but reconstituted orange-flavoured crystals. He drank so much of it that Marianne was worried about the chemicals. She poured it and put a straw in the glass. There was always a box of straws on the kitchen counter, the kind that had a section you could bend like a little accordion. He tapped the air over the glass until he found his straw. Marianne wondered at the tenacity of habits so small they were shadows of real life, but they kept going no matter what happened to the real life's substance. He sucked his juice thirstily until it was all gone.

"What will I do now, Darlene? Marianne? Is it time for my sleeping pill? Will I go to bed for the night? What time is it?"

"It's only four thirty. Don't go to bed yet. Stay up and talk to me for awhile."

"Only four thirty. And I've had my supper. Have you had any supper, Eileen?"

"I'm having a cup of tea. I'll have my supper later on."

"And you have a cup of tea there. That's good. When I was young I had a friend who was the dealer for the Tiger Tea Company. He travelled in every port on this coast right down the Atlantic seaboard to New England and when he was selling tea, if he saw a pretty lady go by, do you know what he'd say? He'd say, 'Look here lady –

> *Today's the day we're giving babies away*
> *with every pound of tea.*
> *If you know any ladies*
> *without any babies*
> *just send them along to me.'*

"That's what he'd do. . . . Now will I go to bed, Darlene? Marianne? Will I take my pill?"

"It's not even five o'clock yet. It's too early to go to bed. The paper's here. Do you want me to read the deaths?"

"Isn't it five o'clock yet? All right then. Lead me to my chair and we'll find out who died."

He sat down in his armchair by the living room window, with the *Telegram* in his lap and his arm around Marianne, who sat on the arm of the chair. He felt her bottom.

"Have you gained weight, Darlene?" Camellia had been on last night's shift. She was slim. Whenever Mrs. Pyle had been on, Sandy asked Marianne if she had lost weight. Mrs. Pyle was fat. Not as fat as Josephine though. That was another homemaker. He didn't like Josephine. He called her "that corporation." She weighed three hundred and fourteen pounds. She wore her hair in a lank ponytail. She was thirty-nine and had a boyfriend who was twenty-one and wore tight jeans and T-shirts and had no teeth. He drove Josephine to work in a maroon station wagon with no muffler. Josephine told Marianne episodes of her life as Marianne put her boots on in the porch in the evenings.

"If you think that's bad," she had said when Julia had become too weak to stand, "you should have seen my mother when she was in the hospital. Fell out of bed at least sixteen times a day. The nurses had to lift her up and she was big bonededer than I am. And sick? My dear. How sick was she? She opened her mouth and the green bile shot out like water out of a hose. It went all over the room. I got covered. And the colour! Green? My dear it was just as green as that sweater you're wearing. Greener." She folded her arms, took a dramatic drag of her cigarette, inhaled the smoke deep, and blew it out in a blue funnel up to the ceiling.

"Now where's the deaths?" Sandy was tapping the front page with his fingertips. "Are they there?"

"No. That's the front page. Here."

"Who's that? Who's the first one? Aylmer? Is it Aylmer? You'll have to read them out because I can't see. I'm blind."

"It's Aylward."

"Oh. It is Aylmer then. It's not Joseph is it? It's not Joseph Aylmer? He used to be on the board of directors at the shipping office with my uncle Desmond. Uncle Desmond Simpson. Is Joseph Aylmer dead?"

"Aylward."

"Oh. Aylward. No. Move on then."

"Becker."

"Mmph."

"Carnell."

"No. Move on."

"Farrell."

"Farrell. Who's that one?"

"Regina."

"Where's she from? Is she from Drake Harbour?"

"Allandale."

"Yes that's it. Drake Harbour is in Allandale. What does it say?"

"Passed peacefully away in her ninety-sixth year . . ."

"Ninety-six! My, she was old. I didn't know her but I knew her cousins. Tommy and Rodney. They were boatmakers. They drank a lot of rum. Tommy married a woman he met in France. He brought her back here but she didn't like it. She ran away again. Back to France. Regina. Regina Farrell from Drake Harbour. Does it say where they're burying her?"

"It says Mount Erasmus Cemetery in Allandale."

"Yes, that's where they buried Tommy. Who's next? Are there any more?"

"Gallagher."

"Hollohan?"

"Gallagher."

By the end of the obituaries, Marianne was hoarse.

"Will you lead me to the bedroom now, Marianne?" He felt her bottom. "You have a nice figure. I like that. Lovable. You're lovable. There," he cupped her bottom in his hand, which was like a claw covered in ancient velvet, velvet so delicate Marianne was afraid it would break open softly like moss, and the claw would stick out, greyish-pink like a bird's claw, clamped around her bottom.

Sometimes he got up from his armchair and shuffled by himself, his hands outstretched and the ends of his trouser legs dangerously dragging on the carpet, to the kitchen. Then he clung to Marianne like a child while she stood with a dishtowel or a spatula in her hand. He patted her breasts and felt her bottom, then he whimpered, and went back to his armchair.

"Marianne?"

"Yes?"

"Can you come here please, Marianne? I know you're busy."

"Yes."

"Marianne? I shouldn't have done that. I shouldn't have come to you like that, and held your lovable body. Lovable. Will you forgive me, Marianne?"

"It's all right."

"But I shouldn't do it you know." And then he would recite *The Act of Contrition*.

> Oh my God I am heartily sorry for having offended
> thee and I detest my sins most sincerely because
> they are displeasing to thee my God who are so
> deserving of all my love, and on account of thy
> infinite goodness and most amiable perfection
> I firmly propose never more to offend thee, to
> atone for my sins, and to amend my life.

"You say that when you're dying and almighty God'll forgive you all your sins. The priest comes in as you say it, puts his hand on your head, and, 'I absolve you,' he says, 'of all your sins.'"

One day he had been eating his chicken leg and saying something Marianne could not catch.

"What's that?" she had asked him. It was *The Act of Contrition* again, but in Latin.

"I'll go to bed now, Marianne. What time is it? Is it quarter to six yet?"

"It's five thirty."

"Five thirty. All right. If it was quarter to six it would be better, but I'll go now anyway. Will you lead me to the bedroom, Marianne? You'll have to help me you know. I can't do it by myself."

When he was in bed Marianne sat on the floor in the living room beside the window, a section of which she had opened so that she could breathe the fresh stream of inflowing air. He never allowed the homemakers to open the windows. In the winter it had been too cold, and now he was terrified of all the bugs that he said were "coming out of the trees. Wait until the screens are up. I'll get Tommy to put them up." Tommy lived next door and did a lot of things for Sandy in the intervals when he had not been banished from the premises. Marianne read from *Seven Years in Tibet*, which she had taken from Sandy's bookshelf.

> *The preparation of a new book entails endless work. The monks must first cut out small wooden boards by hand, as there are no saw-mills here, and then carve the squiggling letters one by one in the birchwood boards. When they are ready the tablets are carefully placed in order. Instead of printers' ink they use a mixture of soot, which the monks make by burning yak-dung. Most of them get black from head to foot during their work. As their subject is always religious the books are treated with great respect and usually placed on the house-altar.... The price of Tibetan books depends on the quality of the paper used. The Kangyur with its commentaries costs as much as a good house or a dozen yaks . . .*

Spots of rain started to fly through the window. They were soft and small, and soundless. One night in mid-February, after two big snowstorms, Marianne had come to work the night shift. That had consisted mostly of preventing Julia from falling out of bed or from trying to get up and then falling. That night Julia had kept exploring the sheets and saying, "It's raining. Are there any snails in here?"

"No," Marianne had said, with the frightening logic of people who are always relying solely on themselves for information. "We've just had two snowstorms. It's not raining. And there are no snails." But when she left in the morning it was drizzling. The same soft rain that was floating through the windows onto her book.

"Darlene! Mrs. Pyle! Marianne? Marianne, are you there? You forgot to give me my juice!" The juice was very important.

"Marianne?" The voice was small. It came out of the bedclothes. "What time is it? Is it eight o'clock yet?"

"Seven."

"And you're going home at eight? Marianne, come here," his arm came out. He patted the bedspread. "Sit down." She did. He felt her legs. "Now that's a nice leg. That's lovable. Are you coming back, Marianne? Will I see you tomorrow? Tomorrow's Easter Sunday."

"Yes, I'll be here tomorrow."

"And Monday? Will you be here on Monday?"

"No I'm off on Monday. I'll be back on Wednesday."

"Oh. I thought Mrs. Pyle was coming on Wednesday. I don't like her. Where's she from?"

"Manchester."

"Oh she's English is she? She doesn't speak English. She's foreign. I can't understand her at all. I think she's Indian. Is she?"

"No, she's not Indian."

"Oh. Very well, Marianne. My love," he patted her, "I'll see you in the morning will I? At breakfast?"

"Yes." She hugged him goodnight.

HIS BREAKFAST WAS three saucers, from left to right; his toast; his egg cup containing his boiled egg; his cup of coffee. That is how it was arranged, and the fragrance, the completeness, the wholeness of an old man's – anyone's – breakfast – happened again. Comfort, simplicity and peace, thought Marianne. How peaceful was the old man's breakfast, as she gave it to him, before he started it. It did not care how old he was, how his spiny testicles peeped out of his long johns, how blind he was, how angry he became. It waited there; toast, egg, coffee; whole and steaming, clean and fragrant – on Easter Sunday. Peace, said the old man's breakfast, like a cat in a window. Be still, my poor, working heart, thought Marianne.

"I'm thinking of the thirty-five names," said Sandy. The names were people who had sent Mass cards for Julia's funeral. "Get Tommy to make me a cheque."

"No. It's Easter Sunday. You should let people be. We can do the names on a weekday."

"All right then." If Marianne was firm he sometimes obeyed her like a child. "I'll sit here and think of all the things that are going on on Easter Sunday.

". . . I used to go along the landwash and beat the mussels off the rocks with a big stick, and bring them home, and Julia would fry them up in pork fat and they'd be out of this world to eat – the biggest kind of mussels. I used to go right along the landwash and beat the mussels off the rocks, and my heart used to dance. . . . Is that my egg?"

"No, that's your toast. The egg is in the middle."

"And what's this? Is this my coffee?"

"Yes."

"What about Mrs. Monahan and the hot cross buns? Did she bring any yet?"

"No, not yet."

"It's Easter Sunday today. She would have brought them by now if she was going to bring them, wouldn't she? I don't think she'll bring any now. Do you, Marianne?"

"She might."

"I don't think so. She brought them for Julia. But I don't think she'll bring them any more now. Is someone knocking at the door? Go and get it will you, Marianne? See who it is. Maybe that's her now with the hot cross buns. Mrs. Monahan.

"Well, was it?"

"Yes."

"It was Mrs. Monahan?" Childishly, joyfully.

"Yes, and she brought a dozen hot cross buns. She said she couldn't come in." Marianne felt as childish and joyful as he did.

"That's all right. And she brought the buns!"

"Yes."

"Will you have one with me now, Marianne?" They were glazed with honey and had pieces of citron peel and black raisins sticking out.

"Yes."

"That's good. I knew she'd come. I knew Mrs. Monahan wouldn't forget Sandy."

"No."

"No, not Mrs. Monahan. Other people might forget. Those nieces. You won't see them here, not now that their aunt Julia has died. And Maura. And Edgar. All of them would forget. But not Mrs. Monahan. No, not her. She's different. Marianne?"

"Yes?"

"Are you enjoying your bun?"

"Yes. They're good."

"That's good. Have another one after you finish that. Today we'll eat Mrs. Monahan's buns and we'll rest, and we'll do the thirty-five names tomorrow.

Will you help me with that in the morning, Marianne? And will you make sure Tommy comes over and makes me a cheque?"

"All right."

"And we won't worry anybody today, will we?"

"No."

"We'll let them be."

"I think that's a good idea."

His breath squeaked and he held his hands out. "You'll pass me one of those buns now, won't you, Marianne? Mrs. Monahan's buns?" She handed him a bun and he bit it. "We'll let them all be. Maura. Edgar. Those nieces. The whole works. None of them will know what they're missing."

Where the Nightingales are Singing

Marianne was going to her parents' house with a box of frozen peas from the corner store when she saw Mrs. Snellen for the first time. Mrs. Snellen was waiting in the bus shelter. She wore a man's skidoo jacket, green trousers, and, over her coarse white hair, a khaki scarf. Her stomach was like Alfred Hitchcock's and her face like Winston Churchill's. She came to the bus shelter door.

"What time is it?" She looked Marianne dead in the eye. "I've been waiting here a long time. I have to be at Eddy's Bus at quarter to five."

"Are you getting the bus to Georgesville?" Georgesville, sixty miles away, was where Marianne had been living for ten months, teaching college students how to write newspaper articles. In Georgesville there was a paper mill, a beach decorated with pink tampon applicators and two Irving Oil tanks, an airstrip, and the college, whose buildings were part of a defunct American airforce base. There was a main street and a Chinese restaurant, a fried chicken outlet and a donut shop. Marianne was visiting her parents in Hell for the weekend. Before she had left the city and taken the job in Georgesville, she would not have thought she would find herself spending a weekend in Hell. But Georgesville was not as big as Hell, nor did it have as much going for it.

It was noon. Her mother's clam chowder was ready for the peas. But Marianne could not resist talking to Mrs. Snellen. Mrs. Snellen's eyes were like Marianne's father's; cold and blue behind their glasses. Her mouth curved in a downward crescent, with lines continuing from the corners downward to meet the line of her chin, so that chin and lips formed the shape of an egg lying down. There were three warts on the right hand end of the egg. A husband, said Mrs. Snellen, was something she'd never had nor wanted. Europe? Marianne was saving her money so she could travel. Mrs. Snellen had had a brother in Australia for forty-seven years, but he came back here to die. What would you want to travel all over the world for when you had a nice home here? Mrs. Snellen had a wonderful home in Georgesville. She had three rooms and a room for the boarder, Mr. Nelson. She had her kitchen and her sitting room and her bedroom, and it was perfect. She had strawberries and rhubarb in her garden, and she wanted for nothing. Marianne must come and visit when she got back. It turned out she lived just around the corner. Marianne stayed with Mrs. Snellen until the bus came. Had it not been so cold outdoors, even on the twenty-third of May, the peas would have thawed by the time she got home.

Marianne forgot about Mrs. Snellen several times, and remembered her several times, until one day she was walking up Mrs. Snellen's street with Claudia, the woman from whom she rented her rooms. It was a sunny day in early June. Claudia had her baby in its stroller and seemed happy to walk on without Marianne. Marianne told her she was going to see Mrs. Snellen. Claudia laughed.

"Her? Well don't run away from home with her, that's all. You have a job to think of. You have responsibilities." Claudia laughed with her baby and went up the street. Marianne turned in the driveway past a cream coloured VW bug and knocked at the door of Mrs. Snellen's little grey house. Her face came to the window. It wasn't wearing its scarf this time, and the white hair stood on end.

"I'm doing my laundry so I'm sorting everything out. Come in, come in." Every surface in the kitchen except the stove and table was covered in piles of clothes. It took Marianne a few seconds to see Mr. Nelson stretched out on the daybed under heaps of linen and scarves and trousers.

"That's Mr. Nelson. He's not very well. He's sick. I expect he'll die soon." Without her coat Mrs. Snellen's body could be seen more easily. Her breasts hung down her stomach, which was huge under the fisherman's sweater. Marianne, conscious of her own large breasts, worried if this might not be the fate of women who grew rhubarb and did not want husbands. There was a low ceilinged bedroom off the kitchen, and a square room with no furniture at the front of the house. The rooms had no doors. The place was more like a cabin than a house. It would have been cold were it not for the wood stove which crackled in the kitchen and threw waves of heat. A pot of bubbling rhubarb jam sat on the stove top.

"Rhubarb jam is good," said Mrs. Snellen. "Good with buns. We need buns." She spoke in a soft snuffly way that made it hard for Marianne to hear anything but consonants. She was saying something else about buns. More wood was needed if buns were to be made. There was wood on the beach. "We'll go in the car." There was a definitiveness in the way she said the word car.

"I carry everything in my car." The driver's seat was the only seat that had not been torn out. So Marianne sat on the floor with her legs stretched out, her feet under the glove compartment which had no door and into which Mrs. Snellen now placed her set of false teeth. "I'm more comortable with my teeth out. Don't need them for driving." The teeth were at Marianne's eye level. They grinned at her all the way to the beach.

Beside Marianne were two salt beef buckets for gathering the wood. The beach was pockmarked with evening shadows. There was plenty of driftwood. The thought of baking buns with it delighted Marianne. She felt like an outlaw. Why was nobody else on the beach collecting driftwood? All cracked and dry among the stones, sea and sky. A gull screeled out loud against the endless speech of the sea. Wind blew through your hair. When the pieces of driftwood thudded in your bucket, when the bucket got heavier, you felt good. You were gathering something useful, something to make fire.

They drove back. Mrs. Snellen took boxes out of her porch to make room for the driftwood. "Garbage," she said. Marianne could not tell the difference between what was in the boxes and the driftwood. She though of her friend Alana whose endless acquisition and discarding of clothes left Marianne mystified as to the difference between a find and a reject.

Mrs. Snellen got a fire going and mixed flour and raisins in a bowl. Baking powder. Sugar. Water. The fire roaring. In fifteen minutes the buns came out. Rhubarb jam and tea. The cup of tea was exciting. It disappeared behind all the steam. The air was cooler than in normal houses, where families lived, and where things lost their flavour. This tea smelled strong like tea poured outside, near a lake, when you were hungry. The soft, snuffly way Mrs. Snellen spoke became much softer and snufflier when she spoke with her mouth full of bun. She was talking about jam made from blueberries.

"I have a cabin at Pond Crossing." Pond Crossing was on the Gaff Topsails. Marianne's father had a hunting cabin there. It was deep in the barrens. There were no roads. You had to take the freight train. Marianne had never been. "For going berrypicking. I'll have to go soon to check everything's all right. I haven't been since the winter. Sometimes a cabin's roof falls in under all the snow. Now if I had someone to come with me. Mrs. Bennett might come, but she mightn't. She hasn't been to her cabin for two years, since her heart attack."

"I could come." Marianne could not resist. After the buns and driftwood she was ready for the freight train.

"I'll check with Mrs. Bennett. She might come with us. Come back next Friday."

Marianne went back next Friday after work.

"Yes Mrs. Bennett says she'll come. We'll leave the car by her place next Saturday morning." Mrs. Bennett lived in Marianne's hometown. Hell. The train stopped there. "She lives near the train station. You can sleep here next Friday night." Two men were patching Mrs. Snellen's stove. They were part of the team of men whom she'd got to build her little house for her. That was mysterious, but Marianne did not ask about it. One was fat and useless and the other was skinny and quick. Mrs. Snellen said they needed more patches. "We'll go," she told them, and she led Marianne out to the car. They drove around the corner and down Main Street, and they stopped in an alleyway next to the tinsmith's shop. Mrs. Snellen knew how to go in the back way that led down the steps to the basement where the tinsmith was working amid piles of sheet metal. He knew Mrs. Snellen and he knew what she wanted.

"Here you go Mrs. Snellen love, and there, and over there look." He pointed at scraps that were just the right size for her stove. They thanked him and took the load home. More buns and jam. The workmen hammered the stove. "Come sleep here on Friday night," Mrs. Snellen reminded her as she was leaving.

It was dark. Mrs. Snellen's house is the only one like it in Georgesville, Marianne thought. She passed bungalows with their violet pulsating windows. Bungalows whose clipped lawns grew a clandestine fraction under the stars. Bungalows and lawnmowers, thought Marianne. Finished basements and bank managers. At least the constellations were not modern. A sickle moon crept along the bungalow roofs sharp and perfect as a golden cat.

"Where've you been?" Claudia, laughing, baby on one hip, eating the baby's food out of a bowl on the counter, tasting it. "Been down at Mrs. Snellen's again? Oh yeah?" A knowing look. Not interested in hearing about it. Has baby, that's enough. Knows it all anyway. Slurp; mashed yam and tinned pear pulp. Almost too good for a baby. Later that night Mick comes home half drunk. Captain Morgan white rum. They have a fight about something he finds in the refrigerator.

"Claudia what is this shit?"

"It's a piece of raw turnip for her to chew on. It's good for them when they're teething."

"Has it been in her mouth?"

"She chews on it all day."

"Why don't you throw it out and give her a new piece? What's a chewed up piece of raw turnip doing in the refrigerator?"

Mick is an engineer with the town hall. He can't stand Claudia and she can't stand him. They aren't married. But they have Claudia's baby. What's in the fridge is one of their favourite subjects to fight about. One time Mick saw something black in one of his ice cubes. It was a black fly. Claudia had forgotten to tell him she had put it there. She had heard they lived on when you thawed them out. Could fly away again. This one lay in Mick's rum.

"Dead." He looked at it for a long time, as if it were Claudia and he would like it to be alive so he could really kill it. Sometimes Marianne found Mick and Claudia entertaining. But sometimes it wasn't much fun, lying on the blue flowered couch on the pink wooden floor of the basement after work, listening to them fighting and the baby screaming. She was glad when Friday evening came. She had a canvas bag of sandwiches and sardines, teabags and chocolate, apples and oranges. Fish hooks. Two thirty-five-cent lines from Arlim's; her dad said fishing was good at the Gaff. A penknife. Her harmonica. She went to Mrs. Snellen's playing *Eine Kleine Nachtmusik*.

"Dig worms," said Mrs. Snellen when she arrived. She gave her a tin and a shovel and pointed out to the back yard. "There, down past the rhubarb." There, under the pink sky that had one silver star glinting low near the horizon, the evening star, lay the Christmas tree from last year, rust red, tinsel glowing in the sunset. Lots of worms in the earth around the Christmas tree. Then buns and jam. Mrs. Snellen wasn't saying much. She was excited about tomorrow. She packed food in a Carnation Milk box. Buns. Margarine. Jam. Tins of beans. Corned beef. Evaporated milk. A box of firewood. You had to take your firewood with you.

Mr. Nelson had disappeared to a cot in the front room. "You sleep in there," Mrs. Snellen pointed to the back bedroom. It was only nine o'clock. But there was nothing else to do.

Marianne lay on her bed and played her harmonica. The room smelled musty. One tiny window looked over the back garden. She could see the two Irving Oil tanks in the distance, past banks of bungalow roofs. Two little stars glittered over the tanks. The sea lay beyond the tanks, but you couldn't see it. The blankets were where the mustiness was coming from. Mrs. Snellen was sleeping in the kitchen. The stove gave great cracks. Otherwise the house was silent. It's always nice being in someone else's house, Marianne thought, especially when they give you a room of your own, and you can rest; real, good rest, out of all the burdens of your own house, where all your possessions lie staring at you in full knowledge of how they got there. Sweet to breathe the mysterious scent of somebody else's blankets.

In the morning they packed the food and wood in the car and drove down the Hansen Highway that led to the Trans Canada. Mrs. Snellen's teeth faced Marianne. The highway was fifteen miles long. Ten minutes down the highway they stopped to fill two big plastic vinegar bottles with water from a clear spring, and to "have a lunch." Mrs. Snellen rifled the foodbox. Buns. Marianne thought of times she had travelled with her parents when she was a child. It seemed as if she had to be half dead with hunger before her father would pull over and her mother would dispense rations from the cooler. Evidently Mrs. Snellen found buns more important than just about everything.

At eleven o'clock they reached Mrs. Bennett's, a tall house with a staircase and yellow kitchen. They sat at the table where Harry, the red-faced and soft boarder, ate a lunch of caplin fried by Mrs. Bennett. Harry was what Claudia's Mick would call a ladies' man, not a man's man. He smelled like sandy, hard soap, and his fingers were like raw sausages.

Mrs. Bennett was like many of the women who lived in Hell. A pale small face with modern glasses, a perm in grey hair, ordinary clothes, neither thin nor fat; you never know how these women feel, deeply. When they meet you they know you quickly, and accept you. A lot of people pass them by, thinking they are insignificant. But they have seen it all, and they are pretty tough.

Mrs. Bennett's house stood near the tracks. Her husband had died in a CN accident years ago. She was a Railway Widow. She boiled the electric kettle and set out store-bought cookies while Harry ate his caplin, daintily tearing off the fins, peeling the backbones out slowly, away from the edible flanks of flesh. The cookies were squares of cardboard biscuit that had holes in it, with four domes of marshmallow on each square, and shredded coconut stuck to the marshmallow. Mrs. Snellen wouldn't eat them. Harry ate four. Mrs. Snellen brought her buns out, and she and Mrs. Bennett sat eating them and drinking tea. They talked, in the soft, snuffly way Marianne could not understand; the conversation of two seventy-year-old people with no teeth and mouths full of buns and tea.

"Whfl fwoothlfoof," said Mrs. Snellen.

"Frff wffl," said Mrs. Bennett.

The telephone rang. "It's Meggs, my sister's daughter," Mrs. Bennett told Marianne. "She works at Zellers with your mother. She wants to talk to you." Marianne had seen Meggs behind the counter. A big woman with red hair and big rings on all her fingers. They said she and her husband ignored each other and that she lived to buy rings and trips to her married children's homes in the

States. She had a cabin at the Gaff too. She was horrified that Marianne might be going to the cabin of Mrs. Snellen.

"Oh no my dear, hers is the worst one there. You've heard of Dogpatch? Dolly Brown? Well that's it." Marianne hadn't heard of Dogpatch or Dolly Brown. "You can stay in my cabin," said Meggs, "or at least stay in my aunt's."

The train was due at two thirty. By quarter past they were waiting by the track with their boxes, stamping their feet against the cold. A solitary flake of snow blew around in the clear wind. There was no shelter. Marianne leaned against the wall of the gypsum plant.

"There used to be boxcars here at the station," Mrs. Bennett said, "where you'd huddle to keep dry waiting for the train." Mrs. Bennett was pacing quietly in her winter coat, her purse and flashlight in one hand, a hammer in the other. She kicked at rocks every now and then. Once she wandered around the side of the gypsum plant and came back kicking a broom along the ground. When she got to where Mrs. Snellen stood, she laid her purse, flashlight and hammer on the ground, picked up the broom and examined it. It was disreputable. Mrs. Snellen thought it was a good broom. "Yes," Mrs. Bennett said, "I was thinking of you." But they left the broom. Too bad they had so much to carry.

The snow turned into pecks of rain. Two boys rode up on their bicycles and started doing wheelies. Christopher and George. George was beautiful, thought Marianne; pale with a coldsore, big-eyed and thin. The train came. The boys straddled over their bikes, watching. It was a big train with a friendly engine. The passenger car was behind the engine. The Gaffers had to battle every year with CN to keep it on. Then there came fifty freight cars. The engineer leaned out his window and greeted them. The conductor helped them on. The seats were red plush and the car was warm. A stove full of coal burned in the back corner. Marianne saw the boys staring through the window. When the train started, George raced it on his bicycle. When he disappeared, still pedaling, Marianne felt sad.

Mrs. Bennett pointed out where other Train Widows lived. She described the deaths of their husbands. They were all gory. The widows were getting old. One had died this past winter. Mrs. Bennett pointed her house out.

"Not dead?" Mrs. Snellen said dramatically.

"Dead and rotten," said Mrs. Bennett. And she pointed out houses that had the deceased's kin living in them, or that had been turned into apartments and rented to families, or been beautified with the RAP program.

"You haven't been in Port aux Basques for awhile Mrs. Bennett," the conductor called from a seat near the stove. That was where the track began.

"No," said Mrs. Bennett, "I haven't seen my boyfriend for a long time, not since before the winter."

"Mrs. Bennett has a lovely boyfriend," said Mrs. Snellen, "but he's old. He's not able to travel much to see her."

"He's dying," said Mrs. Bennett. She did not sound sad. "He has cancer."

"Ya, cancer," Mrs. Snellen agreed.

"I always loved him a lot more than my husband. I don't know why." Mrs. Bennett did not sound wistful. The train whistle sounded. It sank into Marianne's bones. It was an exciting sound. The rocking felt good. You could get to love trains. She moved near the stove. Conductor Bursey sat with his arm crooked over the back of his seat. He wore an expression of challenge. He was about sixty, with a red face. His hair was still dark. Marianne could tell he had reached his conclusions. People like him had a way of appearing in enclosed spaces from which you couldn't escape. She started to back away from the beautiful stove. That was another thing about these people; they were invariably guardians of something too wonderful for them to appreciate. It's too late, he seemed to say; I've challenged you. You can't back out.

"Where did you say you were going?"

"To Pond Crossing." She was pretending she liked him. She knew he would prey on this, and that she was embarking on a course that would mean she would have to acquiesce to more evil as time went on, until she could bear no more and would have to ignore him, whereupon he would feign anger and hurt and puzzlement.

"But where. With Mrs. Snellen?"

"Yes."

"You been there before?"

"No."

He laughed. His eyes bulged and stared at the scene he was imagining. "Well you don't know where you're going."

"My father has a cabin on the Gaff."

"You going there or Pond Crossing?"

"Pond Crossing."

"With Mrs. Snellen."

"And Mrs. Bennett."

"I'm telling you right now you'd better stay with Mrs. Bennett." If he had not been on the job he would have been drinking, and he would not have stopped. Marianne was glad he was sober. He fell into a contemplative silence. In half an hour he had exhausted the possibilities of his vision. He went to pick on Mrs. Snellen.

"This is more serious than I'd thought." Mrs. Snellen did not respond. "Bears have destroyed your camp." He looked back at Marianne. "That cabin is slated to be burnt." Back at Mrs. Snellen. "Your camp is a danger to wild animals." Marianne laughed. Mrs. Snellen had opened her food box and was enjoying a feed of buns and rhubarb jam. She had spread her red plush seat like a table.

Bursey stood in the engineer's doorway. "She has six children you know." His tone suggested that these six children had six sailors for fathers. "And she has a fortune." No satisfaction from Marianne. "Every fall she's up at her camp picking blueberries. And she won't get shot in a hunting accident. Because do you know what she wears when she's berrypicking?" This was his last try. "A Santa Claus suit." He talked to the engineer after that. His voice got lost under the noise of the train.

The Topsails are remote, deep in the interior, among the pond-studded barrens. It was dark when they arrived. Snow was falling, the flakes lit by the train lights. Cold feathers of snow slapped their faces. Bursey stabbed a red flare into the earth so they could see their way to the cabin. Red snowflakes. They were going to Mrs. Bennett's cabin after all. The train had passed Mrs. Snellen's three quarters of a mile down the track. The cabins were dark shapes. One was lit. From it came a young man with a flashlight. He wore a red lumber shirt and jeans. His head had been shaven. His name was Caleb Leblanc.

"You've got your hair cut," Mrs. Bennett said as she pried bent nails from her lock with her hammer. He laughed.

"You been here long?" Mrs. Snellen asked him.

"Since the first of May."

In the light Marianne could see he was one of the French Mi'kmaq the churchgoers in Hell called Jack-o'tars.

"And how long are you staying?" Mrs. Snellen asked.

"Until I can braid this." His hair. He laughed. His wife and two boys were up too. They lived in Hell all winter, near the tracks. In a beautiful house, Mrs. Snellen said.

Mrs. Bennett lit the kerosene lamp on the table. "It's not too bad." There was powdered milk everywhere. Something had been in and dragged the bag around.

"A rat," said Mrs. Snellen.

The four of them filled the cabin. Besides the table, there was a stove made from a tin drum, and, at the back, behind a partition, a bed. The top quilt was soaked, the others damp. Mrs. Bennett rolled the top one back and wedged it against the wall. Caleb and Mrs. Snellen lit the stove. The camp was so tiny you could feel the heat right away. Caleb rubbed his hands. He was handsome. "Well I'll go. If you need anything at all you know where we are okay?" He took his flashlight and went to his own camp.

Mrs. Snellen opened a tin of corned beef. She sliced hanks and ate them off her pocket knife. "Have a piece." Mrs. Bennett took a bun, cut it in half, and ate it without butter. Marianne stripped and got in bed. If you didn't move, your body warmed the air between itself and the damp quilt. She heard Mrs. Snellen and Mrs. Bennett talking beyond the partition as they undressed. They reminded her of bears.

"Did you ever see anyone with two brassieres on?" said Mrs. Bennett. "Ever since the heart attack a year ago next Monday. I can't risk just one bra. I'm bigger. The conductor noticed on the train." Then there was the sound of liquid sloshing. It was Mrs. Bennett shaking her vaginal douche, a mixture of water and vinegar in a plastic vinegar bottle. "You have to taste it, to test it." Mrs. Snellen watched her with incomprehension, eating buns in her nightdress. They both wore nightdresses. Mrs. Bennett got in bed first, so Mrs. Snellen was on the outside. Marianne was glad of that. They could hear snow sift against the roof, until Mrs. Snellen started snoring.

They woke up early. Mrs. Snellen was up first, eating buns and making tea. The cabin door was open. Marianne could see a lot of sky. She stepped out. The fragrant wind blew across her face. It smelled like wildflowers and clouds and lakes with trout in them. The barrens stretched out all around. She felt as if she were standing on top of a great big pie. The tracks stretched to the horizon.

They had to check out Mrs. Snellen's cabin now, because by noon they would have to be ready near the track with their bags packed, and a white flag on a stick. Marianne had almost forgotten they were here only to check the cabins, that this was Sunday, and she had to be back by Monday.

There were huge white boulders in the grasses. They had shadows over their western faces. Their eastern faces were lit. A crow arced above some stunted junipers. His blackness matched so precisely the intensity of the boulders' whiteness that Marianne knew they were mysteriously connected, boulder and crow. They passed Caleb's camp, where his boys were playing with a toy tractor in the dirt. Marianne wondered about his wife. Young, with two boys and a man, out here all spring, summer and fall. Trout, caribou and berries. Dry earth, lakes and flies. Who was she?

Mrs. Snellen's camp was on the other side of the tracks. She had brought the boards up on the train, a few at a time. Some were flamingo pink. The inside was dark because there was no window. There was a pair of dark bunk beds and a shelf, something to sit on, and a wooden crate for a table. To Marianne it didn't look much different from the cabin of Mrs. Bennett. She guessed the difference between Mrs. Snellen's cabin and the others had to it a history that culminated in the present; a present which even now was not fully revealed because it would not really arrive until the fall.

Mrs. Snellen did not do anything to her cabin. "I'll have to get more board," she said. She looked into the darkness for a few minutes, then turned around and went out. Marianne could not tell whether Mrs. Snellen thought her cabin needed serious repair or not. She could not see the cabin through Mrs. Snellen's eyes. They went back to Mrs. Bennett's cabin.

The flies were coming out. Mrs. Bennett found a green woolen hat to protect her head from them. "When the train comes," she said, folding her nightdress, "you have to be ready." She had brought a white dish towel. She found a flagpole in the woodpile. By quarter to twelve they were sitting at the track with their boxes and the flag. They ate buns and drank the last tea before they let the fire go out in the stove. Around one o'clock Caleb Leblanc came over and helped them to close it up.

"If you want to get away from the flies," he said, "you can come in our cabin." The flies were bad. It was hot. Caleb's wife opened her cabin door and emptied water out of a white dishpan. Marianne could see she had sleek, long hair. The doorway looked shady and inviting. Mrs. Snellen was the first to suggest they go in and wait for awhile. Mrs. Bennett told her to go on in.

"I'll wait here. In case the train comes." Mrs. Bennett sat on a boulder, the green hat pulled over her forehead, one hand snuggled around her waist, the other holding the front of her cardigan together. Marianne sat on a flat rock that had blueberry bushes scrabbling up the sides. Each star of leaves had captured a star-jewel of melted snow, and the jewels were shooting off needles of coloured light. Once you had noticed them you could see that the whole barrens was ablaze with needlefires of blueberry jewels. Jasper, lapis lazuli, chalcedony, emerald, sardonyx, cornelian, chrysolite, beryl, topaz, chrysoprase, turquoise, amethyst.

Mrs. Bennett stood up and poked stones with a stick. She started to walk up and down a segment of the track, singing. Her voice was lonely and sweet.

*There's a long, long trail a'winding
into the land of my dreams
where the nightingales are singing
in the white moonbeams*

*There's a long, long night of waiting
before my dreams all come true
for the night when I'll be going
down the long, long trail with you*

Mrs. Snellen was still in the Leblancs' cabin. The flies were getting worse.

"We could go in for a short spell," Mrs. Bennett said. "They might give us some of their Deet."

"You'll want Deet at the Gaff," Marianne's dad had said. No other kind of fly dope would do. "Only Deet and Deet alone." There had been no Deet at the Canadian Tire in Georgesville. She had known better than to buy any other kind.

The Leblancs had finished eating. Caleb's wife had cooked a big Sunday dinner. The leftovers lay everywhere in dishes and pots. A chicken, salt beef and cabbage, turnip and carrots, potatoes, a boiled raisin pudding, dressing and gravy. Mrs. Snellen stood in the corner with a green enamelled tin mug of tea. Nobody offered them any food. The two sons were playing with tractors on the floor. Caleb was cleaning small trout in a gallon bucket. He cut the gutfin off one trout and showed it to Marianne. You could use it for bait. If you had no worms. You only had to catch one trout and you could do that with a bare hook if you had to. After that you would always have bait. He said the place was crowded in the fall. Last fall he'd put orange ribbon around his buckets of berries so he could lay them in a boxcar. When he got aboard the train the boxcars were full of buckets tied with orange ribbon.

"I want to go home," Caleb's oldest son said. Everyone but Marianne ignored him. He concentrated on her. "I hate it here."

Caleb's wife folded clothes and filled the kerosene lamps. She was wearing moccasins with blue and white beadwork. She did not show any emotion. In the corner behind her were four shelves, and each shelf held five or six skulls, the size of skulls of snakes, or rats.

Caleb gave them some Deet. They would soon have to go outside again. The Leblancs were going fishing. Half an hour later the Leblanc family set out single file along the track toward the Chain Lakes. You could see all the way to the horizon, but you could not see any lakes. Beside the white flag

Marianne wondered how far they had to go, and she felt a mixture of deep respect and forlornness as she saw them grow smaller and darker against the sky. Now the three of them were really alone on the Gaff. Marianne tried fishing off the bridge a ways down the track. Nothing nibbled her dead worm. She tried a gutfin. A few nibbles. Around five o'clock the Leblancs had gone. Now it was six. Mrs. Bennett wound her watch. The sun glared on the line of telegraph poles along the track, some of the poles cut off at the bottom for firewood, the tops dangling from the wires. A few pieces of stretched cloud hung in the sky. A wind blew across the tundra flowers, spreading their pink perfume. Marianne could really feel the Gaff's alienness now. She hung on to the fact that the train was coming. In her pockets she could feel some coins. They became meaningless out here. Time was the same. Outside the idea of the train it had no real existence. Tonight stars would come out. And a wind would blow through the opened stars and the closed tundra flowers. The night would smell good. Leaves and twigs would scrape. The moon would spotlight crevices in the rocks for the eyes of no human.

At seven o'clock the three of them were pacing at different segments of the track. When the train comes, Marianne thought, it will be like a beloved animal, or even a person. She told Mrs. Bennett this when they got near each other.

"Yes my dear, that's just what it is like. A dear friend." Mrs. Bennett and Marianne paced side by side after that. At eight o'clock Mrs. Snellen caught up with them. She had something to say. She seemed to be talking to someone inside her head.

"It's strange. How strange. In the fall. To go back home and see no one with buckets. And the reason there's no one with buckets is because no one's picking any berries. That's the strange part that is. People all over the road, and in the stores, and not one of them has a bucket. Why do you think that is?"

"I don't know, my dear," said Mrs. Bennett. "I suppose some of them have other things they want to do."

They came up to a boulder alongside the track, a tall one, and Mrs. Snellen stopped beside it. The surface of the rock had creases similar to those in her coat, and planes on the stone and on her body held the last light in a way that glowed. "I don't see how anybody can stop picking," she said, "until there are no more berries. I don't see the sense of walking around the street with a handbag."

The boulder stood by her in a way that Mrs. Bennett and Marianne could not. "You can't put berries in a handbag," she told it. "Walking around empty handed, that's even worse." She kept near her boulder but the other two kept going. "You want to run up and put a bucket in their hands, but then you'd run out of buckets for yourself. I save every beef bucket I can get my hands on and those people don't care if they never save even one. The whole of Georgesville walking around in the fall with no bucket anywhere. That's the strange part, that is."

French Doors

The taste of partridgeberry jam has bogs and marshes in it behind the sharp taste of fruit. It has the same taste as Newfoundland air that has collected scents from its travels; caribou moss, red blueberry leaves, black ponds, trout and peat moss. Moose and ducks, boulders and juniper. You get that taste in the fall.

There were meadows and thick trees near the shore in Aspel Harbour, but close behind the trees lay the wild barren land where sticks cracked underfoot and fireweed petals lay fallen in the rock crevices, their perfume smelled by no one. Marianne had to wear her red lumbershirt if she wanted to walk to Spur Cove Pond, because all the men were in the woods hunting partridge and moose. The decaying leaves smelled sweet and thick, and the red maple leaves battled the blue sky, the scarlet and yellow-blue grating against each other. Marianne loved the wild smell of the woods and marshes, but she hated it as well, especially the marshes. Once the trees thinned you were in an unfriendly place. You had to know how to be at home there, and Marianne did not. A desire in her soul rebelled against the barrens. She could understand the desert better than this. Here the dry, grey sticks scraped her ankles. White scrapes with blood showing through some of them. The sky blared down a merciless blue with smug puffballs of white cloud in it, and the Indian tea plant with its clothy white blooms and its evil orange furze on the leaves' pointy undersides gave off a sharp, medicinal odour that shrouded every pond.

Women didn't go in the barrens, except to pick a few berries. Mrs. Halloran had told her that at one time the women would be in to the ponds every evening with their bamboos for trout. She said all one summer she had gone in with Mary and Martha and they'd been pregnant, and Mrs. Halloran had had to keep climbing up in the trees to untangle their hooks. But the women of Marianne's generation did not go outdoors. They stayed in, looking after their babies and watching the soap operas, or some of them got in their cars and went to work in the Fox Cove drugstore, the fish plant, or the new communications centre that took signals from aircraft and big vessels far offshore.

Only men went in the wild places now, and they were no company for Marianne. They had no interest in a woman from town who walked in the woods, looking at reflections in the ponds and picking bunches of leaves. They went in with their guns and rabbit dogs, their packs of Export A, and their half-dozens of Dominion. They never directed the slightest sexual energy at her either, so she figured they thought she was good for nothing, or crazy. Marianne thought something had dulled their fire. They should have been full of that fire you could taste in the partridgeberries because they came from the same earth. But they weren't. She didn't know why, unless it was the beer, and the cigarettes, the ten months of unemployment insurance every year, and the fish getting smaller and scarcer the other two months as the years passed. Then there was *Three's Company* and *The Price is Right*, and the soaps. She knew that big unmarried men watched the soaps in their mothers' houses. TV was always on in every saltbox house, eroding the big soul in each inhabitant of the shore. All the days long the soul of the earth called out through the voices of the trees speaking in the hills, while the peat-and-needles-scented breath of the earth stole through the woods. The sea, with the islands in it and the stars over it in the night, was more of the soul that the people had lost. Everyone was timid under the majesty of creation here, Marianne thought. It was as if they had been created by a wizened, meaner god than the god of whom the psalmist had proclaimed, "in his hand are all the corners of the earth: and the strength of the hills is his also. The sea is his, and he made it: and his hands prepared the dry land."

That the wizened god was mean, Marianne could tell by the way he had instilled in everyone the malady of bondage to caution. There was a connection that nobody was making, she thought, and that was the connection between their own souls and the big soul of creation. There should have been an artery through which the same blood could pass between the islands and the people; between the people and the stars; between the people and the stars' creator – who should have been their creator, but apparently was not.

But there was one man in the cove who had star-blood in him, and he was called Larry. He looked like the other men, but he had different thoughts. Everyone said his trouble was that that was all he did; think. He hunted and fished and all the rest of it, but there was no sign of him buying any lumber and getting out of his mother's house to build a place of his own, and he was thirty-seven. He was a real philosopher, they said, and they laughed behind mugs of tea.

Larry was pretty quiet, except when he went on the beer, and then he would cruise along the shore in his truck and torment girls who were walking in twos to the store for a tin of baking powder or a pack of Export A. He would roll his window down and talk to them and tease them until they'd be ready to cry; he didn't know when to stop when he was drunk, just like any of the men. He would keep his headlights on low beam so the girls were always in the spotlight, and he would inch along after them, keeping up a continual banter of good will and innocent intention mixed with an evil persistence, cigarette smoke, and the yeasty smell of his breath. He wore a Greek fisherman's cap, and he always swore he was innocent of everything.

On these fall nights Marianne used to walk south along the road, away from Mrs. Ruby's house and Spur Cove, towards South Bight. The road ended in South Bight; from it ran a trail up into the woods and towards LaManche, which had been abandoned during resettlement after a tidal wave had damaged half the dwellings. Years ago the women of Aspel Harbour had ridden every Sunday from the church in Fox Cove to LaManche on white horses, through the woods and across the swinging bridge. LaManche had been their home. Now all that was left was part of the bridge strung across the ravine, dilapidated but still graceful and lacy.

But South Bight was as far as Marianne usually walked at night. She passed South Bight Pond that lay alongside the road, and she passed a droke of blue trees that spoke to a dark mountain on the road's seaward side. She turned where the road ended and walked down through the white fish shed and onto the South Bight wharf. The wharf was covered by a wooden canopy and had twelve fishing boats tied by green and yellow ropes to its posts. At South Bight you could still see the islands. There were shoals between the islands and shore there, so on a day of heavy seas big geysers would spout up from the ocean. If there was moonlight they were lit up like fireworks.

Now Marianne stood at the wharf's end looking at the Pleiades and the Dog Star. She was searching for Orion, whom she had not yet seen after his summer dissolved in the day skies. A big moon hung. Near her feet on the wharf planks lay seven silver codfish, moonlit, their gills open black, each eye like an olive slice. A fisherman had thrown them down and they had landed in the shape of a sun wheel, heads pointing towards a centre and tails fanning out in a shining circle of rays. She could imagine the slapping noises they had made as they had hit the planks. Near the fish rested a collection of hot-pink buoys, glowing from within under the moon's influence. Marianne beat them like drums; they had a musical "ping" sound within their other hollow sound.

As the water moved under the boats, the taut ropes creaked around their tying-posts. Marianne could smell the dead fish, and she could smell the sea, and the turpentine in the trees on the dark mountain. In the black water that slapped the wharf-head swam spirals of fluorescence, fiery as neon. Mysterious, they appeared and disappeared, silently. Along the horizon moved a ship, harmonious as a bar of Mozart, her soft lights fizzing like drizzle on Marianne's eyes. When she had finished gazing she turned back along the wharf to go home. A truck with its headlights off loomed at the other end. Closer, she could see Larry's lit cigarette end and Larry's elbow resting out the driver's window.

"'Lo Marian." All the men shortened the anne. "What are you at?" He had a beer in the other hand but he wasn't drunk.

She told him the truth. "Looking at the night-sparkles."

"I can understand that. I can well understand that." He took a swig of his beer. "Listen Mar, would you go to a wedding with me on the eighth of October?"

"No."

"Why?" He was laughing.

"Because you're always drunk."

"Get away girl I'm not drunk now. Come and sit in here and look at the moon on the water. Get out of the cold. Then I'll drive you home. Get in, it's cold."

It was. She got in the truck and they sat and watched the moon sparkling on the water, the dark islands, the stars and the creaking tied-on boats, in silence. Larry smoked. She took one of his beers. He turned the heater on. The moon poured gold oil on the ocean. Fir and spruce tree points rose up the hillside against the gold and black water, then against the indigo and rhinestone sky. Larry pointed his beer bottle at the moon path.

"Do you see that?"

"Yes." She thought he meant the light on the water generally. But he meant something more specific.

"No but do you see that . . . not the main part of the path of light but the edges of it! Good god, look at the edges . . . do you see that?"

When you looked at the edges of the moon-path you saw that there were sparks flying off the main path – they clung like drops of condensation to the path's edge as long as they could, travelling, sliding up, and then they clung no longer but shot out like great sparks and flung themselves halfway across the ocean.

"Yes, I see it."
"Do you really?"
"The sparks."
"Yes. You can see it then." He smoked and watched. They were silent together for a long time. Their communion thrilled her. The silence of it. He had to turn the heater off and on to save the batteries. The warm blasts were luxurious. Finally he turned on the ignition. It was past one o'clock. He drove past her house and around the wharf down at Spur Cove, just so they could see the moon-path from there, but then he drove her home. He had to get up at six o'clock. He had a temporary construction job on the road outside Witless Bay.

Marianne had never seen much of Larry's mother. Once she had met her coming out of the woods with a pan of blueberries. She was small, with soft, powdery wrinkles that smelled good. She was stuffed up with the flu, and her hands were stained with berry juice, the cracks in the skin purply black. "The berries are soft," she said. "The frost got into them last night. Are they ever sweet now." Her lips and tongue were blue. Another time Marianne had gone over to her house with Mrs. Halloran. She had made seventeen kinds of cookies and arranged them on a Royal Albert plate. Her woodstove top was rubbed bright silver, and inset in the kitchen wall was a statuette of the Virgin Mary wreathed in plastic foliage and strung with soft pink lights. Her tablecloth had been embroidered and hemmed in hand-worked lace. Her own name was Mary. There had been no sign of Larry in the house whatsoever.

A few days after the moonlit night Marianne heard that Larry had moved out of his mother's house. He was fixing up the shed in the back meadow and was living in that. He came over to her place on a Friday evening to ask her if he could have the broken kitchen chair that was lying in the long grass by the side of her house.

"I could haul the legs off it and set it on a crate." He was snuffling with the flu.

"I'll walk over with you," she said.

The shed was made of pressboard.

"Where did you get the doors?" They were a pale, shell-pink and they opened from the centre with two cut glass handles, like French doors.

"I got them at the dump." He twisted the cap off a bottle of Dominion and stood in the middle of the floor until she sat down.

"They're nice." She chose a torn leatherette seat that had been ripped out of a truck and set on a couple of old tires. He sat on an upturned crate. There was a normal kitchen chair beside the window. The chairs formed a semicircle. In front of them stood an ornate black stove whose doors reached out in an open embrace. The stove had leaves, moons and flowers scrolled in the corners, and from its top front corners two iron gargoyles glared magnificently at Marianne. The stove was empty. They sat in front of it, their hands in their laps, swinging their crossed legs as meditatively as if slow-pulsed embers were cracking and glowing and loving them with warmth. Through the cracked window Marianne could see pink fingers soaking through the pale blue above Great Island. A star soaked through and hung glittering. The island had lit emerald mounds and shaded hollows like a velvet garment on the floor.

"You have a beautiful view."

"Yeah."

"How come you moved out here Larry?"

He drank some beer. "My mother boy. She was driving me crazy." A red bird landed on an alder outside the window. On his head perched a flat speckled cap like a liquorice allsort, the kind coated in tiny blue beads. He let out a vengeful trill of rolled Rs, then shook out his wing-ends like a crone settling down to her tea and sweet bun at a church bazaar. Up came the fat moon like a pound of butter.

Larry hunched forward, clutching his beer, elbows on his knees, gazing into the empty stove. The stove was no good, he told her. It smoked. He'd got it out of Tom Silver's shed. Whoever had dumped it there had done the right thing. Nevertheless, he remained enthusiastic about his shed. There was a current moving through his body even when he was sitting. He sat with his shoulders forward, his feet tapping. Every now and then he adjusted his cap. The shed was his project, and it excited him like an eighty-thousand-dollar pale-blue bungalow in the Pinehaven Meadows Estates outside town would have excited Mrs. Halloran. When the sky darkened around the moon he stood and pulled a chain on the ceiling, and a bulb came on. He had connected his shed to an outlet in his mother's house. The bulb was screwed into a lampstand made out of fancy red glass which Larry had hung upside down from the ceiling. Marianne laughed. He said it was a ruby chandelier.

The window darkened and the silence of the night roared in their throats and ears like air in winkle shells. Marianne thought of all the pursuits in which people involved themselves; all the things they wanted, and the beauty they wanted to attract to themselves. Here was beauty all around Larry, in the stillness, in the simplicity here.

That was true, she thought, if he was satisfied. She wondered if he was.

"I'm going home now."

"All right. Don't talk to any bears."

Wisdom, thought Marianne. Wisdom kept eluding her. Foolishness seemed like wisdom to her in so many places. She had closed the French doors and was taking the path that lay under Larry's mother's kitchen window. The light was shining through frilled cotton curtains patterned with tiny brown salt shakers, salad forks, cookie jars and daisies. Larry's mother must be behind them, she thought, rocking in her chair by the stove where she has laid a covered plate of fresh meat stew and a partridgeberry tart for Larry, knitting him a pair of grey socks, thinking of him out there in the woodshed that everyone is talking about, and feeling ashamed.

The Tree

Marianne was waiting for Ruby's bus to come and take her down the shore. The air above the warm sidewalk smelled of sugar and coconut from Woolworths' bakery. Marianne was sucking licorice mint toffees. She had four ounces in a paper bag. They were exactly the same toffees her grandmother had always bought at Woolworths and today Marianne had seen them for the first time in over twenty years. In the sun people were tripping over the pigeons that lazed about like cats. The pigeon colours were rich; raspberry claws, oil-slick purple and turquoise throats, and eyes the colour of brown beer bottles in the sun. A pair of girls skipped past wearing identical eyeshadow the colour of orange butterflies, as if each had taken an orange butterfly, torn it in two, and pasted the halves to her eyelids.

The Woolworths end of Water Street was full of old women with white handbags and old men in Salvation Army trousers, fat people in cheap summer clothes that showed their dimply-white shoulders and stomachs, and lots of mothers with baby strollers. The expensive stores were at the east end where the cathedral spires and whispering maples and laburnum were.

An old woman walked past with her granddaughter. The woman wore a Spanish scarf, black with yellow roses on it and silver threads sparkling through it. Marianne imagined that the child loved it. Children didn't know scarves like that cost three dollars at the one-two-three-dollar store across the road, where the manager wore a golden crab with red eyes on a chain around his neck. Children thought old people were magic; old women smelled of soap and powder and they always had candy. Across the road one funny one went by; she wore a fuzzy soft dome of a hat that looked like the hats personified bees wore in nursery rhyme books except that this hat was striped vertically; black and wasp-fawn. The woman was a real live pixie with little chocolate legs. Everyone crowded around her looked shockingly drab and ordinary. Behind her an old woman laboured along with a stick, another little girl skipping beside her. Old people didn't seem like invalids to children, Marianne remembered. They knew secrets and stories about Olden Days. And if they walked slowly it was only because that was part of their magic power, their oldness, and their voices that crackled like silver paper.

There was a tree in a backyard along the street. The yard was among the last cluster of wooden houses left in the district. The rest had been torn down in the last five years, and a big hotel sparkled above the little slum with its lines of washing and its unpainted fences. Marianne had noticed the tree one spring day because the new leaves had had light shining in them and were incandescent green against the black-pudding and tinned spinach-coloured houses. She had sat on the fire-escape steps of the black-pudding house and had gazed at the tree glowing with life, and had wept. She had wept over its beauty, and because someone was surely going to chop it down soon.

A whole cosmos of life flickered around the tree; spokes of dandelions springing out of the ground, curtain-ends whipping under the open window sashes, a black cat with yellow eyes upon a crumbling step. The whole collection; houses, yards, tree, took up less than a city block and was so against the new buildings nearby that anyone could see it was about to be replaced one day with rubble and cranes, then with something big for rich people.

The bus was late. Marianne went inside and called Triple Ace Taxi on Woolworths' payphone. Ruby's bus operated from the taxi stand. Yes, Ruby was running late, the guy on the other end confirmed. She recognized his lazy drawl. Once she had waited for the bus at the stand and he had been taking calls and radioing drivers. He had had a carnation between his teeth. His jacket was the very dark blue cheap kind of denim with white stitching, and his hair was Brylcreemed. He was sinewy and brown. The carnation was red. Marianne thought perhaps a woman had given it to him. The flower had transformed the taxi stand.

Ruby would be in front of Woolworths in another hour. Marianne knew it was no use getting impatient. The shore bus went when it went. She went to the cafeteria.

Half the cafeteria was roped off – the orange plastic boothed half, the old half. In the new half the booths were done in what some company had called heritage colours; dusty rose and teal blue. New white-coated managers bustled behind the steam-line ordering the women workers about and maintaining special watch over a new salad bar. On the pillars hung signs that said ABSOLUTELY NO LOITERING. The changes had happened since the last time Marianne had come here, which was about two months before. The salad bar astonished her. Always there had been the same things here; steak sandwich platter, club sandwich platter, fish and chip platter, apple dumplings and strawberry shortcakes, a hot water tank with teabags and instant coffee nearby. Now pots of fresh brewed coffee steamed on a gleaming machine. The salad bar displayed raw baby carrots and broccoli spears, romaine lettuce on ice-chips, and spiral pasta in oil and parsley. There was potato salad and macaroni salad too, and it was these Marianne saw two women spooning onto plates. They did not want to eat raw vegetables.

Behind the steam-line the men in white kept explaining new instructions about tongs and serving sizes and time saving to the serving girls, who were beside themselves with bitten-back fury. They used to be able to slouch against the wall holding their spatulas behind their backs while talking casually to each other, and they could be impatient with slow customers if they wanted. Now they wore green caps and placed metal covers on the dishes of food before handing them to the customers. And it was the same old customers, enjoying the new things as if someone had initiated them for their benefit, instead of to attract better customers. They were the same customers Woolworths had had for years; old dry men in hats with brims and feathers, women with brooches and coats that had fake lambswool collars and big flat buttons.

Marianne saw two young women come in. They had lioness manes like women in shampoo commercials and their waists were slim. Each wore a navy trench coat and carried a navy bag. Marianne thought they looked like flight attendants and that they would pick out vegetables from the salad bar, to the whitecoat managers' relief. She wondered how they had heard about the new Woolworths. But they chose chicken and chips and the club sandwich platter, and they both had gravy on their french fries and ate everything on their plates, so Marianne thought maybe they were from here after all, and maybe they weren't flight attendants. But how were they thin?

A rickety-legged woman in an orange striped shirt and black fur tam sat near Marianne and started eating a seven-inch-high wedge of cake made of layers of cream and orange jello with green things suspended in it. Marianne could see no sign on the woman's face that it was unusual for her to eat such a thing.

Then Marianne saw someone she knew; Sandro Maher, an artist who was always alone. He was only in his fifties but he had bone-white hair and weighed-down blue eyes. Marianne had talked to him before in the Bluebird Café, in the Plaza burger pit at the mall, and here. Sandro was always carrying a copy of the Bible or the Upanishads or a volume of eighteenth-century literature, and he always spoke his lonesome mind. She knew she must greet him or he would sit alone. Once he was invited he would be friendly. He sat down with her.

Once Marianne had stood for an hour in front of one of Sandro's paintings in a gallery. *Sailing on Quidi Vidi Lake.* Ever afterwards she had remembered it as shell-coloured wisps of sails, pale pinks and golds and faint blue over pearl-coloured water. Much later she had seen the painting again and was amazed to see there was only one sailboat. Sandro was enchanted, full of light tinged with the sadness of being alone.

"They're doing a lot of changes to this place," she said to him. He had bought tea and a roll, and was taking a green apple and some dried figs out of a bag. He said people didn't know how to eat; they didn't look after themselves.

"Yes," he said in his soft voice. "Would you like a fig Marianne?" His face was transparent, the eyes trusting and levelled at you yet somehow preoccupied with a sad inner wisdom, like a baby's eyes.

She took a fig and chewed it. Leathery skin and then your teeth sink into the dark sweet part, tiny seeds crackling. "They want us to go home and make room for someone else."

"Yes, they do." He was mournful. He wore a suit, as usual. Marianne thought this gave him some protection from the slightly contemptuous scrutiny people gave someone who was always alone downtown. "But you know, Marianne, they don't realize who is spending money." He bit a piece off a fig, rested his hand on the table and stared into the air. Then he gestured softly with the rest of the fig. "They think it's the rich. But it isn't the rich. It's the poor." As he said this he kept looking into the air, as if he was picturing the poor. He pitied them and he was, at the same time, one of them himself. "It says in the Bible," he said finally, "that the poor are blessed. Theirs is the kingdom of heaven. This place is like the kingdom of heaven. It belongs to the poor. For a little while longer at least." A band of newspaper sellers had come in carrying their sooty *Telegram* bags slung wrinkled over their shoulders. They sat drinking tea and counting their money. A woman sat down with her three-year-old son. She had soup and he had french fries and was crying because he had burnt his mouth. So she floated some french fries in her glass of water to cool them off for him.

Marianne said goodbye and went out to wait for the bus again. It came in ten minutes, with its sliding door and smoked windows. Calvin Ruby had bought it the year before after ten years of going up and down the shore in a yellow minibus that doubled as the Witless Bay school bus. The engine of this new bus sounded smooth and perfect.

The Tree

On the way to the arterial route Ruby would pass the little slum. Marianne watched for it. Even through the smoked windows the tree was lit from within, like green flame. The hotel glinted impassively behind the dwellings. Someone in the slum had hung two men's shirts and a pink baby's blanket on a line strung across a fire escape. Then it was green boxcars in sunlit rows as the bus passed the railyard.

The Incinerator Times

We have the only apartment in Dollarton back of the Spur. I sit on the step hidden behind a tree with the guitar I found at Vardy's Not-So-Antiques. A pretty good Yamaha. I filled the BB hole in its back with plastic wood. I swear the only people who walk past are the guys from the so-called old age home and Linda Naylor the writer. I like her because she let me go skating on the pond with her last winter but I don't go up there any more because my mother says when a woman's got kids you shouldn't bother her. My mother works at the old age home (Dollarton euphemism for mental halfway house) and my stepfather is home like me. He worked there too but one of them had to get laid off, and I'm home figuring out my next move after a year in journalism at Nate Boone College. If there was any point to my going back I would, but you can see just by looking at our local weekly newspaper, *The Coast Line*, that there would be no point at all.

It occurs to me as I pick out *Back in Judy's Jungle* and flip through Kurt Cobain's journals that I could start a pretty good alternative newspaper right here without going back to school, but what would, again, be the point, since no one would read it, much less advertise in it. I could get Patrick to advertise golf balls or Devon Davison to advertise babysitting, that's about it. I've thought about it a lot, actually. When your mother moves you someplace like this even as young as kindergarten, you're always enough of an outsider to study the obvious. I'd make it biweekly to start, and have each issue about what really goes on in one or another hot spot around here. Name it after the first issue, which would be about the incinerator at our dump. I'd call it *The Incinerator Times* and crack some kind of joke in the first editorial about how each issue will be a burning one. I'd do the next one about what goes on in the parking lot outside Murphy's chip wagon. Wait till the third one to cover the ledge under Naigle's bridge where Tony died. I've already done enough silent research on that to write a couple hundred pages, since he was my best friend. I'd use the first two issues to show how it's no surprise to have anyone die around here, that the bridge isn't the half of it. I could do an issue from this hidden step back of the Spur about each person who comes out of there Friday nights. But I'd do the dump issue first.

You'd figure a dump with a rusted out teepee incinerator would be the last place half the kids in town would be allowed to hang out, I mean little kids nine and younger. Bill Sevier's supposed to drive anyone out who shouldn't be there, but he attracts them. Kids from Harbour Duffet get their parents to drop them off at the bridge corner so they can sneak up and get family packs of red Niblets and Juicy Fruit and Glossettes that the truck dumps off at the shack after they expire in Maddy's Convenience. Every kid in Dollarton can tell you Bill's shack has cushion floor with oranges and lemons on it, a card table, plastic tablecloth with brown trains and watermelons, cards with a naked brown-haired woman on the back and homemade crib board. Frying pan, hotplate and jug for vodka and grapefruit juice Bill says is real crystal. He gets a lot of cans of expired grapefruit juice. Outside are a bunch of mangy cats living off baby rats and garbage that doesn't fall in the pit. That's where Vince Power the town manager puts the teddy bears and baby's breath the week after everyone ties them with ribbons to the bridge. Where the cats hang out among sodden hamburger buns and washing machine parts. Vince doesn't have the sense to burn the stuff so I do it. The first time I picked it up there was last year's bears and flowers underneath – Tony's little heap in the exact same place. Dollarton has a seven year plan for getting rid of the incinerator and becoming a green town. If you gave it enough thought you could find a way in all that time to ease the whole town in the fire before the pit closes, like turning a shirt inside out through one of its sleeves.

The oldest biggest dump cat is a grey one that used to be white, with its tail cut off. These cats look at you as if they don't trust you, and Sevier looks at you the same way himself.

His own house on Sevier's Road is decorated with things he got at the dump; half a rear-end of a Chevy pickup rigged up to a hydraulic pump, three spruce sticks with something stuck on each; a mannequin head from Cleary's Jeans 'n' Things, a plastic Christmas tree with fake snow on it, and an airplane.

The reason Bill Sevier looks like he doesn't trust you is that he already lost his job once when Sean Halfyard's mother reported people were paying him in Black Horse instead of mailing their dump fees to the Town. He got drunk on the job according to Mrs. Halfyard but he put in a grievance and was reinstated. He told Brandon Hynes, who's five, he would've been all right if he'd brought the beer home or had it delivered anywhere but the shack. Five years old, that's what I mean. I wouldn't mind if he'd told Warren Hynes instead of Brandon because I could get Warren to do a special freelance report on the whole thing. While he was at it he could write one on their oldest brother Tyler Hynes. The dump's Tyler's warehouse. He moved out of his mother's house after I quit college. She said she couldn't stand another minute of him home now, let alone through the winter. People around here tend to start dreading winter in July. The old man gave him a bit of land behind the Town artesian well and Tyler built a shack he says is a garage so he won't have to get a permit for a dwelling. He gets everything at the dump. Real plywood, no particle board which he says is asking for a mess of carpenters. He says they suck the alcohol in the glue binding the chips together, besides the fact that particle board is for losers. Cement blocks, two-by-fours never used. He made his bed out of two sawhorses, three of Bill Walsh's election signs and a Sears mattress. Irish linen sheets and a comforter he's going to take the stuffing out of and replace with feathers after he shoots a few endangered eiders. All from the dump except the ducks. The only thing holding him up from finishing it by Christmas is that he keeps having to take everything out of it and hiding it half a mile in the woods when the town inspectors come around, which they do because the nuns on the main road keep hearing guns. Tyler says he's going to visit the nuns and give them something that'll make them stop complaining. He keeps Vanilla Coke and cans of picnic shoulder in the brook and has an outhouse made of stolen culvert camouflaged with juniper and old man's beard. He says the juniper doubles as his air freshener. What the nuns are hearing isn't Tyler, it's everyone else in town doing target practice. It's one of those cases where the person you think is the culprit isn't, in spite of other things he's doing. I told him about my alternative newspaper idea and he gave me my first letter to the editor. This is it:

Dear Editor,
I heard you were doing a piece on what it's like to fall in the burning pit. If Wayne Skaines wanted to make a lot of money he could. You wouldn't need to be in the pit any longer than he was if you knew how to get out. He could catch thirty pounds of dope a month when the RCMP unload it. That's if he went there at the right times, which I could tell him if he wants to know. The pharmacy also has a lot of pills they throw down there. All he has to do is ask me and we can work something out since I wouldn't want to go down in the pit myself but I have at least the knowledge to put two and two together.
Signed, you can give him my name but don't put it in the paper,
Dollarton

I'd have to do a follow-up story on Wayne Skaines falling into the incinerator. *The Coast Line* did a six-line piece the week it happened. It read like the parish hall tea. Instead of silver trays there was the rusted but serviceable teepee. The flames were the kind of flames that might heat turkey soup just right. The last line told what the town has in place to keep people safe like it was advanced equipment, not a hook on a pulley that no one ever uses and a sign saying *Children Must Stay Within Vehicle*, as if every kid in Dollarton wasn't chewing Niblets on the shack step.

I'LL INTERVIEW WAYNE over hot dogs in his kitchen. He eats his hot dog in one bite. He just painted the cupboards. They're always painting the cupboards and kitchen walls. It gives the inside of their house a creamy shiny look when you walk in, but it doesn't mask the fact that Wayne only went to grade two and the living room is full of mauled Barbies and the TV is never off. Cheryl eats her wiener skin then mashes the inside with a fork over her bun as her dad talks. He'll say he doesn't use safety belts anywhere. Not even on high steel jobs five hundred feet over Brampton. "They calls me Catwalker." On his left arm are two ghouls made with Cheryl's cartridge pen and a safety pin. Supposedly cat skulls. He got his wife Lynn to draw the second one since the first one had ears and Lynn told him you wouldn't show ears on a skull. Lynn finished grade nine and has two years down at the computer school, but all she can get is volunteer jobs with Dollarton Elementary library.

Incinerator Times: So what happened?

Wayne Skaines: I was lined up behind Brendan Pumphrey and the last thing he had was his Christmas tree, that's from six months ago so you can imagine how that'd flare up. It hooked on the ledge and I tripped on it and fell in, but in a way it's a good thing. If he'd've thrown it all the way in and I'd had to fall I wouldn't be talking to you now.

IT: If he'd thrown it all the way in you wouldn't have fallen over it.

WS: I'm just saying it's fortunate the tree stayed topside.

IT: What saved you?

WS: There was this one area not burning at all, and that's where I landed after I slid over the flames.

IT: Your clothes didn't catch?

WS: I had the sense to haul off my shirt. What saved me was that spot that had no flames, just gravel. It gave me forty-seven seconds to find where the metal had rusted. One spot with day shining in big enough to scrape out. Bill Sevier had the tin and rivets to patch it in his shack these last six weeks. If he'd've got around to it I'd've never walked out.

This is where I wouldn't ask him something stupid from my journalism course, like, "What ran through your mind?" For him to answer, "You mean did I see the face of god or anything? No. I was looking and scraping. I don't think you see god till you start burning." First Year Reporting Strategies: Interview old people. Find out Wayne's the seventeenth one who's fallen in. Find out something about each one to make you care about them.

Make you care about Tony too, though he could have been any of us. Okay I'll tell you telling details about any of us. You pick the one who least deserves to die. One takes his dog to piano lessons. Every Monday at eight fifteen the dog sits in on the lesson and learns dog percussion. They were working on an original composition called *Beef Jerky*. Or one skipped off calculus so he could stay alone in the guys' washroom downstairs, the one with a corner mirror, looking at the infinite line he called "unstoppable mes." Or one is Ezekiel's friend, guy from the home, and has found out Ezekiel makes crows talk. Does he teach them or just inspire them because he looks like a talking crow himself? This is the question he was figuring out last time I saw him. One can beat any of us at chess, and has a chess set he made out of things he picked up off the ground in Dollarton. King's a rusted tie from the railbed. Queen's a partridge feather. Bishops are bleached tampon applicators from the beach. One who failed grade nine twice majors in Classics on his own at home and has spent every cent that passed his way over the last seventeen years on books about Mesopotamia.

AFTER WAYNE SKAINES I'd insert a weekly contest, a crossword or something. Incinerator word puzzle. Anagrams made from names of chemicals the pit spews out. Ten across: What Michelangelo did when he wasn't breathing in polychlorinated biphenyls. Answer: Paint sleepy holy born child. I could have a billion dollar chicken meal deal prize and never have to worry about anyone winning it. Not that an alternative newspaper has to be bitter.

A FAMILY STORY. An incinerator love story. Mrs. Leona Snook. *The Coast Line* would call her Mrs. Harold Snook. A woman you wouldn't think had anything to do with the dump. She says if it weren't for the Dollarton Incinerator she and Harold would never go out, would not have got married in the first place.

Leona: He had to stop in there on our first date to dump a load of shingles from the henhouse. We had to wait half an hour in line so we had a chance to get talking more than if we had gone straight to see *Final Assassination*. I liked him except for the fumes. Though maybe when I look back on it now it's that he seemed all right compared to the fumes.

Now they have three children and Harold visits the dump to pay their babysitter.

"Our babysitter has a picture frame shop. He likes getting paid in old pine or cedar boards. When the golf course changed their fence Harold got enough cedar for us to go to St. Pierre for the weekend. He always longed to go to St. Pierre like he did when he was young. I had a friend who went to St. Pierre and ate green beans in a bistro and brought me back a tiny bottle of French perfume called *Subconscient*. Harold would have told me that what he used to do was rent a scooter and buy French wine and drink it at the St. Pierre dump, if I'd asked him. He'd have explained what he likes about French wine is how cheap it is. When we got there he was sad you can't rent scooters any more. We visited the graveyard instead. They have tombs, not graves like ours. It gave me the creeps but he said it was pretty similar to the dump. There were some small, pretty streets but Harold is not going to go in search of a bistro or a perfume store from back in time."

AFTER ROMANCE I'd have a story on target practice. Once Bill Sevier goes home for the night you might expect Dollarton Incinerator to be deserted, but such is not the case. On Tuesday and Thursday evenings Devon Davison, his mother Sarah, father Bruce and sister Shyla buy a Family Feed Pack at the Chicken Barn, take it to the dump and eat it with the van lights off.

Devon says they started out by shooting from the back window of their house near the dump's east side. "I got a lot of rats just by leaning over my homework table. Mom used the kitchen window. She had to lean over the corner of the stove and said she couldn't get a good shot. Going out was her idea. Dad wasn't fussy about it. There's that little difference between chicken bones and rat bones it makes him nervous. Mom is a serious hunter. She's taking something out on those rats."

YOU COULD PUT A POEM in here about small town life. I might commission it from Ezekiel at the home. Also a free babysitting ad for Devon Davison in order to get more details out of him. "You'd be surprised who else you'll find at target practice. Venus Watson the town clerk and her husband's best friend. Francis Vokey, the principal of Dollarton Elementary and her daughters. Marg Davis who organizes the parish dessert party. They should wear orange vests. Berton Carey the undertaker."

Notes for future editorial:

The ledge is eighteen inches wide, pockmarked and cracked, mossy in places, widens then crumbles at the end where he was lying. It's a normal thing to do. Have a few beers on the ledge. Not the fault of the following:

1. "Nothing to do in this town." There is really plenty to do. See back issues of this newspaper for the plethora of things that go on if you have the heart to participate.

2. Alphonse Whelan who got the town to put a sign over the ball net. The net, a spit away from the bridge, is where we used to hang out till Alphonse petitioned council on account of it being across the road from his fake stone front bungalow closed up except for three long weekends every summer. The sign says INAPPROPRIATE USE NOT PERMITTED. UNTIL 7 PM ONLY. See? This is not a dull town. What you can throw through our net after seven is limited only by your imagination. You have to be fair to Alphonse, it is true we were loud the few weekends he came up, and several of us did fall asleep in his rhododendrons, and there were broken beer bottles and Alphonse's ancient Labrador with white whiskers got his paw cut and had to go around in a cone big as the loudspeaker on Bill Walsh's election van announcing Bill's campaign promise to make his own life more meaningful now that he had retired.

Interview with the basketball net:

Incinerator Times: So how is it? Hanging up there, never anyone using you.

Net: Lonesome.

IT: You have a good view. Marina, boardwalk, occasional beached seal caught on the old railbed. Gulls. Cold, saltcrusted pebbles.

Net: It's all just empty hanging around. A balloon not blown up for any party, sides sticking together. An old widow woman.

IT: There are those who say we are keeping property values up.

This leaves the net speechless. Like people are if I say I was there that night and we didn't know Tony fell off the ledge. We thought he'd gone home safe. Like I am now. You want to know what the only apartment in Dollarton is like, originally here for the Spur owner who now lives in one of his cabins at the Sea View. It's a neat little cubbyhole-ish place, mostly bare except for the toothbrush holder which has fifteen toothbrushes in it while my stepfather tries to find one that doesn't hurt. Sometimes I think writing is totally useless, because all you have to do is take one look at someone and what do you need a writer for? My mother, for instance, is a good woman who has worked hard all her life for bags of potatoes and the electric bill. Her husband, good too, living life behind a hill he peeps around, waiting for it to bury him. Icons of the apartment include teapot, coffee and end tables used for Christmas candy, magazine rack in the bathroom, and the toothbrush cup, a miniature Henry Moore in blue plastic. You don't need *The Incinerator Times* to tell you how any of it is. Inside our place or outside, the whole of Dollarton, all you'd have to do is step in for one second and you'd know how it is. The one exception is this top step, hidden by this tree, neither inside nor out. Maybe I'm kidding myself. Maybe it's no exception at all. Four feet by three, two-by-fours painted white, leaves hanging over it. Just big enough for me to pick guitar and think, with a breeze coming through that doesn't start or stay in this town.

boYs

Derek Matthews has to be the ugliest boy in the class but I like him. I've liked every boy except Barry Pumphrey now. Barry Pumphrey likes me. He tried to kiss me on our step but I said I could see the roof rack on Dad's car coming down Mountbatten Drive. Barry calls me Roof Rack now.

None of the boys I like like me. My status isn't as low as Dwayne Morrison's but I'm not far up the ladder. My parents don't have any idea about the ladder. They are totally wrapped up in keeping the household going and are not interested in me unless they need me to peel potatoes, or it's time to pay for my books, or I've hogged the Ritz crackers in my room. My mother bugs me while my father picks his teeth with the end of a plastic straw he cuts specially. He looks thoughtful but my mother says his mind is blank. I ignore the ladder most of the time. My best friend Denise – this is amazing – has entered the Miss Teen Lundrigan Mills pageant, but I'll get to that later.

How can you ignore the fact that you are almost as low down as Dwayne Morrison? He is low down not for any reason, but because of the atmosphere around him. He moves slowly, he's big and has pale skin. He's no more stupid or ugly than anyone else. Nowhere near as ugly as Derek Matthews, who a lot of girls like besides me. Dwayne Morrison doesn't have as many pimples as lots of other people, and his father's not the undertaker like Clive Skaines' father. Clive Skaines is low on the ladder too, but Dwayne is the lowest of the low. If you touch him, if you even graze his books in the hall, you have to wipe his germs on someone and shout, "Morrison's germs!" Nobody ever calls him just Dwayne. They always call him Dwayne Morrison, like it's important to completely identify him and separate him from every other human. Anyway I'm pretty close to him in status. I could let it bother me more but then I'd become emotionally disturbed and have to go to the guidance counsellor, and I don't see myself that way. Mr. Plumtree doesn't either. He stopped me in the hall one day after World Problems class and told me I didn't realize it but when I got out of here I'd be beautiful; I already was but it was too early for most people to see it. He isn't a child molesting creep, by the way. He's just someone who I guess knows about the ladder and decided to give one of the bottom dwellers a private pep talk.

A few boys have come to my house looking for me. Snoopy is one. Snoopy arrived in our school out of jail. He passed me notes, "Meet me at Duffs Store after shcool," which I ignored until he showed up at my place. My father answered the door. He teaches boys' woodwork at East Side junior high. Whatever he said to Snoopy must have been drastic because I never got another note or visit. That's what gave me the idea to get rid of Barry Pumphrey by mentioning Dad's roof rack.

Dad doesn't know about Tim Whelan. Tim Whelan grabs me by the belt loop in the church basement at Young People's while all the other Young People are upstairs talking about their experiences with God. Selma Forsey recently had an experience with God that was so amazing only certain Young People were allowed to hear about it, because only They would understand. I'm not one of Them. I'm a Young Person that Denise invited so she'd get points, and I keep going back even though I say all the wrong answers like that "Morning Has Broken" is my favourite hymn and they have to tell me it's of the devil. We had an art display and Selma Forsey hung my teapot behind the bathroom door after the head counsellor said it was the best art in the show. So I'm close to the lowest of the low there too, but there's always someone lower than you wherever you are.

Tim Whelan stole ten dollars from me on the ferry the night we had our outing to the mainland. He's from up in the bean, Jellybean Square. It's not that far from where I live, across the road and up Waldegrave Street. Reverend Clydehops came to my cabin with the ten-dollar bill half an hour after I said it was missing. It was my spending money for the trip. Everyone else had amazing amounts, like fifty dollars. Except Tim, I guess. I think Reverend Clydehops is having an affair with Denise's mother, Mrs. Mullett, even though it seems impossible. She cooks burger patties with gravy and onions for Mr. Mullett, who wears brown V-necked sweaters and has silky hair the tan colour of Caramac toffee, and he doesn't do much except watch TV and shovel snow. I saw him watching *Days of our Lives*. Mrs. Mullett is a lot more energetic than her husband. She goes to visit Reverend Clydehops on church business. Once I saw him open the door to his glass porch and let her in. The two of them had this shadowy air around them, like they were meeting about something important and sad.

NO ONE SAID how they knew Tim stole my money. I'd put my ten-dollar bill in my jeans pocket and certainly never felt a thing if someone's fingers went in there and took it. It was too bad Tim did it, because that's what everyone expected of him. But maybe he didn't do it. Maybe Reverend Clydehops just gave me a new ten-dollar bill and everyone blamed Tim. In the church basement I can't get over how hot his, I don't want to say crotch but that's what it is, how hot the centre of him, which is his crotch, which makes it sound bad, how hot it is against me through both our jeans, hot as my scarf off the rad. This only lasts a few seconds before I go back upstairs to the prayer circle, where Selma Forsey is standing up and everyone is amazed at what she has just told them about her and God. I would like the same thing to happen with me and God, but I haven't got a clue what it is. I imagine God has told her a secret that has filled her with relief. Finally she knows what she is doing on this earth. I only wish she wasn't such a snot about it. I really like her older brother Gramson. That seems like a Bible name to me. He carries his Bible everywhere and nobody makes fun of him. When Selma goes to bed at night, I bet she doesn't do what I do in bed, which is imagine Tim Whelan with his jeans off against my skin. I bet she doesn't rub herself real soft until a great relief shudders through her like a heaving sob. I bet that isn't the secret God told her, although maybe it is.

I DON'T KNOW what made Denise sign up for the Miss Teen Lundrigan Mills pageant. Worse than that, she's convinced she will win. She tries to get me to enter it too. Our friendship is one of convenience, I know that. She uses me for a stand-in friend because she has no one else, and I go along with it. We hang out in her bedroom studying for our bronze swim medallions and drying our hair. She has all the binders for the course. When we do the written test, they read everyone's marks out except mine.

"How will it make my hair look?" I ask this while she burns my scalp. I don't have a hair dryer. I walk home from swim class to the creaking sound of my frozen hair.

"It won't make it look like anything." She is irritated. She has begun her pageant research and knows real secrets. If I'm not going to enter with her she isn't going to waste her time telling me any of them. "It's just a hair dryer."

SHE HAS TO HAVE AN ESCORT to the pageant and she finds Tyrone Jesso, who's in grade twelve. He comes to the door for me and my father lets me go out and speak to him. Tyrone asks me if I want to go out to a movie and I tell him he better ask Denise. My mother tells me afterward that my dad is puzzled as to why a guy like that would ask me out. I say a guy like what, and she says, "Your dad thinks he's effeminate."

Everyone knows Denise is entering the pageant but nobody makes fun of her. They pay no attention to her at all. Tamara Manuel is entering and she's so beautiful everyone knows she's going to win. Every time you look at her your heart falls off its little cliff. She's really nice too, not snotty, although she has never talked to me.

The pageant is this Saturday. In three weeks Denise has transformed herself. She gets her hair cut so short she looks like a model in *Vogue*. She gradually stops talking to me. I don't take it personally. It's like she's decided she needs time to separate herself from the ordinary world before she enters the world of French perfume and sashes with her title on them and Kinsmen floats down Main Street. She wears dance leggings and a black angora sweater to class. She would be beautiful if she wasn't in our school. I have to say she's become amazingly elegant even if no one else has noticed.

TAMARA MANUEL WINS THE PAGEANT and Denise is first runner-up. I'm amazed Denise has managed to get this far, but she is furious. She has to sit in the back of the winners' float with the second runner-up, a girl from Presentation, and Tamara in her tiara up front. You can see Denise is furious right there on the float in her white dress with silver sparkles. Her dress is form-fitting, not a flowing gown like Tamara's. Denise feels the judges have made a stupid choice. She pulls out of town and enrols in Bible school in New Brunswick, where she gets a boyfriend right away.

Her mom takes me on the road to see her for Easter break. I can't believe my parents have let me go with her, and I wish they hadn't. Later they will let me do a lot of other things I can't believe as well, like go to Lance Tremayne's apartment, and camp in Lake Ursa Park with Dave Holloway. Mrs. Mullett passes transport trucks when other trucks are coming from the opposite direction. Dozens of times we drive through the corridor between transport trucks with two inches on each side of her car, pasted to the double yellow line. Target Furniture. Doyle and Sons Produce Suppliers Limited. M.M. Kelly Factory Freezer Parts. When we get to the Bible school we hardly see Denise at all. She is off smoking and having sex with Neal Prescott. Her mother goes off somewhere too, leaving me to eat mealy room-temperature red delicious apples on Denise's chair by her stinking ashtray. At midnight Denise climbs through her window with a mickey of brandy and says she has decided to stay at Bible college in case God is real. If he's not real, it doesn't matter – she'll graduate and marry Neal anyway. If he is real, her diploma will keep her out of hell.

Back home Samuel McGill from the other grade ten class asks me to the dance. He has never been in jail. He goes to Young People's but is not one of the people in Selma Forsey's divine seances. He's a quiet boy and handsome in an inert way that doesn't stir up anything inside me, like James Bond and Superman. I wonder if he's asked me because Gwen Aimers or Evelyn Anthony said no. My father picks his teeth silently. Samuel walks me down Mountbatten Drive and up Glendale Heights, which is two miles, and in all that time neither of us says a word. I can't even think of anything stupid to say. My brain's language centre has left the country. We dance a few times, we waltz once. There's no heat from his body and I think of Tim. Samuel walks me home. The first thing he says to me is, "Would you go with me to the next dance?" I drag out of me the courage to say no thanks, not because I don't like him but because I haven't got a clue what he, like Denise, can be dreaming of.

Town with Moses

Leona desperately wants grass seeds for the patch Jeremy dug yesterday to have a look at the septic tank. Moses is watching her. He says, "Kentucky blue grass grows surprisingly well here," though she has said nothing about grass or seed. Some men around here really are named Moses. Janine who cooks and cleans at the home says this one's real name is Mark. Kind Janine, who once warned Leona the dog catcher was trying to catch her beautiful cat. Leona doesn't mind calling Mark Moses if that's what he wants. He is tall when he's walking past to get ginger ale at Morey's store, but short when she lets him in her house. Jeremy doesn't mind him in the house, he's not bossy like that.

On the town map the home is labelled old folks, but it's a halfway house for the mental hospital in St. John's. Most men there are baymen whose mothers died. Their mothers fried bacon, boiled rhubarb, bottled herring, hung long johns from their own sheep on the line, picked bakeapples and died, their sons not knowing how to do any of the work. The sons were all right until the root cellars and Mason jars emptied. After five winters some grand niece brought them in. Moses is not one of these men. Janine told her he killed his parents with an axe when he was young. In Leona's mind this isn't necessarily as bad as it sounds. She doesn't mention it to Jeremy.

Besides being half clairvoyant, Moses is attentive and looks Leona in the eye. Janine cooks pork and potatoes and cabbage at the home but sometimes Leona barbecues him a hamburger and he never says no to a cold beer. He talks while she hangs washing or tends the garden. This morning as she buried tomato plants Hazel gave her, thinking you have to plant tomatoes here in the three seconds before iceberg wind gives way to the stultifying smack of hot lupins, Moses said, "There's two things wrong. One's stagnation."

"I'LL AGREE TO THAT," she said. She'd just got off the phone with her mother, a woman who appears static even when she is pouring coffee or taking curtains down to wash. She does these things with her quilted satin bathrobe rigid and her arms stuck out like oars. Even her eyes don't move, frozen like blueberries in her silver spectacles. She claims to wash her baseboards twice a week but you can't see how she can bend enough to do it. Leona does not have curtains or baseboards. Jeremy, her husband, is not static. She thinks of him as made out of the same stuff as an India rubber ball. Yesterday he dug all day, flies stuck to his sweat. She was mad at him because she knew there was nothing wrong with the tank. The drains in the house were slow for a whole other reason, but try to tell him that. She did not let him know she was mad, since it wouldn't have done any good. This is something she has mastered. In fact she fried steak and onions and mushrooms and bought him a six-pack of Blue Star. She can get on the Fleetline and buy grass seed herself.

She scratches sorrel out of packed dirt with a spoon, having meant to buy a trowel all her life, and waits for Royenne to come on the school bus. She doesn't want to go in the house, where years' worth of *Readers Digest*s and *Herald*s lie undisturbed in the magazine rack. Miss Newfoundland and Labrador in her tiara, and *I am Joe's Liver*, and *The Night my Entire Family got Electrocuted Three Metres from Our Own Front Door*. Leona can't bear to look at the magazines, or even tidy up the rack. She feels they are old, and dark, and frightening. Sometimes she pretends Royenne is her own child.

"THE SECOND THING IS," says Moses "people who won't fall in love – and there are lots of them – never fall into real life." There are times when Moses is not clairvoyant. Times when he tries, but misses. This time he's on her wavelength.

He has Leona thinking while she puts another load in the too small washer, pries fillets apart for this evening and gets ooze out of the crack between the toilet and the floor where Jeremy was fooling around with the system yesterday. It's better than what Jeremy gave her to think about before breakfast, which was twenty minutes of why his compressor is better than other people's. You can't go by horsepower, it's all in the number of the CFM, and his compressor has an unloader that makes the motor idle instead of going on and off, which is the beauty of it. "People buy these dinky ones at Canadian Tire," he laughed, "because they don't know." Sitting with her tea under the dogberry tree Leona does not think about her husband's compressor, she thinks about falling into real life.

"You know what I'd love to have?"

She loves the way Moses gathers all her attention and gives her all his. "What?"

"A good pair of sandals like yours."

Leona got her sandals at Zellers on the wino end of Water Street. They look like Birkenstocks. "They aren't really that good."

"I know they're not the first rate version, but they'll last you the summer. Six weeks."

She laughs with no one but Moses. Hazel is all information on saving your own seeds and how to kill slugs. Hazel cuts slugs in half with scissors. Mona talks about her husband's colostomy. The bag can fall off in his sleep. Jeremy leans out his truck window talking to Doug, both with their engines running, about how they have each fixed rot in a barn, how virtually impossible it is to do, but how they have managed to do it. Leona asks Moses, "Do they let you go to town alone?"

"Probably more than they let you. I only need a letter from the doctor."

WHILE JEREMY READS the sports section she says, "Tomorrow I might take Moses to town for some sandals."

"Are you allowed?"

"They don't own him."

"Who's paying for the sandals?"

"He is." Which she's sure is not true. She'll have to get the bus fares too, and a couple of hamburger platters. "Can you pick up Royenne and give her a snack?"

"What do you want me to give her?"

"Cheez Whiz crackers and milk. Dianne picks her up at quarter to five." Dianne paid Leona on Friday, which is why she has money for Moses.

SITTING ON THE BUS with Moses she wonders is she his keeper or his company. The driver says hi as if she and Moses get on his bus together all the time. Surely the driver would say if he thought something dangerous was happening. Someone would run down from the home and stop them. She should have called Janine. Moses' body heats her right arm.

On the road she thinks how hard this place must be to decipher if you come from somewhere else. She knows the board on the lawn across from Sobeys says Woodfords' Sawmill, but for three years the paint has been so worn not one letter is legible. Other signs have letters blown off: can ilk 99. iced olog $2.99. She's glad she is not a Russian immigrant.

St. John's thrills her. There are stone walls and beds of hyacinth. Moses says, "I know what you mean," though she hasn't said anything. He won't get out by the malls, but stays on till downtown, from where the route carries on to broken, unnamed places. She is heartened by his confidence. With a hand in his pocket and his coat-tails flying – just like at home where no one has coattails but him – he walks past Atlantic Place and the Scotiatower and up stairs to Duckworth where geraniums peep through railings. He says, "No need to get off in an industrial park," and she wonders if he conspires like this with everybody. She sure doesn't. Little parachutes from dandelions float past people's heads like an invasion of unnoticed aliens. He takes her to see Hans who has a perpetual yard sale in the starling alley between the cathedral and Turk's Head Pub. Moses encourages Leona to buy a fifty-cent cake plate. He says she can eat her afternoon lady fingers off it. Alma shows them how a church elm has sucked her well dry, its roots a frantic interlacing around the bottom of the hole. Alma scores the bark each night with her potato knife. Tonight she'll cut the section that will kill the tree. Leona likes to think of the tree stealing all that water while appearing motionless. She can't tell who Alma is, or if Moses knows her. It is three o'clock and she is starving.

MOSES FITS IN. She is the one out of tune. His cobbler is a real cobbler. A gold stiletto slipper advertises in-store dyeing, and behind a wall of sneaker whitener and skate laces are the fairytale lasts and thick-set sewing machines used by shoemaker elves. The Greek proprietor greets Moses as an old-world friend, nods at Leona more hesitant; she has Zellers written all over her. He takes Moses' foot in his hands and measures it, and she notices Moses can make elegant conversation with anyone, not just herself, and feels sad and left behind. She wants to ask if the store has a pair of red shoes. For twenty dollars Moses is to come back in an hour and a half and his sandals will be ready. Moses is the one who asks about red shoes for Leona, and the owner shows her a little pair that would have fit her when she was six.

"Why don't you buy them," Moses says in a quiet voice whose vibration she feels where wings would be. "Just for the . . ." He says just for the *something* of it, she can't pick out what; joy? Memory? She feels his breath on her ear, he whispers but with his voice on the whisper and she wants to chew his lips, so what if he had all his teeth pulled out last year? She realizes she can't tell if he is older than her, or younger.

She'll have eighteen dollars left if she pays for his sandals. Hands in his pocket he leads her out, sniffs easily to the cobbler, "I'll take care of it when I come back."

THEY WALK PAST the coltsfoot-infested ravelled edge between the town and the sea, and she thinks, *this is where all this is leading,* but he doesn't stop here. She wants him to stop here, in the zone of Export A packs and rusted radiators and the town's industrial heap of salt for the roads. Later instead of dirt and beer bottle glass in the grass, there will be ships' lights and darkness. This is the territory she imagines he inhabited before he came to the home. She has trouble following his strides up the Battery to a pink house. Except for the Fisher Price swing set the house is like her mother's. A scrap of scalped turf, pleated lampshades in the window, volumes of sheer curtains with a valance. When Moses opens the door Leona smells warm Alphaghetti and hot electronic innards of a new television. "It's my sister," he whispers. "I might babysit for an hour. You want to come in or see you later or what." Does his sister let him babysit her children?

Maybe Janine was wrong about Moses' parents. Maybe she said *tried* to kill them, not killed them. Leona walks down Signal Hill and gets a medium from the chip wagon outside Atlantic Place. She wishes Moses could have some too while she eats out of her grease-spotted brown bag crusted with salt, the malt vinegar fumes joining the seaweed and sewage smells. She wonders how young his sister's children are, what will happen if she herself shows up back home without him. What she'd like to know is, does he go to his sister's all the time, or just this time. Is Leona heaping responsibility on herself unnecessarily? Her mother's satin bathrobes stand before her; pink, blue, mint green. How would a Supreme Court judge figure it out before and after the murder of the children? She finds a payphone and calls the home. Charlene is working, not Janine. Charlene is younger. Leona can't tell her what Janine said about Moses, it might get Janine in trouble. So she hints around. Is it okay that she's brought him to town for sandals? Yes my dear, that should be fine. Is it okay that he went into his sister's house for awhile? Oh yes, cheerful, an ill-paid worker getting an unscheduled smoke break. The sister might have gone out for awhile and left him with her children. This is so unimportant the worker is silent, waiting to hear the rest.

"I mean, is it okay to leave Moses alone with young children?" Charlene thinks about it. What is going through Charlene's mind? "Charlene?"

"Yes?"

"Did Janine ever say anything that would lead you to think Moses shouldn't babysit small kids by himself?"

"Like what?"

"Do you know her phone number?"

"We're not allowed to give out the wardens' home numbers."

"Could you call her for me? Call her and just ask her what I asked you, and I'll call you back."

"She went down the bay to visit her father."

LEONA CAN'T REMEMBER whether she and Moses agreed to meet at the shoe store or by the salt mound. She thinks of the grass seed and walks way down Water Street West past Zellers and Stan's Tavern and the Salvation Army to the side street where Gaze Seed is. She loves the smell of fertilizer and bulbs. They have small paper bags of Kentucky blue grass seed done up with staples right on the counter, lots of them, as if everyone in town has been talking to Moses and wants just enough for the patch over their septics. She looks at the fish in aquariums at the back for awhile. On the way back she browses in Afterwords and buys three old *Victoria* magazines that have pretty things in them for Royenne to cut out, then walks down to look at the Russian names on the boats, and men soldering in the cavern of a trawler, the molten sparks flying close to her hair. A rat steals across some planks and a police car slows as it passes behind her, and she figures she might as well go get the shoes. The shoemaker hands her Moses' sandals, which smell strongly of new-cut leather, and the red shoes, all unwrapped, as if he wants her to be able to enjoy them as she carries them out on the street. He won't take her money because he says Moses said he'd take care of it. She wants to ask him how well he knows Moses, but she doesn't. She takes the shoes and her magazines, the straps and pages and bag of grass seed slipping around in her arms, to the crumbled edge below Moses' sister's place.

When she gets near the salt heap she sees Moses slide down the bank with his arm around a cake pan. She can see the top half of his sister's Honda in the driveway. The pan is full of rice krispie squares covered in waxed paper. She expects Moses to sit on a rock and haul slabs out of the pan for his lunch, but he doesn't. He hands her the pan. The squares have been precisely cut, she can see the thin sharp rectangles through the wax paper, and he says here, bring them home to your husband. Jeremy loves rice krispie squares, and she never makes them. She can't get her mind around the idea of melting great big marshmallows in a pan without burning them. "You have to use miniature marshmallows," Moses tells her, and they walk and he pays the shoe man with money his sister gave him, and they get the Fleetline home.

Burt's Shawarma

Rhonda has on a cowl neck sweater. Her daughter says no one has worn a cowl neck since the seventies, but Rhonda doesn't care about that. Burt wouldn't know the difference. She has a McDonalds coffee while she's waiting for him. She likes McDonalds coffee more than those pretentious coffees so strong they make her anger grow back. She can see Wal Mart and gas stations at the edge of Pinegate in a pink menacing glow. This is the national teenage suicide capital but her own teenagers seem okay, although she has a suspicion Terry is going to wake up one morning and tell her and Dan he's gay. Dan is homophobic so it won't go over well. Her own farmhouse is an hour away, just past the point where Pinegate Pizza won't deliver. The sheets she put over the twenty-year-old couch and chairs have been there so long they're covered in thread nubbins. Dan's and the kids' elbows have worn the varnish around the pine table so there is a ragged shining island in the middle where the new flower vase sits. She painted the kitchen wall lemon sherbet three years ago, the last thing she did there as if she cared.

"I was the best thing that ever happened to my dad," she tells Burt, "and the worst thing that ever happened to my mother." She is running out of things like this to tell him, but still has a few left.

Burt has Pinegate's original Lebanese cafe, just before the 601 bypass. Three springs ago she ate half a chicken shawarma there after getting a new pair of glasses and when he brought her coffee cream, which was real cream, he said, "Never dye your hair. When it all turns silver, you will look elegant." He kissed her hand, and that was when her anger started to drain away. If his cafe had been right in town instead of on the outskirts, probably nothing else would have happened. But there was just enough distance between Rhonda and the old part of town where she was a little girl; Hennebury's pharmacy and Hoff's fine clothing and the wrought iron fence around Pinegate Presbyterian, that she let it go farther. In fact she let Burt lock up and take her through the door to his apartment in the back, where she discovered that she didn't need to buy shares in KY Jelly after all.

THEY MEET on these outskirts where sunset catches big box warehouse stores, overpasses break up the landscape with big Xs and Zs of concrete, signs are tier on tier of Mall and Plaza and Estates never attaining whatever it is to which their curled, slender fonts aspire. She doesn't care if she never sees rustic, or elegant, or permanent. At home she no longer cares that her vinyl toilet seat has torn pieces that stick up and prickle her butt.

"You can tell about the state of anyone's marriage from their medicine cabinet," she tells her sister Bett. Her own has empty calamine lotion bottles piled in with rubbing alcohol for ears pierced fifteen years ago, ancient antibiotics, blunt useless tweezers and a stack of wrapped soaps with cobwebs on them from the Holiday Inn in 1989, which was the last time she and Dan took a trip together, and that was to bring home a trailer for getting show cattle to the fall fair. She doesn't care about the fence Dan promised to make for her garden twenty years ago. She doesn't care that Dan had an affair when the kids were little, or that there has never been chemistry between Dan and herself. She doesn't even care that the magic with Burt is dying out. Bett calls him an interim phase and that's fine by Rhonda. What matters is that her anger, her poisonous anger, has drained away, thanks to Burt. She watched her mother carry the same anger, panicked when she realized she had it too, knew one day she was mad as hell at her whole life and it looked like there was nothing she could do about it. Burt stopped the time bomb with his hideout, with its cool walls and blue shadows where she didn't have to do things from morning till night in which she had no interest. She will feel relief deep down, be able to breathe deep down, whenever she thinks of Burt even after this is over, which it almost certainly is already, with no illusion of anything permanent. No one has mentioned Rhonda helping Burt run his cafe, but not in the same way that no one has ever mentioned her helping Dan run his farm.

"If I walked away from that farm today," she tells Burt, "I wouldn't get more than fifty dollars." You can tell her all you want about this country's fair marriage property laws, but Dan doesn't own the farm, his father does. "It wouldn't even be fifty dollars," she laughs. Burt has taken all the bitterness out of it. Not Burt himself as such, but her knowledge that there are other Burts, and that she will even be fine on her own, since she has a diploma from Key One Tech, has written editorials for the farm-board monthly newsletter and could find a job that pays enough to live on if she wanted to.

BURT NOTICES when she gets her hair trimmed. Her hair is dead straight and hanging down no matter what she does with it, not in the way people iron their hair these days but in its own way. Still he notices the new lift. He does not think she isn't adventurous enough to cut it any other way than straight to her shoulders like she had it in high school, since he did not know her in high school like Dan did. Dan, oblivious as one of his young beef cattle.

She still thinks of Dan as young, since he has those big eyelashes and he goes around quivering with manly desire for approval, which she would give him if she could. If he ever did anything for her, instead of for his father, the farm, or the cows. Lately Dan has done something for her. This Valentine's Day he went to Pinegate Posies and picked out fourteen tulips. He has told her four times that he chose each one himself. This is where she is tempted to think, how sweet of him. Look, he went in there; the feminine side of him peeped through his overalls, through his hungry hope that Rhonda had managed to make something for supper without broccoli in it, and he asked Danette Muir what kind of flowers he should buy. This is his vulnerable moment, the moment Rhonda is supposed to relent, when all she can think is how stupid he must have looked, and how he probably noticed everything there was to notice about Danette's layered and streaked hair, her engagement ring but no gold band yet, the heart locket that hangs in the hollow of her collarbone. Danette's locket doesn't hang, it floats; it floats there because it hopes Danette will have a good life, and it hasn't come crashing yet to rest at the bone.

"He knows about Burt," says Bett.

"It is strange that he would spend any time at all differentiating between a purple tulip with a pink edge and a fuschia one with a gold edge," Rhonda says. "A mix of open, half-open, and bud. When he could be doing something useful like insulating the barn roof where it drips on the cows."

Dan could pick out fourteen Persian roses. He could throw in some irises and a bird of paradise and a big spray of baby's breath and it would make no difference. Rhonda believes if a person doesn't touch your heart automatically, no amount of trying will change that. The morning of her wedding she and Dan looked at each other and said, "Well, I guess we're going ahead with it," and neither one could see why they shouldn't.

Dan does quiver with vulnerable, animal desire, but there is a weather-beaten garden bench on the verandah that is Rhonda's, and Dan has never acknowledged it, never sat on it. She had the idea that she would sit on it and drink coffee, and gaze at the solitary elm in Hoffmans' empty field, and maybe leaf through the photos in a *Country Living* magazine. She still has that idea. She bought the seat with a hundred dollars her father sent on their tenth anniversary. Dan didn't know about the money, and when Pinegate Home Hardware delivered the bench, which was varnished then, and still had antique-style patina on the back panel of curlicued iron leaves and no rust, he said, "I can't understand why you'd buy a thing like that when we've got to pay Jason McBriarty to fix the leak in the chimney."

The idea she has of the bench always features her sitting on it alone, the empty space beside her inviting someone. Not Sherry Hoffman's husband measuring water levels in his marsh, not Burt, parting a curtain that leads to the other world, a silver-wrapped lunch in his hand as an offering to the dangerous hounds that inhabit reality. How does he wrap those shawarmas with not a wrinkle in the foil? Not Dan, his boots and clothes covered in cowshit, searching for words that don't even touch the surface of Rhonda's thoughts. Why is it she has the feeling he could do it if he tried? "Why don't I get a shower and make you a cup of tea? Hoffman's elm is like us, isn't it? I'm sorry you've been lonely inside. Let me touch you? Not with my paws – with the word *rain*, the colour green, with eating bread and sitting here till a yellow bird comes and eats the crumbs." A noble farmer, she knows, hard-working and unsung, but still.

Burt is not interested in what she might do if she leaves Dan. He does not want to hear about how Drakes' farm is worth only thirty thousand dollars because they lost their milk quota and never got off the ground with pigs because of the protests. He has no interest in envisioning her sitting in the Drakes' bay window, desktop-publishing a groundbreaking new women's farm magazine, and she doesn't blame him for that. Does he have any dreams? She doesn't know. She doesn't want to know. She is terrified of knowing, is the truth, not because of what his dream might be, but because as long as she doesn't ask him, then in her mind she can be his dream. This is what makes her feel good, and as long as it works, her anger does not come back. Now that her anger is banished and prowling on the outskirts, she sees it could easily kill her.

At least they don't have to go to hotels. She leaves her car here or at Burger King or Wal Mart, he takes her to his apartment, and they make love in his single bed with the candlewick spread and lace pattern shadows. Where did he get that bedspread? Did the lace come from Wal Mart, or is it an heirloom from a fourth-century room with walls a foot thick kissed by the cedars of Lebanon? Rhonda can't tell. She wishes she could tell. She thinks a person should be able to tell, but she can't. She imagines a woman older than her, but not old enough to be his mother, bringing it to him from either possible place. The woman is docile, has had curlers in her hair long enough to make waves but not curls. Why is the woman not here now? Is she waiting in the wings?

Burt makes strong coffee in his espresso machine and he feeds Rhonda for free. Even though it would be ludicrous for him to charge her; $6.99 for a shawarma, $4.99 for a half order, $1.99 for a dripping triangle of baklava, this is still how she thinks of it; him feeding her for free. She has to admit one of the things she loves most is devouring his baklava and warm chicken in pita, fresh shredded lettuce and pastry flakes drenched in syrup falling on her thigh and the juice running down her hand, after they have made love and he has stroked every inch of her thighs and belly and breasts and fucked her in his way that is appreciative, even worshipful in the way that one humble god would acknowledge the divinity of another humble god. Never needy. It's like he's celebrating every time how perfect she is, how she falls short of nothing. This does not extend beyond the apartment. He does not ask her to go with him to see a film, or go for a drink in a bar, or get away from the farm for a whole night, and that's fine with Rhonda. This way she will not end up cleaning his cafe floors while he tells another woman to let her hair grow silver.

She hasn't asked him why he does not have a wife because why would any woman in Pinegate marry a mysterious, marginal, dangerous stranger, even if he has been here nineteen years, when they could have a homegrown boy. Sometimes she feels a tickle of fear when she thinks of another stranger, a woman, stopping in at Burt's for a shawarma and falling in love with him. Really in love, instead of just away from lovelessness. Maybe this has already happened.

Every day Rhonda has waited for Burt to think, *you are just an ordinary woman.* This is the day she sees he's thought that all along, but without the word just. She sees it after the sex. Doesn't an ordinary woman have legs like pillars of alabaster, breasts like the sun and moon, pelvic bone called the mound of Venus, and an inner world where she sees visions?

AT HOME THE TULIPS have started to droop, and have that sickly sweetness from being overripe. She sees Burt is not going to change. Burt is never going to stop seeing her as perfect and beautiful. And Dan will not change either. The vase of perfectly chosen tulips will stand there until the water turns green and stinks, and she will be the one to clear it away, and to rub oil on the water ring that has formed on what's left of the varnish underneath.

A True Conductor

Lena Giannou is not an alto who skips practice. Sometimes she is late, as practice starts the moment her shift at Taste O'Ireland ends. In bed after choir she tells her husband things Neil, the conductor, says to make the choir more attentive, until she realizes she should stop. 'I don't mean I'm falling in love with him,' she almost says.

"That phrase *birds in circled flight,*" Neil tells the choir, "keep it rolling, suspended, aloft." He wheels his hand toward the choral room wall which dissolves into a field instead of the music school parking lot. Some choir members are excited more by bake sales than by singing. Soprano Eileen is famous for her cherry cakes, which bring ten dollars apiece, and she can be counted on to bake ten for the choir's fall fund-raiser. Tenor Harold is the heart of the annual flea market. He stacks and labels thousands of old books and records so they look worth buying. Eileen and Harold have been with the choir ten years. This is Lena's sixth month. She had told her husband over and over that she wished she could sing but her father had always said she had no voice. "You don't have to have a big voice to join a choir," her husband said.

When Neil conducts Gabriel Fauré's *Cantique de Jean Racine*, a trap door slips in Lena. She sees Fauré writing the song by a candle in the dark and thinks, *Fauré didn't blow that candle out, he blew it through time, into Neil. Anyone can see the light is right there in him, and he's giving it to us.* She thinks she is foolish to try to explain this, but her husband says, "That's what a true conductor is," and she remembers it's the kind of thing a small appliance repairman knows.

When Neil says, "Don't get complacent about this or that's the end of it," Lena is busy catching and singing out fire. An hour earlier she folded two hundred napkins and served twenty-eight kinds of potato and beer. Denise, the alto at her left, complains you can see the soloist's underwear line. "Somebody should tell her to wear a skirt." This is the week Denise finally bursts with curiosity about quiet Lena. "So where you from? What do you do?"

Lena avoids saying, *I am from music. I do music and am music, if music will only have me. And the soloist has a divine voice.* Lena trembles with the honour of sending low harmonies beneath the sopranos. Denise, greedy for the melody, is always complaining the altos never get a good note.

LENA CRANES to hear Neil say, "When you start that first note you create a whole new set of rules for time." Denise is whispering, "I meant to bring a bologna sandwich for the break and I went and left the sandwich in the fridge and brought the pack of bologna in my lunch tin." What could they be, the new rules for time, that you activate by singing the first note? Lena imagines time slowing around golden notes, speeding between silver ones. Neil knows more than this. He has time's new rules written under his eyelids. He can lie down at night and watch the sacred words float past in their thousands. He can change them just by thinking of a new song. Alice, the alto at her right, looks up at her and smiles a ninety-four-year-old smile. Her hair is in two side buns threaded with plaited embroidery yarn and many hairpins. Alice is one of two people in the choir who've shared scraps of talk in the hall with Lena. Alice practices her alto at home with her great grandnephew, who is seven. She teaches him the soprano part. Lena imagines the room has an old Boston piano, whorled iron stool, a pot of hyacinths. She hears Alice tell the grandnephew his soprano will be straighter than a girl's; it will be as if he and she fling all the silver pins out of her hair and the pins grow wings and can sing. Her alto will ride the fragrance from the warm cinnamon cake on her table. Lena wonders where the boy's mother is; does she think of her son's time with Alice as a divine interlude, or a chance to buy breaded chicken and have her hair trimmed? "Alice," Denise says, "would never be allowed in the choir if he was to redo the auditions today. We haven't had everyone re-auditioned for years." Alice sounds fine to Lena, although she is sometimes on the wrong page. Lena believes you don't kick a ninety-four-year-old woman out of anything.

Lena's other choir friend is Holly, who works in the museum, layering tissue so aged lace will not yellow, gently brushing mouse droppings from hooked mats. Alice, Holly and the accompanist are souls with whom Lena flies into the music. The accompanist is a king's son disguised as a servant. A drop of sweat trickles between Lena's breasts as he plays the piano interval in Fauré between *Divin Sauveur, jette sur nous les yeux!* and *Repands sur nous le feu de ta grace.* In bed Lena ponders things Neil has said, even things less profound than the changing rules of time. *It's all about listening, and making those vowels as pure as you can.* She considers the purity of vowels, pictures them on her fire escape melted and overflowing in beef buckets. *Don't turn the* w *in when into an event. Get to the* e. W in its best shoes going to the cinema when it shouldn't. *We have an antiquated notation system that stopped being useful around Chopin's time and hasn't been useful since.* This idea causes some regret, as she loves to see choir music open on her kitchen counter with those incredibly graceful markings dancing past a bowl of thawing chicken legs. Every week she tries to learn something new: how to read repeat marks, the symbol for *pianissimo*, the almost invisible grace notes. *You've got to break habits all the time.* She loves that idea, takes a can of beer out of the fridge and fries sausages in it. She kisses two dimples in the small of her husband's back that she has noticed but not touched every night of their lives together, wonders if he knows this kiss is because of choir.

Everyone, even Denise, knows the tenors are not ordinary humans. Once Neil accidentally addressed all the men – basses and tenors – as 'men and tenors.' The tenors are crumpled puffins about whom the whole choir is tender when they dress to perform. Then they are ironed, their tufts combed. On performance night little collections of them practice in corners of the lobby. Broken bars of music hit tables, smash against brick corners: fragments of audible stained glass. The tenors' suits make them less absent-minded, and they do not sing through the women's part in *Mairi's Wedding* nor through the *Grand Pause* in the 56th measure. Neil does not have to shoot them after all. Between songs Neil mouths to the whole choir, "Sing to me, not the people behind me." *I will sing to you only and forever, have never sung to anyone but you,* Lena manages not to reply. *My conduit to immortality. If what passed between us during a song happened alone in a room we would be Christ and his bride.* She wants to go home with Neil after choir, lie on a flower-lined balcony with him, new music in old music's arms, ask him everything about each note and every space between. She wants him to tell her everything he knows until the last star goes down and the first warmth makes steam rise from earth. *I just care about the music, you understand,* she'd say. *Songs written in rooms like Fauré's, crowded with prayers.*

With the music over, Neil is a friendly mortal, the divine breath gone out of him. Lena knows his angels leave him alone until he invites them back. After the concert he tells everyone they did a good job. She is not sure he means it, and the following week choir is cancelled; he has resigned. The executive committee hires a replacement who thinks music begins on the page like a recipe for layered sausage and potato. She jumps on a chair, bullies the choir into spitting hard *K*s. She says, "I will not tolerate soft consonants."

FAURÉ CAN BLOW OUT a thousand candles and no one will know. The new director tells the choir to put Fauré away and take out a medley from *Guys and Dolls*. The second sopranos remind each other how much fun it was when they did this before, in '87 or was it '89, and they even wore costumes. What horrifies Lena, next to losing her true conductor, is that no one notices the difference, except maybe Alice and Holly, who have never spoken to her about the metaphysics of choir. Lena fears bringing it up in case she has imagined their sympathy. She considers quitting choir, wonders if she should stay just to keep learning about time signatures, slurs, staccato. Maybe even this stomping new director will let drop a few details about the history of music, the minutiae of composers' lives. Lena starts searching the choral room itself, and the music building, for scraps of the nourishment Neil used to give. She sees a portrait of a famous soprano, for-sale signs on the bulletin board: a cello, a full-sized keyboard. She scours locations beyond the music building for signs of the world she fears she has lost. On a shelf over sweaty jackets at Second Time Round is a chipped plaster Beethoven head whose curls spill past his collar like Neil's. She buys this and places it between her jewellery box and tin of postcards.

One evening Taste O'Ireland's mechanical cheese grater breaks down so she has fifteen extra minutes to wander the halls of the music building. It doesn't have chandeliers or keystones or round walls, just bulletin boards and huge orange doors, but music escapes through the doors and she is frozen by each set of notes: a student playing an organ, a quartet's scrap of Christmas a capella. She follows violin notes through a stairwell exit. Over the banister she sees the hair and arm of a student on the next landing down, her music sheets spread over the radiator. Even Lena knows the mathematical star paths of Bach. She imagines this student has had violin lessons since she was a child. Can pick up her instrument and fling notes up the echoing stairwell and open the doors of heaven while Lena sits, her bum on the cold tile and rubber edge of the top stair, not daring to move lest the student catch the smell of fried onion from her hair.

The music carambolas up, down, and across the stairwell, then collapses. The student has made a mistake against which all the former notes and the few she can't stop from coming after lean and fall, and the music crashes like the tenors' broken music in the lobby before the concert. Lena knows how that feels. It amazes her that this broken music happens every time the choir practices, right up to the last rehearsal, then in performance somehow the music stays intact. It's a miracle, that's the only thing it is, and here it is, the same breaking happening to the violinist. And the violinist doesn't mind. She picks up the notes, strings them on her violin and spirits them into Bach's constellations all over again. You can do that if you know how.

In choir Lena misses Neil over and over again. Denise can't say enough good about Ms Stomping Consonants. "She's always been a musician," she says. "Neil was just a nursing assistant till he was forty."

"He was?"

"He didn't get his music degree till the second year he was with us. He was just a student conductor his first year." Lena wants to ask Holly if this is true, but can't bring herself to do it. Instead she asks her, "You have to have a degree to work in a museum, right?" You have to use a certain, soft-bristled brush for the hooked mats. Place acid free tissue between layers of lace. Be able to tell by its pattern the year the lace was made. It's the kind of thing Neil knows about music, the kind of thing Lena knows about nothing. Music's mystic part she can barely apprehend, then come the technical details. Roads and roads down which you wander and study, roads so long you never come to the end. Holly has tea bun crumbs on her lip. She says yes she did get a degree, as if she was saying yes she had a small pet mouse, a white mouse that mostly hid in her bed. Not a significant mouse. It was almost an apologetic mouse, really, Lena will think as she notices the beauty of rain-shattered streetlights in her window on the bus home. She knows somewhere in this building there must be a reception desk with forms people fill out to come and learn the whole works. She wishes she had the guts to ask Holly how much you need to know before you start.

Eating the Bones

When I get the call, the only thing near me you could link to the word home is the potato garden mat I'm working on. That was sold before I started it.

Mary Hannah's daughter says, "She left you an old picture." I tell her that picture's the only home I ever had. It's every mat I've made. It moves while I remember it, something like the hologram of crab habitat my husband cut out of *Canadian Geographic;* anemones, pincers, sea glass; but soft, not sharp. What might be kittens or light is skittering down two girls; me and your foster girl Mary Hannah Vardy. Curls down our frocks or music in your kitchen? In my hologram we wriggle. Cat claws click and hitch our skirts and collars.

Last time I almost got that picture back was ten years ago. Your nun daughter called saying your house was gone. It got left to the wrong child who had Jefford's Excavation bulldoze it. Sister Beatrice took courses in Vermont that said to get over something you have to go through it, but her voice said let's get this over with.

You can have a husband and two children thirty years and they can be a pretty good husband and children, but nowhere as good as by-the-way things that weren't even supposed to be. So when Beatrice said come get a few things George has in his barn across the road, I drove down and stood on the gravel where your house was, an unbelievably tiny patch.

HALF A PLATE in the rubble has a whole ironstone rose. Your white rose bush is gone. The one blowing petals on us that day you gave me my second cup of tea and waited for me to find your ball end of green yarn in it instead of a teabag. The house isn't gone, I tell the cabbage garden. I rip the air over this square of gravel and see you turn a herring in the pan, fry it till you can eat the bones. Eating the bones is easy; fry them crisp, tear bread. Eating the bones is something no one does now. There is no step between stopping bone-eating and stopping herring-eating. No one eats herring in the other houses. They eat boiled ham, peanut butter, cheese slices not sliced from anything. This square of gravel was sliced from something. It's the crumby heel-end of your house, herringless. I, Anne, swallowed your rafters, mat frame, bed posts, hot birch junk. Persian rose wallpaper, lace on the landing over the screaming turre islands.

I didn't swallow your neighbours. They're happy to watch schools of uneaten herring leave the cove, bones in the millions, impossible to remove; you never tried to remove them. The herring are glad enough to leave the cove since you were the only one left who knew how to eat them. The glittery leftovers you wove to the cove with your mat hook. Nothing would be more lonely for the herring than hanging around while your loops unravel. People think not eating herring is of no importance.

The last silver, pink and green herring slip behind alders. Their scales illuminate the last stories your house wanted to tell. Crumb and heel-end stories, lit the way lightning lights a night garden; one white rosebush, not the red one. Two delphiniums, handle of Loyola's blueberry rake, not the statue of Mary. Spot on the kitchen wall where you had my picture. I was always going to come back for it.

I haul a paling from cow parsnip smothering Loyola's cabbage garden. One of these palings was my toy husband and another one was Mary Hannah's. We kissed them goodbye every morning and laid them in grass by the gate. That meant they were gone to work. At five o'clock we brought them in again and stood them up for their suppers. Mary Hannah's had a black crayon moustache and mine had orange sideburns. They were pretty good husbands. Even then I cut my pretend turnips like yours, in rectangles so it looked like someone gave them a lot of care to get them looking nothing like when they were found. You said they're boiled enough when the edges are blunt.

At our house my mother forgot to put soda in her dumplings and to keep the waste from my father she hid them under the big rock by our rhubarb. It rained and the dumplings greeted him by the back door in the morning. They boarded me with Liz and Eddy Mowbray next door to you. Liz and Eddie were old. Store bread squat around thin bologna, orange crystals in a glass of water. After my dinner there you gave me mashed potatoes chicken and gravy. I could see my teeth marks in your bread and butter, then you sent me out with the brush for my job; scrubbing your mats on the fence. One day Marg Vokey had to go in for tests so you asked me to draw a cat out on a brin bag and said I was a better hand to draw than she was.

Between the houses and the water is that big meadow where the Mowbrays cut their hay. Keegan Aspel's bat's in the grass from where he grew up a million summers ago but Ron Tibbo's shack is not there any more.

It made no difference to me and Mary Hannah that Ron was the town drunk. You could learn a lot from Ron. Wear a singlet all year, not just September to June. Carry an apple in your pocket in case you meet a horse. Know where you have left your nails and string. Never leave home without a bucket. If you don't bathe for more than six months you don't smell any more because of the wind and sun. We looked out through Ron's ragged curtain at the gas station flag, at Goat Island and Hallorans' place and Loyola bringing water to his pony. After Ron's cat had kittens I beat a path to his door twice a day to play with a patchy black white and orange one. Ron said I could have it when it was old enough to leave its mother. He had a green pitcher on his table full of warm Freshie he'd pour when he wasn't lying down. We dipped coconut bar cookies like pieces of burnt box in it till we got sores on our tongues. Ron had two hens that walked in and out of the shack like Min Halloran going to bingo, and one morning we went in and he had his arms up to his elbows in a kneading bowl, he asleep making bread and the hens standing on his table pecking dough.

I told Liz and Eddie Ron said I could have the kitten. They must have told him off because when six weeks came and I went down with a baby quilt in a mustard pickle box Ron said the mother had taken the kitten away and hidden it. That was when he took the picture off the wall over his table and gave it to me. I don't know what Ron Tibbo was doing with a picture like that. I brought it back to the house and Liz wouldn't even let me keep that. She said it was too filthy to clean but it wasn't. You cleaned it for me with a piece of Loyola's shirt in a basin of Sunlight and vinegar. The frame was like the piping on Marg Vokey's niece's wedding cake dipped in gold. You scrubbed down into the ridges with a toothbrush. The glass had a BB hole in the corner. "That glass is no good," you said. You fitted half a storm window in the frame, hung it by new wire in your back kitchen and said it was mine. Every grocery day I put lemons in a bowl with a doily under them to remind me of the lace frock on the girl that was me.

When Ron's shack fell down you fed his mother cat even though you hate cats. Ron went to live in half the post office. The post office was on stilts in the water. It had two doors. The boat came in and passed mail to the postmaster in one half. When me and Mary Hannah opened Ron's door his room would be half filled with fog. He'd be on the daybed and we couldn't see him till he sat up. Everyone fed him boiled ham and scoops of potato salad through the week and beef and cabbage on Sundays. I visited you once after he died and you said, "Poor old Ron, I wonder did he go to heaven?" I was drawing your stove and blue oil lamp in my mat sketchbook and you warned me, "A mat's no good without a bit of red in it."

George is out in his boat and his wife says there wasn't much in his shed. She says he was going to have a yard sale. I play hopscotch in the gravel patch. Here's the end of the back kitchen pipe to Loyola's spring. Frozen nights you let the tap drip. Here's where the wood stove was; bread before the moon sank, crossbar Loyola hung from sick on his daybed, pan where you flung the cat's turre scraps, codskin, bacon fat.

This gravel is too small to have held white clapboard, red marine paint door, stairs. Sister Beatrice hated the stairs and the inconvenience of your top front bedroom. Nowhere to hang clothes. You've got nice dresses, she said before the Mother Superior came to visit. Get rid of that brown cardigan, go up and put on what I've laid out on your bed.

You threw the birch junk for warming your sheets downstairs, screaming every time it thumped so Sister Beatrice thought you broke your neck. I said what does she expect in a house where Jesus hangs over the kitchen door Scotch taped to his cross. But she's mad at me, you said. I said that's what comes of always calling your own daughter Sister. They put cheese on fish in the convent, you said, I never heard the like. But she is a Sister. I should treat her the same as any other Sister. That didn't stop you from telling your lobster joke to everyone at the Mother Superior's wake. The one where Bill tells Joe he's sorry, they found Joe's wife on the bottom drowned, her body covered in lobsters. You shouting over and over again, and Joe said to him he says, pick them off and set her again. When you died Sister Beatrice told me the whole time you were tending Loyola you had a tumor of your own as big as a pineapple. Now that's something you never saw in your life, a whole pineapple.

George says he doesn't have my picture. I want to get out of his shed and go look in his kitchen. If he doesn't have it I know it could only be Mary Hannah that does. George has: your blue oil lamp, dented; money box from when you had the store, Japanese sugar bowl, garden cherub, English nickel teapot.

Not hot tea with two spoons of sugar and buttermilk buns. Not the photo of you in the wedding dress your mother made out of a silk parachute she found on the barrens after saying nineteen novenas to St. Jude. Not your story about riding a white horse over the swinging bridge before the tidal wave made everyone move to Parsons' Cove. Not your mat hook. Not a plank of the orange crate with the rooster I copied on burlap for Sister Beatrice's Christmas mat. Not your frying pan with two frilled eggs.

Not that you were warm or ample. You filled one kitchen drawer with jam crusts for pudding and half the time me and Mary Hannah ate them before you could put them in to soak, and you roared at us over that. You cried over the electricity bill to me who was no more than fourteen. The foster children leaving lights on all the time. You who always had enough of everything, buckets of herring, saucers of fat scraps, afraid over money.

MY HOUSE HAS NONE of that nonsense and I hate it. This house is what my children and husband wanted; a water cooler that heats water as well as cools it, the microwave, no window the right light for a St. Joseph's coat or a geranium. Nothing humble can live here, not even a kettle. The more I said I love it small the more my husband kept building on; sunroom, new master bedroom, bathroom for the new master bedroom. He gave me money for take-out breakfasts with hash browns on the weekends, the table full of ketchup packages and the children whining how come I ordered sausage patties not bacon. I only ever completed one mat the whole time I was married; the Captain's wheel from my husband's crab boat, *Northern Voyager*, with a border of things I imagined clinging to his crab pots.

My new mat is made of my daughter's Brownie tunic cut up for the drills, sweatpants Ellen next door gave me for the potato plants, and a silver scarf from Greenland for the caplin on the ground. I warn people about this house; the living room is full of rags. They think I mean there are a few rags on the piano stool and the floor, maybe some on the couch. The rags are up past your knees. My husband couldn't stand it when I made the *Northern Voyager* mat even though it was for him. Bad enough shrimp fishing in Greenland without being covered in beads and sequins and foam and eels when you get home. When he was home he wanted all oceans hidden. Not his wife swimming around waving rags and hooking them into bits of sun and moon and fish that speak. I threw my rags out and hoarded tricks I learned from you. Things no one could trip over. Rub the end of thread between bars of soap to get it through a needle. Fling water out of a teacup to mop the floor. Turn an armchair round so it looks out the window. Things I use now my children and husband are gone. The chair-back I always lean my latest mat against in its frame so I can see if the design says what I want it to. If I had Ron Tibbo's picture I could hook how the cat sat on the frock of the girl that was me. How I twirled my hair round my finger on your step to make it glitter like hers.

MARY HANNAH'S DAUGHTER wastes no time. She comes Sunday after mass with the picture. I unwrap it when she's gone. It is a Victorian picture of a woman leaning out the door saying goodbye to her soldier husband. It's not my picture. Then in the background there's a daughter sitting on the floor; one girl not two, and she's playing not with a kitten, not even with a puppy, but with a full-grown spaniel I begin to remember. It is my picture, but it's nothing like what I came to think it was over time. For the purpose of making mats that picture is of no more use to me than the four rolls of film Sister Beatrice has in two albums of you standing stiff as your ash shovel on the Basilica steps reading for the Pope's visit. All these years waiting and longing for my picture, and now any mat I make that has to do with you and your house I guess I'll have to make from out of my own head.

Jerome Hepditch

Nick has several divorced friends who go to repressive regimes looking for docile women eager to come to the west. These men seek pen pals in magazines or answer ads requesting essays on Why I Want to Teach English in Korea. They all have lovers here but without the right compliance. The lovers could tell the imported brides a few stories, like this one about Jerome Hepditch. His wife Diane was my friend for years and she told me things Kim Hye Soon must not have known or she would not have married Jerome in Boston in April. Kim Hye Soon must not have asked herself why Jerome was whisking her from the airport to the magistrate without landing on his home soil first, or why he invited only my husband, none of Jerome's daughters, not even the four who do not accuse him of anything. Perhaps she does not know he has seven daughters. Though he prides himself on being an honest man.

"Yes," Jerome's voice is lowered since Kim's daughter and parents are clearing dumpling grease off plates in the kitchen alcove. "We did have daughters, Diane and myself, but you have to understand in our culture, the things that once held people together are not considered so important any more." Like building a house in the burnt woods nine miles from any other house then telling your wife you've changed your mind about getting her a car.

During the three years Diane figured out how to get her own car and a job, we met maybe seven times at Parmesan House over veal and all-you-can-eat iceberg chunks with Kraft Thousand Island. Veal is mysterious, isn't it? You wonder about it in a place like Parmesan House. When our lunches started Diane had just got her last daughter in kindergarten and I had my first one in part-time daycare. We had noon until nearly one and she was the talker. Before I ever figured out what gave the salad dressing its colour she always turned its exact smouldering orange, lowered her chin two inches from the table and said, "Guess what I caught Jerome at last week."

I have to tell you what you would see if you met Jerome anywhere but in his own home. You would see a man who calls other men gentlemen. "I met a gentleman today who says he knows you," and he is referring to my septic tank sludge digger who rolls a partial plate around on his tongue and shows his bum crack while bending at his gas tank. You would see a man dressed in a ginger tweed jacket and wide striped tie, cleanshaven ginger hair and half inch sideburns. When he comes to visit Nick after his divorce he tells me something he would not tell just anybody. Perhaps he senses I am a woman to whom more than a few men have confided a hidden identity, which in his case is a living descendant of the vanished Beothuck tribe of Newfoundland. "I wear only what I feel they would have worn themselves," he tells me of retracing their lost hunting paths along the Exploits River. "I rub the red ochre on parts of my skin that would be exposed too much to the sun, and I make a loincloth out of the soft part of birch bark tied with caribou moss and moose sinew." He dries stomachs of wild animals on a stove rack on his roof and cuts strips of sinew which he uses for bows and arrows as well as for his wardrobe of, he tells me, fourteen loincloths. In the trailer before he built the nine mile house his wedding photo had foot-long hair and an Ozark beard. Now he wears white ankle socks and pretty, pointed black loafers so thin you can see his toes.

"Telling Gerard Walsh he loved him." Diane tells me these things about Jerome as if he were not her husband but a ridiculous neighbour down the street. "I know it was Gerard because I answered the phone myself. Before Jerome hung up I heard him say, 'I love you too'."

"Did you say anything?"

"I laughed. He hates that. He hates it when I laugh at him."

"Did he try to explain himself?"

"He said I thought for a second I was talking to you."

"He didn't get Gerard to phone then give the receiver to some woman he's having an affair with?"

Diane laughs even harder. "I never thought of that." This is the way lunches with my friends go. Me offering plausible explanations for outrageous events. I don't know why I do it. The next thing she tells me is harder to account for. "He started moonlighting taxi. I never saw any taxi. He said he made eight ninety-five the other night. He took it out of his pocket and showed it to me. Eight dollars and ninety-five cents. Two nights ago I followed him. He walked to his office, that's a two and a half hour walk. He stayed there two hours, then he walked around Crowberry Pond until four in the morning. He went back to his office again and I didn't see him till five. Lately he's been locking himself in the attic and pacing back and forth. He keeps his guns there and I'm half expecting one to go off. He never says a word to me, not a word. Did you notice him when you came to get Penny that time?

How red his face was? I thought you'd say something about it. He's depressed." This was in the old days, when her family was still going to the Independent Baptist church, when a visitor would share a boiler of spaghetti or platter of potatoes and meat and cabbage with all seven daughters, when Jerome said grace and had not told me about his loincloths. I thought maybe Diane was driving him crazy with her incessant talk, as he was a quiet man. No matter whom she discussed it seemed to take her a maximum of thirty seconds to reduce them to a rubble of tragic events and twisted motivations. I thought there was a thin possibility she was the one on the edge. The blue powder she told me about, for instance. Had she made it up? Right after the second night of pacing with the guns she said she had forced open their bedroom cabinet which for several weeks he had locked. It had her hymnal in it, her diaphragm and hair combs, and on his side nail clippers, Q tips and cortisone for the chronic coldsore in his left nostril, his father's green melamine shaving kit and a couple of Eat More bars. Now there was a plastic bag full of baby blue crystals which she tasted and could not discern soap or sugar. He could have made up anything when she asked about it. There was no label. He could have said it was bubble bath or Freshie but he lied, she knew when he was lying, and said he'd ordered it out of the back of a magazine and it was a crystal drink to increase sexual prowess. "There was never, ever anything wrong with his sexual prowess," she said over a forkful of the veal, which I don't think was veal.

The story remained ominous but kept its lid on until the part where her brother gave her the down payment on the Tercel and told her to take the kids and run for her life, which she did. Jerome sold the house and moved to an apartment over the Cast Iron all night café downtown, which I thought was very Bohemian of him, and not at all coexistent with the Independent Baptist Congregation or the Beothucks. That was the last I heard of Diane because now Jerome started phoning my husband as if they were the ones who had been friends. He corresponded with several women on the Internet and settled on visiting Kim Hye Soon. He came over and showed us pictures of weeping willows in Seoul, and said you could get McDonalds there but the government was promoting the eating of dogs. I left phone messages with Diane but she never phoned me back, and meanwhile Jerome cemented his way into our house by showing up with lacquered boxes and kimchee and hinting that he would need Nick's help at the wedding. He bought Nick a plane ticket to Boston, a white shirt and a bow tie that did not fit around Nick's extremely thick neck.

It's hard to get details out of Nick as he is an event person and does not see particulars that tell the story, but he did give me this. The new bride showed up in a gorgeous red dress with a plunging neckline. Her daughter wore a white leather mini skirt and white go-go boots, and was tragedy-struck and lonely. Nick took the daughter for a hot dog while Jerome and Kim ate rice cakes with barley and mugwort in the airport terminal. I worried slightly about the daughter and my husband but told myself Nick is a good man.

Since the wedding, a year ago now, Jerome has not phoned us. It has occurred to me that we are supposed to phone him, were supposed to phone him within a week of the event to say hi, welcome Kim Hye Soon. I keep wondering if she is thinking it is a strange thing never to see the best man again. I know Jerome took two weeks off work and then left Kim alone in the apartment each day. The daughter went to school and Jerome kept his boarder, a 34-year-old computer systems manager who isn't sure if he wants to stay here or go back to North Carolina. I imagine the boarder crossing the psychic pathways of the new family to get to the toaster or flip his egg, and I wonder if Kim has said he has to go.

I know Kim gets so lonely in the apartment that she shakes, and once she went out with a garbage bag to clean Starbucks cups and newspapers off the street, and that Jerome told her she hasn't to do that. The one time Nick phoned to ask how things were going Jerome told him these things. He said she can't stand the empty streets. I know what she means. People do not go out in the streets here, not even downtown. There is no understory, no mind behind the streets that says, "Centuries-old daily market life," or, "Working class people get together for a smoke," or, "Washerwoman throws carp bone to cat," or even, "Someone cared to plant scrap of marigolds." Kim goes out on the doorstep and looks past the cafe and the parking meters and the string of lawyers' offices, and she cries. I know she has kept her little apartment in Seoul which has been in her family for generations. Her parents are still living in it. The only piece of encouraging information I have about Kim Hye Soon is that she has that place to go back to if things do not work out with Jerome. How can you know, when you set off in your red dress, that you will miss more dearly than your own girlhood the sound of your neighbour Lee Kyong Ja clacking through a vat of snails, hearing them drop in the basket, watching brine drip from Lee Kyong Ja's fingers as she sniffs to find out if a snail is fresh and alive.

There is a little book store I go to near Jerome's apartment, and every time I go there I look up at the window to see if Kim wants to come out and play. I would suggest a small washing line in the back, and ask mischievously how Jerome is. I have lost his first wife as a friend; maybe I could gain his second. What do you think? Do you think I should knock on the door, introduce myself as the wife of the only guest at her wedding, and warn her about blue powder, guns, the whispers of Jerome's daughters, loincloths? Some of it hearsay, you understand, from one woman to another, in a land of unreal, empty streets. Or do you think by now she has figured her new husband out all by herself, no matter how hopeful she was at the beginning?

Rock Talking to Bone about Light

Brunch waitresses gathered around the cash register eating *Pot of Gold*. I didn't want to ask one to take my dirty plate so I could load a new one but I asked anyway. The smell from the barrens outside town couldn't get in here. Fermented partridgeberry juice, bogwater, sweat of Woman of Little things in her transformed state. The day's sad edges crept around a whole salmon that had olives in its eye sockets flanked by mirrors bearing cut cantaloupes and croissants, steam trays of omelette covered in melted cheese, a teenager in a chef's hat slicing a side of beef. A waitress cleaned pennies out of the chlorinated wishing fountain with one hand and held a chocolate with buttercream filling hanging out of it in the other. I blamed the mirrors for much of the sadness, their reflection of each element as it was; here a side view, here upside down. Seeing salmon and artificial plant fronds from all angles hardens the message that you will never get more here than what you see.

The brunch musician had his own sad edges. A miniature version of our already tiny premier, he played four chords in a yearning medley of Irish songs cemented with bits of Pachelbel's canon. He was the premier's unsuccessful brother. The waitresses had uniforms like uniforms I have had. They paid for them out of their first wages, and when they are not wearing them, when the uniforms hang among their jeans and sweatpants and Indian cotton dresses, the waitresses hate their stiff black and whiteness and the fact that they have to be clean and pressed. The park after brunch was no different. The willows heal and the beeches have plentiful nuts and bark that sings against your hand, but the prophet Isaiah on a bench asks for a cigarette, the mental hospital visible beyond the beeches.

"Laughing Brook," said my husband Raymond, "They gave you the wrong name." He has no idea Isaiah has seen me naked and copulating on the barrens. A lot of freefloating denizens have seen this. Most of them are birds; crows, jays, mallards and one or two of the park swans who know how to get out of the granite pond and feast on bog toads before the wardens know they're missing. I know my secret is safe with Isaiah. Denizens have a healthy demarcation between what happens outdoors and what happens domestically. I'll slip Isaiah a Djarum cigar on our way back to our car, envying him his lack of a car, his having no choice but to let freezing wind crawl up his secondhand trousers. I know Raymond would like a happy wife. He has said so many times. "I just want you to be happy." After a while I realized he meant, "I just want you to shut up." I also knew he did not mean shut up in an insulting way, he meant shut up so he can see the access road to the new hardware store. He meant don't smash glasses of wine. He meant shut up in the sense that he is a good man if you don't make him uneasy, and I can appreciate that. My friends secretly tell each other if it weren't for him I'd be sitting with Isaiah shouting poems. They think I'm lucky to have Raymond and keep saying so to my face. I mean circumstantial friends here, mothers of kids my children go to school with, wives of guys who work at Raymond's store. A store whose biggest seller is black street numbers on gold peel-and-stick backs, but which sells other kinds of numbers as well. Raymond is not the reason I am still in the world of the living. The reason is a woman I consult regularly to keep from slitting my wrists. Raymond knows her only as Rosa, the assistant general manager at Wong's Laundry where I take a couple of garbage bags of his socks and the girls' jeans when the pile gets overwhelming. At least I think he doesn't know any more about Rosa than that. If he knows about her, things aren't the way I think they are at all. Rosa is the Woman of Little Things. She says little things and does little things that are just the right things.

For instance she will give me a bread plate, not a dinner plate. On it, one layer of rice, one of beans or meat, one ladle of red curry sauce. Just that difference — eating it off a smaller plate — lifts my trap door.

She tells me anyone can see it is ordinary after fourteen years of marriage and a couple of teenage daughters to fall apart at the sight of a salmon corpse at a hotel brunch.

She lights licorice root, says the harvesters' songs stay in the smoke and overrule porridge stuck to my pan, telephone messages about taxes, the competitive tension of Raymond and me together.

She finds me a rock. The rock radiates heat to my bones; rock talking to bone about light. When I come home from sitting on the rock Raymond is relieved with what passes for my happiness.

BEFORE RAYMOND I was married to Pascal, an artist. Early on I thought the reason Pascal had no compassion was that he spent it all painting the soul of humanity in cross-sections of hill and roots. But there was no compassion in his paintings. It was one of those things I finally had to admit. Being an artist

Rock Talking to Bone about Light

did not make Pascal more compassionate than anyone else. Neither did being an artist make him any more feminine than boiler mechanics and cement finishers I passed by to get to him, though his soft hair and eyes fooled me at first. In fact the boiler mechanics were more feminine, turning into girls when we made love. They brought me to tears. Raymond, whose store smells of metal dust from his key-cutting machine, is almost that tender sometimes. The Woman of Little Things listens. When I tell her things I only have to tell her once.

"Yes," she says, "the most masculine men are like young girls."

WHEN I SNEAK AWAY from Raymond and walk past railings and old maples and the vacant lot that used to be the Presbyterian churchyard, she makes love to me. Rather she changes into beings who do. My favourite one of her beings is a bull moose. Our game is this; I have wandered to the east hill beyond the vacant lot and am with an unnamed friend who shouts, "Look! It is charging us," and flees. The Woman of Little Things has become such a large and angry wild animal I know there is only one way to stop her from goring me with her antlers, stomping me to mush with her hooves. Knowing I am ovulating I turn my back to her, pull down my jeans and lift my haunches. At my smell she whuffles and slows, questioning, sniffing for a second, then pushes in the huge penis with its good scratchy hairs. Tamaracks scratch my knees and send fumes of popped gin-berries. Her forelegs are surprisingly gentle around my shoulders like waves over a rock. Her penis rumbles, climaxes, then can't throw me off, and I grab her side hairs and ride under her belly until I slide off in a cranberry bog miles down the shore. Her semen smells like fresh bean sprouts, same as men's. I become pregnant and I know the offspring will be shaped like a young moose but without the hair; a flesh-covered slender and beautiful young human moose. She dances, this moose child of mine, with waves as her backdrop and rain as her curtain, the Great Bear and sun her limelight. She drinks rockwater laced with small fish.

THE WOMAN OF LITTLE THINGS understands when I tell her that by none of this do I wish harm to Raymond, whose name almost means light of the world if you put ray with the French word *monde*. She sulks. The light of the world has nothing to do with him, she says, he did not cause his name. She concedes there may be a spiritual reason for him having the name he does, and watches me go back to him. I have gone back to him countless times. He says, "You look pensive." Woman of Little Things says it's not his concern that keeps me with him, it is the way he decides to make jam for the first time in his life and stands stirring caramelized berries while his solitary hand waits for him on the table undemanding as an old friend at the pool hall. Simple company is addictive, says Woman of Little Things, and she takes me on a walk that would be small-town suicide if it were not for the smell of meat frying. Sniffing breakfasts between people's yards keeps me going. Edges can creep as sadly as they like; if someone is frying bacon and making coffee I will be saved. Woman of Little Things reminds me that Raymond, light of the world, makes coffee and bacon every Saturday morning. She is and is not interested in convincing me to leave him. I go to see her a little too often, and she likes to have Saturday mornings off.

I TOUCHED THE SALMON. Its skin stuck to my finger. I considered taking the olives out of its sockets. Would they make a sucking sound? Would hotel security men with glittering buttons stream from elevator doors? I put my coat on and Raymond followed me to the park, where he watched me suck the olives until they fell apart in my mouth and the pimentos slithered down my throat slippery and whole. Raymond doesn't like any kind of insinuating, happy or unhappy. He likes me to tell him straight out that I am the happiest woman on earth, constantly, because of him. I do this when I can. They say in women's magazines that you should do this because men are easily shattered. So we went home, and Raymond went downstairs to file his chainsaw and I microwaved some sausages for our daughters then went in the garden to watch evening primroses snap open. I have several kinds of snapping flowers. Snapping turtle-flowers explode when you touch mature pods. It is their way of tossing their black seeds over the soil. If you fondle an immature pod it will slowly unseam itself. The seeds, white instead of black, cling to the pod. Evening primroses are a flower-a-day species like day lilies. Seed catalogues say they have been known to burst open with a fluorescent flash, and I am waiting to witness this. I also have snapdragons. Raymond doesn't know I have snapping flowers. He doesn't know I can sit in my garden for two hours doing nothing but waiting for them to snap. He thinks I am cooking, because of the sausage aroma, which the microwave takes thirty seconds to create. He thinks I am weeding, then reading the paper, none of which he minds, though he has asked me to do his books, as if he believes I have time I am not using. I used to fry sausages by hand but my children don't like the little black bits caused by a real frying pan. I have a secret theory that if I microwaved myself for an infinitesimal time period every morning, my family would look at my plump shining skin and assume I have become happy.

I have two recurring thoughts, one happy, at least it seems happy to me. It is linked to flowers. It's that inedible plants don't have to smell good to us but they do. There's no reason why irises and dogberry flowers and alder pollen should smell good to us, but they do smell good. We have the necessary receptacles to report a good smell, when it wouldn't matter if there was a bad smell, or no smell at all. I find this encouraging. Woman of Little Things, who is surprisingly practical at times, says the plants smell good because they are trying to suggest uses to us that we haven't yet discovered. I haven't told Raymond about the plants, even though you'd think I'd want to tell him something positive. You know what kind of thing Raymond likes to hear? He likes to hear, "I took the video back to the store." To him, this is evidence of a happy woman, contentedly sealing up small loose ends that would fray a hole in the world if she left them undone. Why did he marry me? Why didn't he marry Deb Gallagher across the road, for whom he could have cut plywood toadstools to tole paint, or Moira Hann next door, about whom there's a hint of something more exotic than her job distributing lotto tickets to all the Mini Marts would lead you to believe.

The other thought I can't shake is that Raymond is not married to these women because he likes being married to someone who monitors flowers for their fluorescence, who has sex with women transformed into wild animals of the barrens, who breaks under the strain of the artificiality of a hotel brunch. What I wonder is, if he knows where I go, knows even about the silken moose daughter, my pact with Isaiah and jays and crows, does he slip this knowledge in an unconscious pocket, the way the wind slips fallen partridgeberries under pillows of caribou moss, or is he taking the time he needs to make other plans? And what could he be planning? I mean if I was Deb Gallagher or Moira Hann and I was married to Raymond, and say I knew Raymond was having an affair with a cow moose who was really his friend Barry Whelan who fills the Pepsi machines at the pool hall, what would I want to do with that information? The thing is, I don't believe many things but I believe one thing and it's this; that the way you do one thing has everything else you do within it. I mean if Raymond had a secret life I would see it when he eats his porridge. The way he could have seen mine, if he'd wanted to, the moment he watched me disintegrate those two olives with my tongue.

Cremona Has a Secret

Win wants to know who "they" are, but does not ask. Her mother, a kite over the sea, would falter, perhaps fall. "They" are so many and pervasive, it would take a lot of mental backtracking to list them, when there is sky, wind, flight to enjoy. Win can backtrack if she likes, figure out who "they" are herself. At home in Sulfur Mills, "they" are pitiful at orchestrating the backdrop of life; where they should put waste bins along Main Street, there are Burger King wrappers in the gutter. They have put up no Victorian lanterns and no pots of fuchsias on the lampposts in summer. If there is a need for fireworks, they provide only Roman Candles and a few Rockets; no Catherine Wheels, no Exploding Glories. There is a general lack of knowledge about gentle, manicured order. They change bus schedules at whim, once leaving Vivian Baikie standing in front of the Co-op Grocery for forty-five minutes with a bag of live lobsters before she decided they must have cut the one pm stop.

Win would be all right if she could understand her mother's "they" to mean the town hall and municipal workers. But "they" transgress municipal boundaries to include bigger things; "Oh, they've added five fifty onto the Canada pension," – and things that have no size at all. Win puts it down to her mother's childhood in the war in the industrial north of England, when they could order you into an air raid shelter while bombs flattened your school and Sharpe's Butcher and Ridley's sweet shop. They could dictate the number of raisins you were permitted to bake in a pudding. After the war, in Vivian's seaside town of Amble Sands, they built an amusement park at the pier. The real source of her mother's concept of "they," Win decides, is the carnies who operated the bumper cars, the roundabout and the Ferris wheel. This was joy, colour, festival. It had a season, a time limit, a manageable orbit and a pink ticket that held your thrill until the carnies tore it open for you. Win decides her mother's "they" are the carnies who operate the great roundabout of life.

Back and forth "they" go over the Atlantic, for here "they" are in Cremona, Italy, where Win and Vivian have taken a hotel room because Win wants to see the birthplace of Stradivari. "They've got to have more than that going on here," Vivian says to the concierge at the Astoria, who speaks no English at all.

Stradivari is a dreary prospect for Vivian, fresh from holiday in Rome and Florence with a frivolous day-trip to Pisa, where she laughed at the way they had plonked the leaning tower on its scrap of lawn without any sort of platform.

"I think I'm starting to understand Italian," Win said as they passed a newsstand. "I think that headline says Fish Eats Person from Pisa: Great Tragedy."

"I can't get over how the tower is situated," Vivian said, and walked all the way around it in the searing heat, while Win sat under the one shade tree and ate cherries out of a bag, and watched young Germans take photos of each other posed so they appeared to have caused the tower to lean by pushing it, then with the camera tilted so that the tower appeared straight and it was they who leaned.

"MEN DON'T FOLLOW YOU when you're in your seventies," Vivian said the fourth time she had to wait while Win told a man she would not go for coffee. By the Trevi Fountain Vivian said, "As you get older you don't want to have your picture taken. You'll notice that as it happens to you." It has already happened to Win. She has to have had a deep sleep, she has to have shuddered with release or spent a morning drinking coffee and eating croissants in the sun, or be sitting near an open window with a lace curtain listening to rain hit the street, for her photo to be soft. Otherwise she is gritting teeth or frowning or tightening the cords in her neck. Win sees her mother has put away the sorrows of her lost beauty. She has folded them like table linens and put them in a drawer, if sorrows are what they are. Vivian is matter-of-fact, not sorrowful. "What do you have instead?" Win wants to ask her, for her own sake, not her mother's.

She knows her mother is still chasing some balloon of promise. Vivian is not bound to the way things are. In Florence, when they opened their window to look out on the Mercato Nuovo where throngs examined leather and glass and a dejected boy sat in his derelict wagon of sliding doors, Vivian said, "This, with the window open and the market outside, reminds me of New York. Not when we were there, but the illusion of New York. Aren't they hilarious with that pig?" At the front of the market, right under their window, was Pietro Tacca's bronze pig cast from the Greek boar in the Uffizi gallery. While the original pig sat unmolested behind protective railings, the market pig constantly had its nose rubbed by visitors for good luck. At three o'clock in the morning Win and Vivian could look out their window and see someone rubbing its nose. Now, at two in the afternoon when sensible Italians rested behind their shutters, there was a hundred-yard lineup in front of the poor pig. It was an oxidized black except for the snout, rubbed to glittering.

"What do you mean, the illusion of New York?" This was the second time the illusion of New York had cropped up for Win. The first time was at a concert by the Florentine Chamber Orchestra. The first half was the world premiere of a composition by the conductor. Win felt violin notes fall on her like blossoms. Real new Italian music from the composer himself. The second half was his arrangement of *West Side Story*. What? Italy, nostalgic for the memory Europe had of itself when it reached the new world? Win enjoyed this question, a dream of a dream of a dream, over several siestas.

"Well," Vivian said patiently, "The people are completely unpretentious, and the place is full of *romance*. I can't understand why there isn't any here." New York, the only place where things were as they should be. How had this woman ended up in Sulfur Mills?

Win is aware, on this holiday, of the part of herself that is like Keith Baikie. This part spends hours looking at Galileo's instruments in the science museum while Vivian sits waiting for her on another floor doing her best to ignore several tons of pickled human brains, uteruses and skeletal fragments from four-hundred-year-old laboratories.

The balloon of promise is gone for Win. She already has a husband; romance is limited to things she makes up herself, like how his hand when he's asleep curves into the angles of God's hand in Michelangelo's *Creation of Adam*. Even little romances of being alone are not as strong as they used to be. A ribbon of steam does not catch her heart. One white pigeon is not a magic omen. She is more intrigued by an old woman crossing the street in a headscarf that looks as if there is a coffee table under it. Another woman, who looks like a man, carrying a flat of tomato plants near her head. Win has become interested in props and scaffolds and odd burdens old women have. She feels she is closer to their state than Vivian is. She can imagine waking up one day and finding a coffee table on her head, which she must cover with a scarf before she goes out. She likes the idea of buying a flat of tomatoes and carrying them along the street. The sun will light their patch. Worms will work the soil. Children's voices will sail over the leaves. Win likes to see old men play cards outside taverns. People her own age are invisible; she is invisible, except to a remnant of men and to Vivian who is faithfully interested in her, although Vivian becomes different on holiday.

"I mean you must have something here besides Stradivari," Vivian says to the concierge as if he is a member of "they," and personally owns an arm or a finger of the dead Stradivari. "He's been dead for five hundred years."

Who does Vivian become? Win thinks it is Vivian at twenty-one, in 1952, barely grazed by forty years of marriage to Keith Baikie. Vivian was Vivian Waugh, and on holiday she becomes Vivian Waugh again, and Vivian Waugh has been unknown to herself since she was a stenographer, since wartime newsreels showed a New York full of romance. She knows things that have been in the papers. There has been lots of psychological development of Vivian's married self. What's missing is psychological development of her individual self, Win thinks. So that when she leaves the house where she has been in a routine defined with Keith Baikie for forty years, she is not a seventy-year-old woman. She is a girl who could have been played by the young Audrey Hepburn. Inside her, on the Italian street, float the illusion of New York, the balloon of promise, the bluebird of happiness. Vivian is having more fun than Win is. In Florence she drank tangerine rum soda right after breakfast. She carried her sandals and walked barefoot over filthy hot cobblestones. "Watch out for the horse droppings," Win warned, thinking blisters, blood poisoning, long waits in Italian hospital corridors, payphone calls over the Atlantic to her father: "Your mother thinks centuries of European civilization instantly decimate any germs those horses could leave, ha ha ha," while Win tries to find the clause about flying your dead body home in her Air Canada insurance pamphlet. It's true that her grandfather, Vivian's father, once told Win in an airmail letter that he believed Keith Baikie liked hillbilly music.

THOUGH VIVIAN is not interested in Stradivari, hillbilly music is not what she wants to hear in Cremona. The brochure the concierge gives her lists the only musical event this week as an operetta in a barn fifteen kilometres outside the town.

"I'm not going to suffer through third-rate performers in a barn."

"A violinist plays every violin in the Stradivari museum every morning." Win decides to invoke "they." "They can't leave the Stradivaris in glass cases without exercising them or the violins will lose their voices. The violins will die." Nothing much thrills Win any more. Maybe someone could play her like that. Ecstasy spilling through her openings, no one can help it, anise ferns grazing the walls as someone wheels a cart down the street.

"I'm telling you, they've got something else here. Cremona has a secret and I'm going to find out what it is." Vivian has hinted to Win that she thinks all of Italy is keeping a secret. They are keeping their natural Italian passion under lock and key. Vivian stops and stares at men dressed so formally, buttoned from their shoes to their necks. "Isn't it the men who are supposed to be staring? And the women – you wouldn't want to get on the wrong side of one of them." Win agrees about the women; their makeup concealing lips sharp as knives.

Where are the Italians Vivian's father told her about when he came home from the war?

"They threw fennel on the streets to carpet the paths of English soldiers. They gave us lamb and artichokes on skewers, and sang *Pagliacci* on balconies."

They aren't singing it now. The only place Win and Vivian heard any incidental music at all was in Pisa when they got stuck in McDonald's waiting for the train, and that was only Andrea Boccelli.

"He's overrated," Vivian said.

"CREMONA IS the birthplace of nougat," Win offers after one of her solo trips around the piazza. She takes her own lone walks; shadow-play of a man dancing and smoking his cigarette through jeweler E. Fantini's night door on Ponte Vecchio. Light glittering on a glassmaker working with a calculator surrounded by Florentine glass fish, cockerels, butterflies. A *duomo* in Perugia with steps, towers, ramparts, bridges and windows made of chocolate. She finds little histories and keeps them to herself. "Along that bridge where the goldsmiths are," she did not tell Vivian in Florence, "there were tanners soaking hides in horse urine." The main headline Vivian was looking for was where you could get a good cup of coffee. Win was constantly coming in with new coffee reports.

Vivian said, "It's never hot enough because they insist on putting it in glasses, and there's either too much milk in it or none at all, or you have to have chocolate floating on the top and it costs six dollars. I can't understand what they're thinking."

"Italy is only the good cup of coffee capital of the world. Italian coffee machines."

"I'm dying for a good hot cup of instant."

"So nougat," her mother seems curious about Cremona so Win breaks her ban on little histories. "There was a Cremonese princess who had everything, and the king gave a party and offered half his kingdom to the guest who could bring her a gift she didn't already have, so this poor guy boiled up some stuff and put almonds in it and made nougat. I think it was in sixteen hundred."

"It's not nougat. There has to be something else. I'm going out."

On her own meander through the streets Win watched a confectioner tie ribbon around a cake, the customer walk down the street with the bare cake in her hands. If only her mother could be content with a ribbon edge, the surface of marzipan. Nothing, Win remembers now, has ever halted Vivian on her quest for something else. Vivian walks with her head forward, body trailing behind through an ever-uninteresting present, into her own golden elsewhere.

VIVIAN PUTS ON A PAIR of freshly washed underpants, wrung out but not dried. A carriage horse in Florence gave her that idea in his wet burlap coat in the hot square. If Vivian is going out Win will have to go too, although she feels this is the time to slip under a cool white sheet and let Florentine and Cremonese scenes slip deliciously past her eyelids for an hour or so. In Florence Vivian went out while Win rested. To find her way back, Vivian asked people in the street, "Where is the bronze pig?" She charaded rubbing his nose, getting her picture taken.

"His snout sparkles," she told an old man coming out of a shop with a bag of lemons. She made sparkly movements with her fingers beside her own nose and considered oinking. Win had been proud of finding their *Albergo* in the first place on the tiny, unmapped Via Calimaruzza near the famous Piazza della Republica. Vivian returned limp but brave after drinking two bottles of water and using a third to replenish her underpants. Win was still contemplating shades of white under her cotton sheet. "I'm really sorry," Vivian said. "You must have been so worried."

WHEN VIVIAN GETS AWAY from Keith Baikie she treats shopkeepers and taxi drivers as if she wants them to believe she has been ordering people around all her life.

"Take us to the River Po."

The taxi driver considers this.

"Po, look. The river. Just take us to it." To Win she whispers, "The Po will have cafes. We'll get out of this heat. There'll be things going on." The driver makes what seems to Win like a doubtful start up some westbound streets, then along the very boulevard Win knows can lead only to cement guardrails, dried mud flats with old newspapers and oil cans sticking out of them, galvanized fences with clanking signs that warn *Pericoloso*. But it does not lead there. The cab comes out onto dappled light, weeping willows, box hedges containing old aloes and young oleanders that have begun blooming. It pulls up at *La Lucci La Trattoria*, where Vivian sinks into a white chair under parasols.

"I'll have a papaya granita."

The waiter brings Vivian the granita with a platter of fried shrimps and scallops.

"This is more like it." *There are always white chairs to recline in. There are always granitas and scallops, we just don't realize it. The world has a courtyard if you know how to get in.* Vivian has the key in her heart, on a green cushion. Win had no idea.

While they eat and drink Win notices a creature engraved all over the trattoria. It looks disconcertingly like a grub with wings. On the parasols. Over the door. On the half gate. The grub looks like the kind of thing that would love to hide at the bottoms of trattoria saucepans, bury itself in the food so it appears to be the end of a tagliatelle or an engorged rice kernel. It's not the kind of thing Win would want her clients to be thinking about if she owned a trattoria.

"What do you think that is?"

"It's a firefly," Vivian says, and Win realizes that's what *Lucci La* means; *Lucci*, lucid, lucifer, flight of fire. There are no fireflies in Sulfur Mills. Children do not run through meadows at dusk lighting their way with jars. No fireflies, no weeping willows and no papaya granitas. There is one oleander, which grows on Vivian's doorstep in an Italian pot, and it never flowers.

Music floats over the hedges. Vivian orders two minced clam tagliatelles and a litre of white wine. When it gets dark she decides to follow the music. It leads to the biggest fairground Win has ever seen, much bigger than the one at the pier end in Amble Sands, infinitely bigger than any tattered ring-toss that has stumbled through Sulfur Mills. A lit-up pirate ship rides the sky. *Luna Park* is written in roller-coaster lights. Vivian walks the perimeter of carousels, Ferris wheels, red and gold trains, hot candied almonds and Cremonese nougat. A balloon seller with gas balloons hypnotizes Win. She can't look at anything else. The people choosing balloons are hypnotized too, they point to a silver dragon.

"No that one." A funny red and yellow car.

"But the clam shell is so beautiful." The people start to bob back and forth as if they too are on strings in the balloon man's hand, filled with helium. Win tries to keep up with Vivian, who goes deeper into the crowd. *Effervescent, that's what my mother is, and here she is effervescence in the midst of effervescence. How easy it would be for her to dissolve.* But Vivian does not dissolve. She emerges beside the nougat tent, ready to go back to the Astoria. She looks like she's had a good big sigh, the way everyone feels when they've had three glasses of chilled white wine on a hot day. Which Win and Vivian have had, but Win knows that's not it, it's something else. Her mother said she was going to find something else, and she did.

Black Petunia

It's all right for our small town liquor store to sell turkey platters and dresses from warehouse fire sales, but it's not all right for an old woman to see if a blouse fits before she buys it. I'm here buying a six-pack for my husband. He's sweating because his cement mixer broke and he had to mix the basement floor by hand. I hear one cashier tell another, "We get them all the time, people stripping off in the store trying stuff on. Last week a woman stripped off to try on a blouse and she must have been nearly eighty for God's sake."

I bet that woman didn't take her bra off to try on a blouse. I ask myself what's wrong with seeing an old woman in her bra. I can picture her. She has come from down the bay to see doctors who will tell her which scopes they want to stick down her and up her. She'll tell them they won't get near her with a scope, she's too old to fool around with that. But she will ask for cream for the ulcers on her leg. She figures no one is watching her as she peels off her blouse behind boxes of ABC detergent and slips on the sheer silvery one that reminds her of herring skin. She likes it and may wear it to bingo but she thinks blouses these days never fit you around the bust. They make them for women who have no busts. Captain Morgan looks down at her from the liquor shelf and agrees. "Get yourself a good big blouse girl," he tells her. "Get one that fits."

"The men from the Russian trawler stripped to their underwear," the cashier says. "Trying on jeans." Her tone says, "Garlicky Russian man. Skinny, sunburnt, foreign Russian man. Legs like chicken wings. Russian man whose next move you never can tell."

But the boat was Ukrainian, not Russian. The Ukrainian men were trapped here after fishing shrimp for an American owner who would not pay them, or send them home, or come for his rusting boat. For three months the men walked from the boat to the little fish and vegetable market and corner store. They carried bags bulging with grapes, melons and broccoli back to the ship, and made phone calls home from the town hall. My friend Margo took them tobacco and paper tubes. Margo and the Ukrainian shrimp fishermen are the only people I ever met walking in this town.

I am not such a young woman myself. I tried on a pair of shorts in the second-hand store down the shore last week without going into the dressing room. I slipped the shorts under my skirt, slipped the skirt off over them, then back again. Are people talking about me now?

There is no dressing room at the liquor store. I figure the old woman did her best. Why are the cashiers so uptight about her? Same for the fishermen. I say if you don't like their underwear don't look. It'll all be over in a minute. What's the fuss about? Man from the foreign country of Ukraine. Woman from the foreign country of Oldness.

Now I am in the swimming park. There are hundreds of people. It is the twenty-second of July. My husband is sitting beside me. My red-haired four-year-old pours buckets of water in the sandbox. I love swimming pools. People of all sizes not caring what they look like. Humongous women standing by the water in black bathing suits with petunia skirts. Huge teenage girls drying their ankles while their cleavage hangs in yellow and green spandex. Twelve-year-old boys pelting each other with water bombs, their bellies hanging over wet trunks with dangling strings. Then the perfect people. Blonde lifeguard in a blue bikini, her skin burnt carrot brown. I'm glad for her sake that it's fake. Student with a sunhat over his face and a book by Charles Dickens beside him on the grass, *Our Mutual Friend*. Skinny boys under twelve. One has a pointy chin and ribs like a sparrow's. He yells sly nicknames at people he hardly knows then runs fleet as a young fox, like a boy should run.

I finish my twenty minute breast-stroke down to the silver birch and back. I am shuffling back into my clothes under two towels when a boy comes up to me on the grass. I can't figure out how old he is. Maybe sixteen. Maybe he is a young man. The Beatles are starting to seem like kids to me.

"I'm sorry madam," he says, "but you should go in the dressing room to do that."

My underwear is in my hand under the towel. I am working on getting dry one half at a time. The dressing room is a soggy wooden hut across two hundred yards of gravel and a bridge. I wouldn't dream of going there unless I was in the middle of my period. I do not say this to the small young man, who has freckles and blond hair. He squats two inches from my face. I say, "Go away." Of course he doesn't. He does not introduce himself. He seems to be the self-appointed modesty police. He says there are a lot of people here who I might be making uncomfortable. I decide he must be a lifeguard. Maybe he feels he is guarding the lives of the fat thirteen-year-old boys whom I might be about to rape all at once. I tell him to get lost. He turns red and leaves, shouting, "Use the dressing room next time." I look around to see the people I have offended. They are tearing butterscotch doughnuts apart with their teeth or running after youngsters in the wet grass. Behind me a stiff woman in a Tilley hat is looking. Maybe she has been watching. Maybe she is offended because she knows I'm half naked under my towel. I decide not to think about her.

Later I tell my friend Margo. I'm starting to think maybe I was indecent after all. I tell her I've been getting dressed under towels all my life and nobody ever complained before. What does she think? "We'll get a bunch of us ladies in our forties and do it," she says. "Together. All of us. Just give me a call when you're ready."

She knows this story is about the country of Oldness. The country you visit then can't leave. The country youth does not want to see in its bra, not even an accidental corner winking past a too-small towel. "I'll be ready," she says, and I love her for it. That's what I call a friend. Someone who sees as I do how frightening we women become, just sitting on the grass by a river as time passes.

Nothing but Bethlehem

This is one of those suppers when a surface crack in the household can turn into a structural one. Louise thinks talking to Martin about his muffler created a surface crack. It would have been a crack even if she had said only, "I'm concerned about that muffler, Martin," and not mentioned stupidity or asphyxiation. In a minute his rabbit news will crack right through the house, though you might get Martin and Louise to agree the crack was there all along. They agree about many things. The heart of the marriage is hanging together, and they love each other, though Louise thinks Martin regrets that she is not more contented. They agree that a corn supper on a wooden table with steam floating up from it is a beautiful thing. That they are lucky to have a shady yard in summer. That ten thirty is a decent hour to go to bed, and it's good to have musical instruments in the house. They have each lost something old because they let someone borrow it, and they both like a window open while they sleep.

* * *

GRADE THREE: Jemma is in her painting smock at school. She is standing up telling the class about her rabbit and her dad's hens. The teacher has a sturdy little body that sways like she's on a raft as she holds a large book about African animals. The teacher makes cake from apples that grow in her garden. At Jemma's home there are yellow silk curtains, through which can be seen a glossy cooked ham with netting over it. No one is in the room with the ham. One parent, either Louise or Martin, is in the garden. I don't know which one, though I know what the parent in the garden is doing.

The garden is not an old garden like the teacher's. It has no fence, no apple tree, and that is part of the problem, though the builder did leave a trembling aspen. Louise is a cold name. I know it's wrong to say anyone is cold. Louise has a spirea bush, but it is not a bridal wreath spirea. A bridal wreath spirea is that bush you see everywhere in spring. It spills veils of lovely white blossom. Louise has an ordinary pink spirea whose flowers are static. She went to the plant store and asked for a spirea, her heart full of the thought that finally she would get the lustrous thing she wanted, and they gave her this one. She assumed it was her heart's desire until it bloomed seven months later. She has cooked a ham for the same reason that she wanted the white spirea; to fill her life with wholeness. The father, Martin, is part of the plan. Jemma's father has a false tooth which he sucks onto his tongue and plays with as he talks. This makes people like Louise more than they normally would. He is one of the men who work in hard hats on hot days with jackhammers on the road. He eats two-for-a-dollar hot dogs at the gas station and tells stories about growing up in Quebec like Roch Carrier. His stories have farmhands in them, and sisters with moustaches, and boys whose fathers call them by the names of wagon parts because they can't remember all their kids' real names, and maples that are always being pruned or tapped for syrup, with limbs and trunks falling on people's heads along the way. Martin's stories comfort Louise and turn Jemma into a child everyone loves.

* * *

BY GRADE FIVE Jemma has divided her home into two worlds. Her mother's contains old dishes that were not made in England. Her mother, Jemma feels, is a person who is waiting for her dishes to become English, and whose clothes and books and tins of powder take up all the cabinet space. Her father's things lie in their own refugee piles all through the house. Jemma knows her father is a gypsy in the house and her mother is the person who really lives here. Going on twelve, Jemma feels she is pretty much formed. She will refer to grade five as the year she was grown up; will look at ceremonies of old faiths and proclaim them right to mark the coming-of-age at twelve.

SO THE LITTLE FAMILY is eating corn on the cob. The corn is fresh and they don't feel the need to have anything with it. There are a dozen cobs on a platter. Martin has corn in his stubble. He rolls his cob in the butter dish. Louise slices kernels off with a steak knife and eases them on her fork in double rows. Jemma is eating and thinking about how Plumberry is alive even though he's going on nine and her *Caring for your Dwarf Rabbit* manual says dwarf rabbits live about five years. She says, "I can't get over how Plumberry's still alive, and how good he looks," and she's thinking it must be because she has been good to the rabbit, cleaning his cage, putting vitamin drops in his water bottle, taking him out in his harness to run in the grass and eat weeds. The manual says a dwarf rabbit can die instantly if you drop it, and she has laid Plumberry down gently, all these countless times.

Her dad puts his cob down and says, "Honey, we replaced Plumberry. He did die. He died one day when you were in school and we didn't tell you. You were only eight." He sounds impatient. Jemma has said a few times now how she can't get over Plumberry being so old. Her dad doesn't like being stuck on the same terrain. He's known all along that Plumberry isn't really Plumberry, though the original lie may have been his wife's. Martin lies all the time, though everyone would agree he's a good man. If a supermarket clerk asks him how much an item is, he says, "Two forty-nine," so he won't hold up the line while she phones in a price check. Jemma has seen a clerk ask him if that papaya juice is good, a new kind Jemma knows he's never had before. He said it was great. When Louise noticed Martin's small lies it made her wonder if he was telling big ones. She became good at reining these thoughts in. Jemma feels there is a lot her mother doesn't know.

It's true there are things Louise misses. When she sees Martin make himself a grilled cheese sandwich an hour after this supper she won't think, hey, he made a grilled cheese sandwich the day the rabbit died too, because she doesn't know about the other sandwich. She knows he likes fooling around doing stupid things with animals. She knows he'd like to have a couple of cows, and that he catches the rooster and brings him next door to show Mary, just to show her a big fat rooster crowing murderous threats in the crook of his arm. Mary is scared to death of the rooster.

JEMMA WATCHES MARTIN go down the basement stairs without taking his plate to the sink, breaking Louise's house rule that says it's slatternly to leave dirty dishes around. Jemma has looked slatternly up and read it means slovenly, to spill, slop or waste, and that a slattern is a woman. The word is from the seventeenth century. Louise uses old words honestly. She learned them from her mother, who heard them from her own mother. I'm sure Jemma won't be able to resist using some of them herself. The seventeenth century is not all that long ago. Louise keeps using the old words even when she knows parts of their meanings have worn off and decisions have to be made about how to speak of a man who now might be expected to clean up his own plate of melted butter. Jemma is sure her father cares about none of this.

It's her mother who faces her across the table, the power of words coiled inside her. Jemma has figured out that her mother has words about how things should be, her father words about the way things are. Her mother's words are more threatening, and Jemma takes this to mean that they are more powerful. Jemma has learned the power of a few well-chosen words herself. She asks, "What did you do with the body?" Louise goes on eating corn off her fork, without any butter. Martin is filing his chainsaw in the coolest part of the house downstairs, between the hooks with his work shirts on them and the corner shelf that has his duct tape and all his screwdrivers and nails on it. Jemma has begun to suspect everything is a pack of well-intentioned lies.

"I don't remember," says Louise, and maybe she doesn't. The body is right where either she or her husband left it, under the boulder by the juniper where the bog starts, beyond where Louise is trying to grow hollyhocks. It is now a collection of white bones arranged the exact same way they were arranged inside Plumberry, only flattened. You couldn't draw a more graceful arrangement of tiny rabbit bones with a soft pencil and good rice paper. In spring, notes from the songs of loons and thrushes drop by to grace the bones, and in winter good thick snows come up to the boulder's top, surrounding the little grave with a blue-white curtain. It's a nice grave. It's the kind of grave I wouldn't mind having myself one day. At this point Louise would like to think about the bones, have a peaceful conclusion, but there is the new rabbit to think about. The one that has been made to masquerade here almost four years as Plumberry, but who is not Plumberry. Louise got used to it years ago. She is the one who spends time with it every day. She is the one who sits on the couch with it licking salt from the inside of her elbow with its hot little tongue. She did those things with Plumberry too, and a lot more besides.

"What killed Plumberry?" Jemma sees Plumberry was four when he died. Louise remembers what it felt like to lose Puffy when she was almost twelve. Puffy looked like snow with a patch of asphalt showing through. She saw the car approach slowly. If she had been older she would have known to wave, point, stand in the road. There would have been plenty of time. The driver would have seen her. She composed new words to "O Little Town of Bethlehem" which she sang every day walking home from school. Everything fit perfectly when she changed nothing but the town of Bethlehem.

O little dog of Station Ridge,
how still we see thee lie.
Above thy deep and dreamless sleep
the silent stars go by.

Orion glittered above Norman's Building Supplies. Louise wept tears that covered a lot of things besides Puffy and dried by the time she got home. Jemma does the opposite. She weeps and wails over phone and TV limits in front of her parents, is analytical and tearless in private over things of the heart. Jemma would have strode in the road and stopped that car before it killed Puffy. Louise says, "Honey, I'm not sure what killed Plumberry." It sounds to Jemma like her mother has said, "There are a whole lot of reasons why he died." Louise does have an infuriating way of veiling things. She is thinking about all the times she took Plumberry to her little office at the back of the newspaper building. He was hard to catch when she wanted to bring him in from the car. He hid under the driver's seat eating crumbs. He looked so perfect the day she found him lying in his wood chips. She has wondered if she damaged vital organs. He loved being in her arms once she caught him.

Jemma says, "He would've only been in his fifties if he was a person." Louise hears "You're almost fifty Mom, you are close to death too," though she knows hearing this is unreasonable. She has the urge to say Plumberry would be dead by now anyway. When you've got over a sad thing you don't always console someone who has just found out about it, even if you know how it feels, and even if the someone is your child. People assume mothers are perfect. Not their own mothers, but mothers they see and hear about.

"It's no use trying to make me feel guilty," Louise says, "I already think everything's my fault," and she gets up and scrapes the dishes. Jemma picks up the impostor rabbit as if it is the one in all this who needs comforting and brings it to her room even though it has chewed through her phone wire twice. While she's gluing her September collage she can smell her dad's latest grilled cheese sandwich and she's glad when he brings half of it to her. They sit on her bed together eating and he plays with the rabbit's ears as usual, plasters them tight to its head so it looks like it has no ears, and he says nothing at all about what happened, only, "This one here, he's a beau rabbit, he don't want you to care which rabbit he is," which gets to the point in Jemma's mind. Her father can always be counted on for that. He shows her how rabbits can't resist grilled cheese sandwiches, leads the new rabbit across the bed by holding a piece in front of its nose. He can do that without feeling bad, since the main thing is love is almost back.

That night when his wife turns out most of the lights and they're sitting on the couch, he tells her what happened with Plumberry and the first grilled cheese sandwich. How he was getting a kick out of leading him all over the house until the rabbit fell down the basement stairs into a bucket of lemon cleaning solvent. Unbelievably, Louise laughs. They both do, and she sits on his lap, which she doesn't do very often. Martin is so full of comfort, or is it that he is empty of self-condemnation, that he can absorb all the blame for Plumberry, for everything in the house that falls short of happiness.

Room Full of Blood

I have my new baby but we are still attached to the hospital by a needle stuck in my arm feeding some clear nutrient I have lost. After a night with this vein extension I scream and threaten to yank it out. It is attached to a frame tied to the wall. By it I feel the whole psychological content of the hospital swim in my blood. A nurse comes and I expect her to be angry but my screaming works. She doesn't know I am afraid that if I yank it out all my blood will spurt over the room and the other three new mothers in it, leaving me a spent balloon. She gets the doctor to say okay, detach her. The three new mothers do not seem to mind any of this. They have their own problems. We observe each other's dramas. When it gets too much there is always the curtain round the bed.

I did have a baby before, and can't remember anything like the trauma we have in this ward. With that first baby there were prenatal classes with placards showing abdomen and fetus cross-sections, labelled with the head's distance in centimetres from the cervical opening, and dangers like placenta previa. All any of this told me was that someone had thought it not the least bit upsetting to show a roomful of pregnant women another woman's abdomen and fetus sliced in half. We received little pieces of paper folded like paper in fortune cookies and had to read them out; either "vaginal" or "Caesarian." This was to show us one in six deliveries in our town was by Caesarian section, a national record. I nearly had no delivery at all. One day I bled little spots and a room full of interns learned what a third month uterus feels like when you shove your arm in and grope around. Their director, a gynaecologist named Doctor Kum, said, "Wild night in bed last night?"

"You realize you won't get to have this baby," said an eighteen year old with his arm inside me. I had not realized it, and I walked home and had a rest and had that baby just fine.

THIS TIME I AM OLDER, but not as old as Mona, who is forty-seven. Her bedside is a tableau of the Madonna. Her husband and adult children stand like shepherds over the tiny baby in her arms, reverent. The baby is a pulsing white baby star amid old planets, giving them new light and hope they never dreamed of. All the work, surprise, unexpected change in plans, is sooty dust at their feet. They extend an envelope of quietness around them, with a transparent membrane off which creaking trolleys, electronic beeps and corridor murmurings deflect. If you talk to Mona between shepherd visits, she talks back in a melted voice like someone who has just spent a month sitting in front of the television eating buttered toast and cheese slices in her nightdress. Nothing bothers her; look what she's gone through. You can see her arms hang like they've forever held grocery bags at bus stops, but the wonder and love of the shepherds, we feel it in the room and know the holy family will hold together as long as Mona doesn't get one iota more tired out than she already is. "I want to get my tubes tied in a couple of months," she told her doctor, "after I get back my strength."

"You might as well get it done now while we've got you in here," he said.

"I want to think about it. I feel so good just like this."

I HAVE A FRIEND who won't be my friend any more after this visit. At home Gorda comes to my doorstep at supper time with her children. I have seen her feed them turkey skin and old baked potatoes cut up and fried. Her children are starved when they get to my place. Nothing is about anything other than Gorda. I have closed the curtain around my bed because of something that has happened with Melanie, the second other mother. A curtain is something Gorda will never see as a skin of privacy. She drags a chair through it and sits to tell me she has come to the hospital not to visit me and my new baby but to request a tubal ligation for herself. "I," she says with a superior downcast gaze at my amazing redhead with midnight eyes, "have decided the world is already too burdened with ill-conceived youngsters to risk adding accidental progeny of my own." She goes on for half an hour about her careful weighing of this decision, glancing at my baby now and then not to ask how it is or how I am, but for confirmation that the world is too full of breeders and their spawn. New mother hormones flooding me with patience and understanding have saved you this day, Gorda, but I'll get you back. I will tell the world you lunch at Bruno's Trattoria on baby endives with virgin oil, then feed your children turkey skin.

MELANIE IS UPSTAIRS trying to nurse her baby whom they have put on a four-hour schedule. Melanie was in her last stage of labour when I called the nurse. "She's been here a week moaning like that," the nurse said, and left.

I yelled, "If you don't take her to the delivery room she's going to have her baby here in about fifteen minutes." The nurse called in a doctor and a team wheeled Melanie out.

That was when Mona told me, "Melanie is homeless."

Daphne is not homeless. In the third of our four corners she has to stay put three months until her baby is due. She won't wear a johnny coat or eat hospital food but has metallic-yellow maternity bell-bottoms and eats foot-long Subway sandwiches brought in by her rock band husband and four-year-old mermaid daughter. Her wax paper rustles as she drops fragrant crumbs and onion shreds on the bed. On everyone else's end cupboard crowd Kleenex and bedpans and sad foil balloons and mortuary chrysanthemums and plastic cups half full of warm orange juice with sticky rings under them and bent straws, but on Daphne's there's a bottle of wine and a candle and a tumbler of daisies, lupins and wild roses.

Gorda finally leaves and I look at my curtain and go over what happened to Melanie.

A social worker in navy-blue trousers sat with her clipboard at the foot of Melanie's bed and said, "You know of course we can't allow you to keep your baby." The rest of us clutched our babies. We hadn't known they could take your baby just because you didn't have a place to live. This seemed outrageous on a thousand levels, all of them outweighed by the clipboard. We each knew someplace Melanie could stay with her baby. Mona knew four places and I knew three.

"She could come and stay in our basement if she doesn't mind hanging out with a pile of amps and drums," Daphne said. "There's a fold-out sofa and two windows above ground." We did not realize we were telling each other this, and not telling Melanie, until she came downstairs crying.

"They feed him formula when I'm not there. They pretend it's okay for me to nurse him but they're making him not want my milk."

NURSES WHEEL MONA out to get her tubes done. "There's an opening in his schedule," they tell her. "You'd be a fool not to take it." My doctor comes to decide if I can go home. She doesn't want to let me go yet because of the clear nutrient problem. And because I've been here only a day and a half and am almost forty. She asks me again, "Have you had a bee em since the baby was born?" I know what she means because they are crazy about bee ems around here. Every nurse who comes in asks me if I've had one.

"Yes. Two as a matter of fact. Remember I told you it's because I brought my own beans and rice." I show her a disreputable container of half-eaten basmati, which she plainly finds disgusting. I have to walk the line between getting rid of her and pissing her off too much. When she's gone I say, "The thought of spending another night here makes me feel like a prisoner. I am a prisoner."

"One night's nothing," says Daphne, who will be here longer than the Arabian Nights by the time she's finished. "When I had Joanna they did the car seat test and she failed it seven nights."

"What's the car seat test?"

"They wake your baby up at three o'clock in the morning and put her in a car seat that rocks. They leave her there for two hours and check her vital signs. If they get anything irregular you can't go home until the baby passes the test."

I know that if they did this to my baby I would wrap her up and escape with her into the parking lot. It crosses my mind that the staff are onto me. They know I have forgotten to bring underwear, have forgotten one pours with blood after having a baby and needs underpants to keep a pad in place. I had to ask a nurse to find me an ancient menstrual belt in the antediluvian caverns of the basement. If any of the staff have spoken to Gorda they must suspect I have the kind of friends who do not know how to feed children correctly. I noticed when my doctor got here just in time to catch my baby she shuddered when my blood splatted her green gown. I was uncooperative about the clear nutrient. I didn't even make my first visit to this doctor until I was six months pregnant, a fact she found unbelievable, and for which she punished me by informing me my fetus had a suspiciously small head, which turned out to be untrue.

But a nurse comes in and says, "Doctor Trueblood says you can go home this evening if your husband brings your car seat up for inspection."

"I forgot somehow, to bring a bag of clothes for the baby. Can I take her home in one of these?" All our babies are wearing flannelette blankets donated by Woolworths when they went out of business. Red sleds, green reindeer. This is July.

"What if we lose the blanket? What if you don't bring it back?"

"I'll bring it back," my husband says. "I'm a town councillor's nephew." The town is a couple of thousand miles away. The room is getting crowded. I phoned the hospital chaplain to come and see Melanie, and now he's here. Melanie has not forgotten to bring clothes for her baby. In a panda bag in her cupboard are fuzzy sleepers with feet in them and a Fisher Price rattle. The chaplain is young, has just left seminary, and before that softball, asters, old fences, one or two sheep. He knows nothing about screams, blood, or social workers with a clipboard in one arm and Malanie's baby in the other.

"Make sure the authorities know myself and the other women in this room have a list of twelve homes where it is possible for Melanie and her baby to live," I tell him stupidly.

"Yes," he says.

"What's your name?" I ask the social worker. When she tells me I try burning it in my brain so I can make calls when I get home, but when she goes out the door her name disappears.

AFTER HER TUBES ARE TIED they wheel Mona back in. A tube comes from her nose and she sleeps groaning. At six the next morning she tells a nurse, "I'm not sure if I can still nurse my baby." Her life force is stuck behind the knot. "I was doing fine wasn't I?"

"Yes," the nurse says.

"I would never have let them do it if they'd told me I'd feel like this. I can't even think about my baby." Yesterday she could think of nothing else but the joy of him.

The nurse comforts her, "Shussh now," but there are no shepherds.

Dismissals checks my car seat, which I bought for two dollars at Salvation Army. It is coffee-spattered, its industrial belts twisted. The car seat is all Dismissals can know of what will happen to my baby. In it, can they see whether there will be kale leaves mushed in a baby food mill, absence of perverted uncles, a warm house? There is a new smell on the car seat even though it is old, because of the belts, the certified plastic. It is a carcinogenic smell. It passes.

I BEGIN TO SEE DAPHNE once a year at the bowling alley birthday party of Charmaine, whom our new daughters know, and whom mine hates because Charmaine won't let her in her club at daycare. We read their bowling scores on TV sets hung above alleys lit with black lights. Our children wear white shirts, sneakers and lip gloss that glows white-purple. There is pizza, and cake made by Vi down at the mini mart who hangs her hundred rented pans beside duct tape and tire gauges. Copyrighted Little Mermaids, Pocahontases, Dalmations. I don't say more than hi to Daphne. She glows with surplus vitality that puts me off just as the soap-opera and Export A-induced torpor repel me from the other party moms. I lean against the Pepsi machines in my own little hell of isolated motherhood, waiting for the game to end. The year our daughters are five I finally ask Daphne what happened to Mona and Melanie.

"We found a place for Melanie," she says, "but then she went to live with her sister in Alberta under social services supervision." Daphne's Holly runs up to her crying. She dropped the ball on her toes. Daphne yanks her on her hip, swings her and lets her down and she runs off. "We all had to move out of our room after you left. This other woman came in and there was something wrong with her dressing and her pads, and there was always blood all over the little bathroom floor and sink. We complained to the nurses that it was unsanitary. When we complained loud enough they moved us down the hall."

DAPHNE AND I LIVE on a sprawling shore that has sulfurous smokestacks and a terrible weekly newspaper with nothing in it but death notices and council minutes and a birthday announcement page called "Waves." Starved for meaning, we get an electric charge from this exchange, information about the blood-filled room. Who is the bleeding woman, and why is she left all alone? Did Mona ever find her stolen happiness? Does anyone believe a word Melanie has said since I yelled that her labour pains were real? As soon as my daughter rests her pizza crust on her Dixie plate I tell her, "Let's get out of here."

"Where are we going, Mommy?"

"I parked at Pipers so we can walk a little ways."

"But I don't want to walk. And I forgot my loot bag."

"I'm sorry, honey."

"Can we go back for my loot bag? Why did you park far away?"

"So we can get some exercise. So we can get some fresh air."

"But I had some exercise."

"I know. You were running around like crazy, and the air's not that fresh is it?" I walk on the outside of the dirt shoulder clutching her hand. A Holsum bread truck passes us, and a backhoe going thirty kilometres an hour, and a guy on a dirt bike revving up and trying to overtake the backhoe, and a caterpillar of cars all the way to the lights, and a white limousine full of prom girls. Outside Pipers stand three shopping carts full of lilies and roses people buy to put in graveyards because some saint's day is coming up. Some lesser woman saint who does not mind that the lilies are plastic and the rosebuds frayed nylon. There is a bin of dishcloths. Someone has taken the time to fold them and I lay my hand on a green and white one because the sign says they are one hundred per cent cotton, and I want to feel if this is true.

Violin Woods

Rowena walks to Velma's Minimart for the fat pork instead of taking the truck, on account of the swinging flesh Martin played with on her arm this morning. Not that walking makes your arms thin. Pork is always needed in the house, this time for rabbit stew to give the man who wants to buy her mother's bit of land. She'll cut a quarter pound slab off the five pounds she'll buy for three dollars, with the knife Winnie Whelan gave her for a wedding present in 1956. A knife Martin grinds in the shed twice a year. Pork fat; white, pure, heavy, common as the day is long, though these days it's dark at four thirty. There's snow under the spruce and birch. Same clump where she saw the thing that made her nearly give up last winter.

"I don't know what you mean," she had told Karin, spelled with an *i*, woman with small boots, when Karin phoned and asked her to keep Martin away from her. "Martin and me have been living together as man and wife over forty years." But she'd seen them standing in that shady spot right here. Martin's voice muffled in the snow, him scuffing the tracks that showed their boots meeting, saying someone will see the tracks, someone will know. He always noticed any strange tracks in the cove himself.

Rowena overheard him say her name to the girl. Row, he says it like a boat you get in and tow wherever you want to go. She, Row, makes a great pot of rabbit. She's a good woman, I'd never hurt her, but she has her limitations. Not like you.

No my dear, not like you still in your thirties, from the city, though you know how to chop wood and milk cows or he'd never have bought you those boots on our farm card at the feed store. One hundred and twenty-nine dollars plainly marked on our monthly statement.

Rowena's own boots are black rubber with a red diamond and no liner, $12.98 from Morris's store, and she bought them herself.

The birch and spruce is what Rowena would call a nice rabbit spot. She is glad to pass it by. She did say to Karin what lovely boots you have my dear, where did you get those. Karin had the decency to look down at Rowena's linoleum patterned with red sticks and green stones and little yellow dots while she chewed goulash made by Martin's wife in boots the wife recognized as

Martin's gift. Others before and after Karin had no decency at all, though Karin is still around.

Rowena passes the bakeapple marsh speared with starrigans, her mother's house behind it. Past the house is the spot she's started longing for now her mother wants to sell it. Edge of her mother's land, it's on the north side of what is really a mountain if you take sea level into account, eight hundred metres below. It's a cold, dark spot if you go at the wrong time. When Rowena was a girl there was a draw to it, a green room in the ancient spruce and sparse maple. The summer she was ten she met a man there while she was picking fiddleheads. He was from away and she was used to that. Hikers came from all over the world to see puffins and cormorants, thousand-year-old misshapen black spruce, white corpse pipe plants in the caribou moss, chanterelle mushrooms. This man cut bark and pieces of wood and put them in a leather backpack. He told Rowena he was picking fiddleheads too but not the same as hers. This here, he flung his arm, is a real violin woods. He was looking for the right spruce for violin bellies and maple for their backs. He said the wood on a cold north hill had closer grain than wood in warm woods. It made brighter music. Rowena brought him home to her mother who liked strangers, gave them tea and asked all about themselves. It was her mother's way of finding out about the world.

The violin maker had beautiful hands. Did he have one of his violins, Rowena asked him. No. She knew what kind of violin he would make anyway just by looking at him, even though she had seen only one violin in her life, the short necked one old Bill Winter scratched in the parish hall at Christmas and fall fairs. The violin maker would not make one like that. He took time to tell her how the bridge and scroll weren't for show, they had to swirl for the music to work. He showed her the bridge has a heart at its centre like people do. He said the violin would make no sound without that heart.

After he went away Rowena took notice of anything to do with fiddles. She paid attention, which nobody else did, when old Bill Winter muttered the names of his songs; Singing the Travels, Marrowbone Waltz, Running the Goat. She wanted her own fiddle but there was no way that would ever happen. She fantasized that the violin maker would send her a parcel and there would be a fiddle in it. Months after he had gone Rowena went back to her mother's hill, picturing the spruce and maple changing into violins. She heard sounds the woods made; north wind in needles, stony water trickling. The violin maker said he heard violin woods before he saw them; notes and sighs for every air you could play on a violin. She remembered other things he said. How you made violin bows from tails of white horses. She watched for the horses to appear in the trees, and he said they weren't here, they were in Mongolia. Where was that? She asked her mother. Her mother got angry. Stop thinking about him, she said. People come here and they go.

The violin woods in winter was a place where icicles hung low, met bogwater and froze in hollow shapes. One was a seahorse. She visited it every day and, with a tablespoon, dug bogwater and froze it to the sides in thin layers, to make it less like a seahorse and more like a violin. The feel of a violin was in her. By New Year's Day she had her ice violin in the woods; all it needed were strings and a bow. There was old snare wire in the woods for strings. If there were no white Mongolian horses there was Jerry Parsons' Newfoundland pony and her mother's shears. She tied pony hair to a chokecherry bough and broke spruce boughs to sit on. Before she ever bowed the strings the wind got in the ice violin. The sound was a skirl, an idea the wind gave.

She visited her violin every day until her brother Jim followed her and smashed it with his gaiters. He said it wasn't anything like a violin, it was a piece of garbage. It lay broken and dripping in the bog.

She made other things after that; clay squirrels, juniper rabbit houses, not another violin. That was something the woods had begun, not something she made out of the big nothing inside herself.

* * *

GOING FOR THE FAT PORK is the first walk Rowena has had in three weeks, because it is the first day in that time that her new baby grandson is with its mother and father instead of with her. Baby Jared on the floor in his plastic rocker while she boils partridgeberries, renders the last bit of pork fat for rabbit joints while Martin roams the woods in his best green oilskin with new caribou cuffs. He came home with the cuffs sewn on with real sinew by that young woman's hand. That Karin knows herringbone stitch hurts Rowena, who foresees her baby grandson will grow up to be no different from his father or grandfather. She hates that the hurt is wasting her time. Her mother is ninety because of bakeapples, a cold bedroom, well-used walking stick; because of the solitude old women get, quiet air in old houses. If Rowena can become old things will be all right. Not this haircut, these lines that ruin her face but have not grown deep enough to hold spells.

There are spells in the driftwood washed up below the main road. On her way to the pork fat Rowena explores the meaning of washed up. Dishes. The bathroom. Her own self. For her old mother washed up means mysteries of the ocean, as it should mean. Her mother has a lovely name; Carmelita. She never told her mother about the ice violin. She never mentions it. She figures that's why the violin woods are the only thing around here that has any make-believe left in it at all.

SHE LOOKS AT KIDS' SURNAMES spray-painted on the guardrail. The seven sisters look down on her from their disguise, the day blue sky, and consider Rowena as they have considered a great many women before her. The seven sisters; Maia, Taygete, Alcyone, Electra. Celoene, Sterope and Merope, know what to do with an ice violin. They each own one that never melts. The strings are made not of snare wire, but of frozen light. You can't say the sisters have sympathy for Rowena. They try to cast imagination over a woman like her but it never works. Such is the gulf between woman and star. If only Rowena had a clue, they think. But Rowena heads for Velma's. She picks up a pack of plastic dish scrubbers, a sponge, a bottle of pine cleanser for the crack between the toilet and the floor. The pork fat is in buckets of brine between the door and the sacks of turnips. There is satisfaction in ladling a thick piece out with a slotted spoon and slipping it into a heavy plastic bag. She discovered during Karin that Martin worried he would lose the house if he left his wife. He said in a little voice in bed in his yellow underwear, Row, if we ever were to part, you'd never try to take my farm would you? He said it tenderly like he was saying you'd never steal my heart. She had laughed at him and he was too cowardly to admit he wanted a real answer, so they had left it at that. The farm is his heart, at which she laughs. This is something the Karins of the world will find out in their own good time.

The ice violin glints in her mind, saying something. Her mother was right, the violin maker did not come back. People were always coming here with big ideas; crowberry wine, international seabird sanctuaries, cranberry plantations. They never came back and did these things because there was always someplace where you could do the same things a lot easier. If you think about it, her mother had said, how would you come here and make a thousand violins, and take them away again and sell them, and keep doing that over and over again? You'd have to be cracked as a pisspot to think seriously of doing such a thing.

A crowd is supposed to come to Rowena's at five thirty. They will have the rabbit stew. This man who wants her mother's cold north hill for a summer house, will he know to watch for sharp bones? Rowena's mother will take out the surveyors' papers and legal titles over tea buns. Creamery butter. Partridgeberry jam. Rowena is a woman whose tea buns fluff high, whose linen closet has towels big and small, white then cream then a few green and rose and blue. Everyone loves how her sheets smell, are folded, ironed. Their love of this is a tiny burst finished before they know it bloomed. Rowena would like to tell them this, but they would think she has gone crazy. Everyone enjoying her work in great gobs of mouths, in one towelling of a face, a turn of the body in the bed at night. The rabbit stew can be counted on to have the right amount of wild taste and fat, but this is not considered important. Everyone will sign the papers, her mother with quiet indifference, and the violin woods will be gone. Last time she came to examine it Rowena couldn't see she had any legal claim on the land herself.

She does clean the bathroom because she likes the smell of pine cleanser. She likes to see thin lines of brown come away from their cracks and know there'll be no germs for awhile. She does joint the rabbit cleanly with a sharp knife, renders the pork fat, sears the rabbit brown. It is when her son comes home with the baby that she surprises someone. She wipes her hands on the red houndstooth cuptowel and raises rocker and Jared up off the floor. "I'm not looking after him any more. I've got too much else to do."

"What?" says the son.

"You look after him. He's your son."

The new landowner and legal papers are the official business of the evening, Rowena and her rabbit stew the unofficial. Her husband and son look at her sideways, don't know why they feel uncomfortable. She knows why. She knows her son was asking, what the hell else have you got to do. Grown children ask this about their parents. Because they ask it silently, Rowena feels no need to answer out loud.

Old Games

Cassie waits for Stacey to come out next door, now that last fall's leaves rattle on the road to wake this year's leaves. She's had the winter to ask herself why she didn't let Stacey in the house last summer. What unspoken order was she following?

She's in her window seat again. She paints it white three times a year to keep the clean smell, loves the thick semigloss. Between coats she flicks it with the feather duster and wipes it with a rag from Bernard's car washing stash. There are hopscotch marks on her paved driveway.

IT WAS LAST JUNE she saw Stacey mark hopscotch lines in the dirt next door. She remembers she laid down her crocheting and watched. The girl had green shorts on and a shirt the same blue Bernard likes on his tools. Stacey made her squares all scotch and no hop. Cassie went in moved-away Bernard Junior's room and found a can of chalk where it had sat for seventeen years under Hardy Boys and Meccano. She went out and stood on her grass where it met Stacey's dirt driveway.

"You don't put double squares all along."
"I know."
"You keep putting one square in between and that's where you hop."
"I know."
"You can mark with this over here if you want," she alarmed herself. No one had marked on Cassie's and Bernard's blacktop before. Her window was hidden behind spruce Bernard sheared every spring so they huddled dense and creepy. The varnished sign near their door even said, *The Creepe's*. There were lots of Creepes in town, but Bernard and Cassie were considered part of the family tree snipped from the rest like ends of Bernard's bushes. Stacey took the can of chalk but didn't come over. She fixed her old hopscotch with a stick. A couple of rainy mornings Cassie saw chalk marks dissolve on her asphalt.

IN JULY STACEY CAME TO HER DOOR with a wood-handled rope. "Do you know any skipping rhymes?"

Every object in Cassie's house cried from its stillness for her to close the door. The white cherry jell-O on an ironstone plate in the kitchen. Bananas. Her husband in his La-Z-Boy by the unlit fireplace – Bernard did not like ashes. The chain flame-guard, the poker in its stand. The soft snick of seconds in the battery-operated wall clock.

Cassie baby-stepped to the frontier of her welcome mat holding the screen door before her and the main door behind. She'd special-ordered the old fashioned pine screen door thinking how its breeze would kiss the backs of her knees all summer, but Bernard kept the inner door shut. "I might just remember parts. Parts are no good." Stacey stared as if Cassie were lying. "I could remember how to play marbles if I thought about it. If you came back tomorrow." Though it looked as if Cassie did nothing but sit in her window seat crocheting, there was a schedule, and she didn't know how she'd keep to it if the girl came back, but the invitation slid out. Even now she was off schedule. If she did not turn the fish fingers the breading would burn, and she was already considering two drumsticks that needed thawing for lunch tomorrow. You couldn't get the skin off them frozen. Bernard had his drumstick boiled with no skin. Neither she nor Bernard ate any other part of a chicken unless she roasted a whole one. She sometimes tried to imagine who was buying the trays of thighs in the store. She and Bernard ate the fish sticks or drumsticks with a banana, a glass of milk and jell-O or pudding. Cooking was not what took all Cassie's time. Space took her time. The space between the sofa and chairs and the gold fire-brush stand did not want to be disrupted.

There were a lot of sunny days on which Stacey did not come back. Cassie watched her line Barbies against the basement wall, mix and match their outfits, bring her guinea pig cage on the lawn and read *Archies* near it, and go off to town in the car with her mother. In August it clouded over and the Big Ben doorbell chimed through Cassie's house. Stacey was on the step holding a box with half its dominoes missing.

"I don't know how to play dominoes," Cassie said. "My father used to play it but I never learned." Her father had played it with men at his corner tavern. She had glimpsed through the pub door a scene she envied: golden light, back-patting and leaning in together, everyone wearing blue and white suspenders.

"Did you remember marbles?"

There were shoulder chops cooking in her speckled roaster with a can of soup. Cassie calculated they could stand fifteen more minutes. She had thought about the marbles. She remembered the thrill of playing for an Emerald Fire or Ruby Glimmer, marbles older, dangerous players owned; Wilhelmina Wiseman and Dan Malty. She was surprised she remembered the players' names, and realized she viewed all kids as the same sort of creature now she was old. And they look at us the same way, she thought as she held open her two doors and described a marble hole, and rules for Turn the Spindle. It was Sunday and every driveway had one or two cars in it. It surprised her how many were white.

"It's no good drawing it in the air," Stacey complained. "You gotta show me." So Cassie got a tablespoon, sneaked past Bernard tilted in his chair like a corpse, and went out. She knelt in Stacey's driveway feeling little stones through her pantyhose, and dug.

She marked spindle lines with the spoon end. "Have you got anything for counters?"

"Like what?"

Cassie looked round Stacey's yard where no one had planted so much as a red pom pom dahlia. She went in her own garden and picked six low hips off the Alba rose bush her sister gave her. She believed Alba meant morning, and thought it fit the roses still blooming on top, which were white.

She remembered the rhyme from the old game:

Turn the spindle
rainbow road
Turn it once for a marble gold
twice for green and three for blue
any other shade and you turn back two

She remembered the spindle was yourself. You stood and turned yourself. But she couldn't remember why, or how you got marbles into the hole, or whether you kept your eyes open. Stacey looked like she finally trusted her, so she made it up. You shot a marble from five paces back, like this. You didn't look at the colour till after you rolled. That's when you turned the spindle. You had to hit the first marble with another one from whatever place you ended up.

"But how do you win?" Stacey asked, and Cassie couldn't remember that either.

"You have to get one of every colour in the hole," she lied. "If you get more than one the same, you have to give the doubles away."

"You can't play it alone?"

Cassie snapped dust out of her pantyhose knees.

"It's stupid." Stacey scuffed out Cassie's lines and kicked the rose hips in the dust.

"I'm sorry."

"I'm going in to see if my mom made some jell-O or somethin'."

Cassie had chilled lemon cloud in her kitchen. She had canned cream and jam. She knew Bernard wanted things well weighted down and stuck together. Boiled carrots, turnips, potatoes. Not peas or corn off the cob. Jelled puddings, not biscuits or pound cake or anything that might make crumbs. Porridge and cream of wheat, not cornflakes. Cream pie filling without the crust, without coconut.

She stood on the edge of Stacey's driveway watching Stacey open the aluminum screen door, then the hollow plywood door painted scrubby white with three teardrop windows. As Stacey disappeared Cassie stood at the edge of her own garden looking for the reasons she couldn't ask Stacey in. The reasons stood up, a line of grey soldiers who'd been lying in the grass until now. They were stiff as pipes on the organ at St. Agatha's where she was married, and did not speak or move. They were guards. She wondered what were they guarding.

As long as she'd been married, Bernard had not invited people home. Bernard Junior had not had friends home when he was growing up. He'd never asked to have them in, and neither Cassie nor big Bernard had said anything. Not one friend. The thought began to astound her, until by the time she heard the muffled TV go on in Stacey's house, it hammered inside her the way people pounded their windshields driving behind big Bernard.

INSTEAD OF GOING in her own screen door – she loved that door – Cassie walked on the cool lawn, past the hedge Bernard kept clipped tight. She felt his clipping made the spaces in the bushes darker than they needed to be, caused the bushes to broadcast some threat she could not make out. She often helped him clip them while he directed.

Here were the dahlias that weren't next door in Stacey's yard: dark red. You could almost wonder what the colour red was doing, allowing itself to go as dark as that, like it didn't want to be red at all. The dahlias were spiky as glossy plastic windmills on sticks at the supermarket checkout, but they didn't blow around. As she passed them Cassie became aware, in spite of the pipe organ soldiers who had not entirely lain down again, that the supermarket was the only place she had been outside the house for forty-seven years. The soldiers threatened to bob back to attention but she told them to relax.

"I'm just going over by the white rose bush to sit and think," she said, understanding the soldiers did not like to hear this. She realized she knew how they felt about most things, though she had not acknowledged them until today.

She sat with a white rose in her lap for a long time. She and the rose exchanged ideas. She dared to imagine the house without the Bernards senior or junior all those years. The rose whispered, "You should come back in four days and see what he does out here."

A cold evening draft worked through her cotton sweater, and she saw from her watch that the soup and shoulders would be congealed unless he'd got out of his chair and turned them off. She stepped over the soldiers to go in and they acted like they were asleep. Her dinner was arranged on a heatproof plate on a warm burner with a dish over it. Bernard had eaten his and washed up his dish and the pan. He was watching Hollywood Squares. "You managed all right," she said. He had a mug of tea and a square of chocolate she'd hidden in the pantry. He didn't respond. It occurred to her that other people answered each other.

The next Saturday she kept her eye on the backyard and saw Bernard suck the fullest roses off the bush with his blue Shop Vac. He vacuumed the edges of the driveway and worked his way up to the screen door, which he hosed with his water blast attachment. He hosed and vacuumed anything the wind might blow.

AT CHRISTMAS when Bernard Junior phoned, she heard her husband refer to her evening out on the grass. "Your mother's fine," he said. "She's been fine since you last called, except for one brief cameo disappearance."

When he hung up, she said, "Were you worried?"

He sipped his tea and swallowed with the big "Nkeh" sound she had heard over four hundred thousand times. "I saw you out the window."

"Did you ever think there were grey men like soldiers in the grass?"
"No."
"Did you ever feel like something like that might be there?"
"I might if we still had the septic tank."
"We haven't had the septic tank for twenty years."
"Right. There's nothing to worry about in the grass any more."
"Bernard?"

"What?"
"Do we have to always clip the hedge?"
"It's not really a hedge."
"But do we have to keep clipping it?"
"Does this have something to do with the soldiers?"

CASSIE QUIETLY WAITS for the right spring day to invite Stacey in. Over the winter she remembered more of Turn the Spindle, the intricate parts that tickle a girl's delight in broken patterns. She remembered Grandmother's Footsteps, Old Ball, One Two Three O'Leary, Cat's Cradle, and elastic skipping. She sat in her window seat and wrote them in an old scribbler from Bernard Junior's room while Bernard Senior blew snow off the driveway with his turbo spout adjusted beyond the manufacturer's maximum angle away from himself. Each flake suggested to Cassie ways she could work small particles into Bernard's path. As she passes him napping, she drops dust from the upstairs windowsill, barely enough to fill the Life line in her palm, onto his face.

SHE SWEEPS MAY SNOW with her broom, wanting the earth bare in the sun. She refuses to hold the hedge or the clipper handles for Bernard. When he naps she props the screen door open, letting in moths. She marks *Old Games* on her scribbler and keeps it ready on the window seat.

A couple of times Stacey comes out of the house next door with her mother and they drive away. Cassie thinks Stacey looks much older than she did last summer. She thinks Stacey is too old for the games, but keeps them ready anyway. Getting them right was a lot of work. When she wasn't sure about an old rule, she played the game in her mind till the rule unwrinkled and stretched out like new. She walked past Bernard, ate with him, plotted his final breath by spilled dust, desiccated coconut, the introduction of pie crust. She steam-ironed a threadbare pillowcase she'd saved to boil puddings in, stuffed it with goose down and slipped it under his sheets.

She buys chalk in the school supplies aisle and works outdoors perfecting her games when the street is quiet. If anyone sees her, they see an old woman walking on her own paved driveway, bending down, shuffling back and forth, never hopping, standing politely straight when she hears a car, as if she is checking the marigold border. Nobody pays attention to such a thing. She waits for Bernard to stop breathing in his sleep, for Doctor Lynn Wells to find a plug of phlegm and feathers the size of a golf ball in his lung. Surely Doctor

Wells will think it unusual for anyone to breathe in that much destructive material. Will say the part of the brain that alerts a person must have been unaware in Bernard. Cassie imagines herself replying, "In Bernard's case, Dr. Wells, it was worn right out."

The History of Zero

I hate wedding photographs but I have one of theirs, one Veronica didn't want. It shows the essence of Veronica; Veronica snow laden with a zillion flashing pieces of confetti, batting off the confetti which looks like pure, zinging energy, a flood of purple and blue lights pooling in her dress. That dress. It is night, and she is lit, and laughing. Graham, the chosen husband, is nowhere near her. It could be something other than her wedding. It could be her initiation into the fiesta of laughing swans.

Graham is the most apparently rational husband I have ever met. At first and second and third glance, Graham is sedate, conservative, steady, ready to smile. But ready, one notes the fourth or fifth time, to smile only at his own take on the world. His own very special take. He shares this take with you if you are a person who will absorb it, which Veronica is not. Veronica has no time for conversations about the transduction of heat, or the instability of Chinese taxi services. Are you kidding? Veronica does not want to talk about that. Veronica wants to talk about champagne flutes, about the London version of *The Lion King* and not the Toronto version, about the New Year's Eve ball descending on Times Square. About being inside that ball, yourself, in this one and only life you have. Graham, Veronica thinks, acts as if he has many more lives lying in their packages in his sock drawer. What's more she knows that even if he were raised from the dead he would never, ever use them. He would keep washing and ironing and putting on this same one he is living now, with her, because he likes it. Or does he? It seems he does. He seems happy to hoist laundry up and down the basement stairs. He fills the car with gas and never complains. He eats whatever artistry Veronica comes up with in the kitchen, and Veronica comes up with a lot of sophisticated concoctions. He eats them. He does the dishes. He inhabits Veronica's decorating decisions more than Veronica does, and these are glazed as well, like the red Chinese lacquer console which holds the stereo, music and back issues of magazines to which Veronica subscribes; *Today's Parent*, *Marie-Claire*, and *Chandelier*, a quarterly fusing interior design and social architecture in the world's great cities. Veronica bought the console when they were on a family holiday in Washington. She took one look at it and had it shipped. The red is punctuated by asymmetrical painted orchids.

"It looks sticky," Graham said, "like a candy apple at the regatta."

"It's perfect," said Veronica, which is what she had said about the ebony coffee table, the green doeskin couch and the interior paint, whose colour swatch read dove grey pink. She said this about anything that gave her spirit a lurch upward. God knows this happened rarely enough, though over the years she had managed to ride the euphoria of seven or eight obsessions which included music, furniture, and singers whom she worshipped from afar. She had passionate affairs with these singers in the privacy of her mind, using a vibrator her friend Gwendolyn Cardoulis gave her for her fortieth birthday. What bliss with Andrea Bocelli in the Tuscan hills, although always with the forlorn, lonely ending.

"This looks like a slice of salmon going bad," Graham said to Wilhelmina the thousand dollar dog as he applied the paint above the picture window, and Wilhelmina shot him a beam of dissatisfaction from her divan. Graham had no desire to live with stray hounds and horse-hair daybeds as he had done in his youth. He had no intention of visiting his mother's old house unless it was to dig her a new well or otherwise raise her standard of living. He dreaded bumping his head in her doorways, finding crumbs and even jam on knives in her cutlery drawer, watching her St. Joseph's Coat asphyxiate in her curtains. Last time he had slept there he spent ten minutes unsticking his toe from a hole in the quilt and an hour nailing tacks in the stair carpet so his mother would not break her neck. Veronica had not accompanied him. She had put her foot down early about going to Shoe Cove.

"I can't go to a place," she said, "where they keep a Carnation milk label tied with a rusty twist-tie to a clothesline over the stove because it has a recipe on it for bologna stew."

It was not bologna stew Graham feared. He was all right with bologna stew. If truth be known he wouldn't mind a slice of Maple Leaf bologna now and then, and in fact he went down to Velma's all day breakfast once in awhile and had some. What Graham feared about going back to Shoe Cove was being swallowed by the incompetence and lack of imagination that had allowed a Colgate toothpaste cap to block and render unusable the upstairs bathroom sink since 1979. You now had to brush your teeth in the bath that had rubber daisies along the bottom. You had to kneel on the floor with a double layered shower curtain wound behind your back and spit your toothwater toward the plughole, smelling the unwashed toilet as you did so. None of Graham's four remaining brothers had fixed this, and he knew they never would. Anything lovely about the house in Shoe Cove, such as the lilac that filled the house with perfume and scratched with soft, aching insistence on his boyhood bedroom window, was cancelled out.

THERE IS A PERSON Graham talks to in Bowring Park. Graham is a member of the deep breathing club, which is a group of people who go outdoors and take the fullest breaths possible, believing that proper oxygenation along with eating half of normal western food portions can make a person live one third longer. Graham is not a club sort of man, so he uses the club as a springboard for his own solitary actions. He attends monthly and during the times when other members have their weekly meetings he walks around the green areas of town breathing deeply. He is not having an affair with this person, Celia, as she and he are both demure and proper persons walking their dogs. Though he is aware a camisole edged in ivory picot peeps from behind her second button, and that he could tell in one touch whether it is pure linen, he knows he will not touch it. He knows he and Celia will at no point leave the park together. But he takes more comfort in her than he acknowledges, because her blouse is a pale, washed blue, a blue in which he could rest, and she listens to him in a way Veronica will not or cannot. He can talk to Celia about paper fractals, about orbits and gravitation, about magic squares and the history of zero, and while he is talking a field opens in his chest and he has fallen into the field and is flying a kite on its hilltop. He runs with the kite. Back near his body on the park bench Celia's hand is white and small, inches away from his hand, and he feels like enfolding the little hand but he does not, and she asks him the very question about magic squares that no one has ever been able to answer, not Plato, not Archimedes, not Einstein.

"You ask good questions," he tells her. "I wish you were in one of my classes."

"Don't your students ask good questions?" Her voice is tiny and intelligent. Something weightless and golden has blown into her collarbone and she does not know it. It is some kind of colourless flower a field guide would call insignificant, but it has landed there and he can see it, and it is not insignificant to him. "I have one student who asks good questions. Cyrus Hamlyn. Who really gets into it, you know? Who you could get into some interesting theoretical discussions with. I'm lucky I guess to have that one."

VERONICA WENT OUT for wine with her friends on weeknights after work. It gave her bags under her eyes but she went out anyway to save her own life and dabbed her eyes with concealer. She stayed at work until nine or ten, then ordered in something from East Side Mario's, then met Gwendolyn Cardoulis at Swinton's Wine Bar or the atrium at the Fairmont Hotel. She had tried to come here with Graham but he hated it.

"I feel," he said, "like all these plants are going to grow around my legs and tie me to this chair. I don't like it here Veronica. I don't like the grand piano that plays by itself, and I don't like that loud waterfall. It makes me want to pee."

It was at the atrium, while waiting one night for the others, that she heard a new obsession, a singer she could worship right here, the Tuscan hills be damned. He was not the lead singer of the duo. The lead singer did nothing for Veronica.

"He sings through his nose," she told Gwendolyn Cardoulis. "But the other one. Look at him. He's perfect."

The back-up singer, whose name was Steve, had honey brown hair, beautifully washed, down to his elbows, and at no time did his voice or his bass guitar move out of second place, behind the nose guy, and in every moment his harmonies were restrained and never before heard no matter how you had longed your whole life long for something like them. You had to listen with your whole body to catch them, and his body, well that was focused so wholly on producing this perfect background for the nose singer that you could see the current vibrate through him, and Veronica knew if she touched Steve the shock would fling her against the bar.

"My God," she said. "The only problem is he's at least ten years younger than me."

"That's not a problem," Gwendolyn Cardoulis said, and it got Veronica thinking. Or more accurately it connected her with the live wire she now felt had always powered everything in the world. Her own life had previously been powered by accidental jolts of it, very hit and miss, whereas Graham, she realized now, was running on the barest residual trickle and would soon die if something was not done.

"Well I'm not plugging him in," she told Gwendolyn Cardoulis after explaining her new theory of the universe, a theory that might have perked Graham up had she been able to back it. He might even have found her some polynomials, but she did not think about that now. "I'm not dragging him out of his doldrums," she said. "I'm sick of trying to get him going. He needs a kick in the ass. He needs artificial resuscitation and I'm not interested in anything artificial any more. I want the real thing."

"Way to go," said Gwendolyn Cardoulis.

THE DAYS SHORTENED. Celia's husband came back from his work term in South Carolina and the park was not the same without her. Graham fed the swans glacé cherries, though he knew you are not supposed to feed them anything but bird seed, and he walked his favourite path, the one down by the water where you have to walk under the weeping willows, and a loneliness seized him. Not the dreaming solitude for which the willow walk was designed but a loneliness that made him want to go get Veronica from work early and have a baked potato with cheese and cheese sauce at Wendy's and then maybe drive up Signal Hill and watch the city lights go on over a couple of paper cups of hot chocolate. They used to do things like that and it was all right. It wasn't earth shattering but they would put Radio Two on in the car and Veronica would say the voice of Danielle Charbonneau was melted chocolate and he would not argue, and she would lean into him and they would sit for forty-five minutes. They watched weather in the distance. Veils of rain striping from faraway cumulus, pockets of gold, sheet lightning. Then they would descend, and going past Dead Man's Pond Veronica would say she wondered if there had really been dead men in there long ago, if their bones lay on the bottom, the bones of one man or half a man, and Graham would argue with that. He would say no, Veronica, there are no dead men in there and it isn't anywhere near as deep as people think, that's just one of the stories everyone likes to exaggerate. He'd say that, and Veronica would not mind. And they'd go home and make love. But not these days. He had told her she looked tired. She knew he meant, "If only you would put on your comfy pyjamas." His concern and the truth of what he said made her more tired.

ON HIS WAY HOME ONE EVENING Graham noticed the city had strung its snowflake lights on the poles along Duckworth Street. Now Veronica would really be after him to install the illuminated penguin on the lawn. Did she think he could not hear her through the bedroom door talking on the phone to Gwendolyn Cardoulis, to her mother, to any woman who would listen, about this new man, this back-up singer who sang down at derelict holes in the wall like Roxy's and The Spur? He would be alone again tonight, he knew, with her Zen fruit bowl and Toulouse Lautrec dining chairs.

He decided to go into Fred's Records to get himself a CD that he himself might like, instead of Andrea Bocelli or the Finnish Vocal Ensemble singing Abba, but he was out of practice and he did not know what to buy.

"Could you give me some advice," he asked Alistair, who had worked there many years. "I want to listen to something wonderful. Something with profound majesty."

"Can you elaborate a bit more?" Alistair said.

"Maybe I'll go look. Can I bring a few selections to the counter and get you to help me choose?"

"Sure."

Graham came back twenty minutes later but Alistair was not truly happy with any of his selections. He led Graham to the back and found Beethoven's Sixth Symphony. "What I would recommend for you," he said, "is the fourth section. Do you have a minute?"

"Yes."

"Do you mind if I just tell you what Hector Berlioz said about it?"

"Okay."

"I've got it right here." He took out his personal notebook. "Listen," he read, "to those gusts of wind, laden with rain; those sepulchral groanings of the basses; those shrill whistles of the piccolo, which announce that a fearful tempest is about to burst. Are you still with me?"

"Yes."

"The hurricane approaches, swells; an immense chromatic streak, starting from the highest notes of the orchestra, goes burrowing down into its lowest depths and seizes the basses, carries them along and ascends again, writhing like a whirlwind which levels everything in its passage . . . Can I go on for one more little bit?"

"Sure."

"It is no longer merely a wind and rain storm; it is a frightful cataclysm, the universal deluge, the end of the world."

"Wow."

"So I think you might like that. I can open it up for you. Would you like to put the headphones on and give it a listen?"

"No, I'm going to trust you."

"Really?"

"I don't want the frightful cataclysm to hit me in a public place. I'm going to unleash the universal deluge in my own private mausoleum."

WHEN GRAHAM GOT HOME a truck was waiting for him in the driveway with a teenager and an eight-foot glass tank in it.

"It's cold," the teenager said. "We have to get this guy indoors right away."

"Pardon?" said Graham. In the tank stood an iguana. "Did my wife arrange to have this brought here?"

"She never told you?"

"I don't remember hearing about it. That tank is as big as Snow White's coffin."

"Because we have to get him indoors real soon. His temperature is regulated."

Graham and the teenager took the front door off. They moved the lawn penguin out of the porch and carried the coffee table down to the basement, and the teenager gave Graham a list of acceptable food with thirty-eight items on it, modest things like celery, carrots and radishes. Their modesty made him warm up to the iguana.

"You can let him out of his tank," the teenager said, "once he gets used to the place. They have a bowel movement once every two weeks. The best thing to do then is put him in the bathtub. He's due for one now. You'll know. He's immobilized right now because of the cold but when he's ready to go you'll see a lot of activity."

Graham settled in among Veronica's decanters. He fed the dog, then he decided to have a drink, which he didn't usually do alone. Usually he and Veronica had a couple of drinks together, or they used to. Everything in the liquor cabinet was what Veronica liked. He put Beethoven on repeat. He poured himself a flute of sparkling rosé which was not as sweet as the blueberry wine. The blueberry wine was syrup, really. Everything in this house was sweet. He decided to feed the iguana. He cut up a carrot and found a few leaves of iceberg lettuce and some green onion stems. He laid these in the tank in a stack like they give you in Orlando's, Veronica's favourite restaurant.

"How come," Veronica had said to him, "you order a western omelette every time we go out to eat, no matter where we go? Don't you ever get sick of them?"

"I like western omelettes," he said, "I like them a lot," and it was immediately after that conversation that she settled on Orlando's.

When he finished the wine he rooted around in the cabinet and found the Southern Comfort Veronica kept for when Gwendolyn Cardoulis came over. At eleven Veronica phoned, breathless.

"My god Graham did you bring in the iguana? I completely forgot about it."

"Yes."

"Really? Oh my god thank you. I'd die if anything happened to it. Did Jordan leave it on the step?"

"He was waiting for me in the driveway when I got home."

"Great. I'll try to get home soon okay?"

"How come you think it would fit on the step?"

"What do you mean?"

"Have you seen the iguana?"

"No. My boss just told us she needed an emergency home for it for two weeks. What do you mean how come I think it would fit on the step?"

"How big do you think it is?"

"I don't know. About the same size as the one Gwendolyn Cardoulis' son owns."

"You mean Newton."

"I don't remember its name."

"I remember it because he named it after Sir Isaac Newton, and it's a newt."

"How big is the iguana, Graham?"

"It's a fairly large animal."

"Just tell me."

"You'll see when you get home."

"I might not get home until after you're in bed and I don't know what I'm going to face."

"I might try a couple of experiments with him. I'll probably still be up when you get home."

"Are you drunk?"

IN THE SILENCE after her call Graham would have given anything for Celia's phone number. Why in the name of god had they never once, on that park bench, asked each other their last names? He decided to place a blueberry farmed in Quebec on top of the iguana's stack. Blueberries were not on the list. He wondered what would happen. He wondered if Celia had ever tried to reach him. He wondered if right at this moment she was in the same situation he was. He decided to try Veronica's wedding dress on the iguana. She kept it in his side of the closet in a zippered bag. It would be good to get it out of there and on the iguana. When he got it on the iguana he felt a real sense of accomplishment. He helped the iguana sit on the couch, and he sat beside it.

"I want to show you," he told it, "how fast you're moving."

The iguana contemplated this.

"You think you're motionless but you're not," Graham said. "I want to show you how fast you're hurtling through space."

"Okay," said the iguana.

"You need to know that the diameter of the earth is thirteen thousand kilometers."

"I knew that."

"So, I'm calculating from Venus. You have to calculate these things from a fixed point. You are going twenty-one thousand miles in twenty-four hours, at eight hundred miles an hour."

"Wow."

"That's spinning. So our orbit is a hundred and fifty kilometers. Did I lose you?"

"No. Go on."

"So, if the earth came to a crashing halt, you would head out into space at over thirty thousand miles an hour. So you're not really stationary are you?"

"I guess not."

"So the next question is, how come there are two tides in one day?" Graham took a swig of Southern Comfort. "I haven't got that one quite figured out. The moon causes the first one, and I think maybe that swish, that centrifugal force of the earth, causes the other one."

GRAHAM NOTICED that the lawn penguin, propped up in the hall, glowed halfheartedly with solar power it had managed to absorb in the porch. If it were glowing more brightly he could put it outdoors right now as a beacon for Celia, not that she would connect him with it, or with any part of this house. What was he thinking? That Celia was out there searching for him, pausing outside every house waiting for a sign? His euphoria was fading. This wasn't a house, it was a home furnishings emporium and he was the night watchman.

The penguin looked like a giant bowling pin. It was guaranteed to withstand the elements for five years. Beethoven's immense chromatic streak was winding up again, getting ready for the universal deluge, and Graham decided to find out how many elements the penguin could withstand. He rooted around in a drawer and found twelve mouse-shaped silver place card holders and was surprised at how they ricocheted off the penguin, which he realized was made of fibreglass. He brought the penguin forward and threw some decanters at it, and a couple of the Toulouse Lautrec chairs, one of which crashed back into Snow White's coffin sending spectacular shards everywhere. There was some blood, and when he had checked to make sure it was coming from himself and not the iguana he passed out on the floor.

HE HEARD VERONICA talking to the operator and he said, "You don't need to call anyone." It took him a long time to convince her. "I hate being alone," he said. "I'm sorry." He tried to warn her about the imminent bi-weekly bowel movement, and at the same time wondered if it was too late. "I'm sorry," he said, "about your dress."

"It's okay." She was leaning over him now.

"Is it ruined?"

"Don't worry about the dress, Graham. It's okay. Everything's okay."

"Is the iguana okay?"

"It's okay."

"It didn't get down and walk on the glass?"

"It's okay Graham."

"I like that iguana. It doesn't ask for much."

"Graham we have to get the blood off you and see if the bleeding has stopped."

"Okay."

She washed the blood off him and put on a couple of bandages and helped him go to bed. She stayed up all night and cleaned up the whole works. The next morning she made boiled eggs in the smallest Paderno pot as she did every Monday, Wednesday and Friday, but she did not crackle his shell gently for him so the egg would lie still on his plate while he cut it in half and scooped it onto his toast. She put the egg on his plate and it rolled around, and she did not sit down with him.

"Veronica . . . are you . . . ?"

Veronica took a new static duster out of the package and wiped water stains off the clean wine glasses in the dishwasher. They came off only if you used brand new cloths on dry glass. She did not let him do this. It was part of her own system. She did the glasses and he checked the back of the cracker cupboard once a week for mouse droppings. She had to remind him to do it.

"I'm not going to be late for work over this." When there was a whole lot Veronica was not saying, her voice grew thin, high and clear, and it used to shatter but not any more. These days it went out the door with her and did other things. Graham had a feeling that today it would go with her to Home Hardware and cut a brand new set of keys. He imagined the sound of the key cutting machine, which he loved. You couldn't get more definite than a freshly cut key. Veronica sat down and beheaded her egg, and salted it, and spooned the crescent of yolk and white out of the lid, then started on the main body in its brown egg cup. Finally she said, "I'm taking the lawn ornament back to the store."

"Do you want me to install – I can – if – did we ever get that extension cord back . . ."

"You obviously hate that penguin, Graham, and I honestly don't care that much about it. I do not want to see it on the lawn after last night. Can you imagine looking at it all through Christmas?"

"That was a real heavy duty extension . . . Veronica. Jesus. I don't want this." He pushed his plate away with the egg rolling around on it.

"I have eight meetings today, Graham. Eight."

"Okay. So when you come home do you – I mean I guess we'll have to – I mean this was a wake-up call for me . . . right?" He extended his wrist to examine a blot of blood that had soaked through one of the bandages. "See that? It looks like a – a guy on a horse. Imagine how hard it would be to try and paint a horse as – I know I'm – Veronica?"

"Graham, last night might have been a wake-up call for you, and that's fine. But I'm not going to question that right now. Right now we have Christmas to get through."

"But that's – my god, more than a – a month and a . . ."

"We have Christmas to get through first. My mother's coming, and your mother's coming, and we're having Gwendolyn Cardoulis and her husband over tomorrow night and my work party the next night, and I've got a ton of Christmas shopping left to do, and we've got our regular open house on New Year's Eve, plus there's a million things to do at work between now and January, not to mention that iguana, so I do not want to deal with this until we get through that whole thing. When all of that's over we can talk about your wake-up call."

"You mean, in January?"

"That is what I mean, yes. If you want a specific date and time I can do that. If you want to talk about your wake-up call at eight fifteen on the morning of January the sixth, I'll put it on my calendar."

"But the sixth is – that's Old Christmas Day."

"If that date has sentimental meaning for you we can do it the following day."

"So you want to just keep – I mean now, for the purposes of . . ."

"January the seventh then. Is that all right with you, Graham? Can we call January the seventh our day of reckoning, and can we try to make every day between now and then a day like any other ordinary day?"

Binocular

Every now and then someone tells me a complete story, one where I don't have to imagine any details, and this is one of those. My friend Ann and I were driving home from the MicMac powwow. I had gone in the sweat lodge and she had stayed with the firekeeper and eaten Indian Tacos, which were bread dough griddle-baked and filled with ground moose and grated cheese and taco fixings which people kept in Coleman coolers around the powwow grounds. She ate a lot of KitKat bars as well. I was hypnotized deep in my blood by the circular dancing that had gone on for two days. It was a long drive home but Ann makes a long drive short the way she talks. This story came out pretty much exactly this way, although I know how crazy it is to say that, and how this story will be pretty much unrecognizable to Ann by the time I tell it, even though I am going to be as true as humanly possible to what she said. Memory and facts and logic are tricky. For instance despite filling her face with tacos and chocolate, Ann lost nine pounds at the powwow. But now I'll get on with her story about her friend Debbie.

I think Debbie was a soccer mom, something like the mom of my husband's first child. My husband's first wife is a woman I respect from afar, because she has several pairs of clean jeans and cuts her hair at the barber and imports some good henna for herself from Kensington Market. I saw her once open her son's school door on a Sunday for some soccer event and it was a heavy door and she opened it like a man, and I liked that about her. I picture Debbie as the same type of woman. Debbie had a baby, a daughter, to whom she was devoted. The child's father was out of the picture. The last thing he did before he left was get an egg salad ready to take to a pot luck. He decorated the salad with paprika sprinkled through a stencil of his name, which he had cut out of cardboard, and he was proud of this creation but he was of course drunk.

So for four years there was no guy. Debbie did not want a string of men coming in and out of the house while she brought up her daughter, but then somehow Stephen came into the picture. He was ten years younger than her, and he was beautiful. He was quiet and artistic and self composed. He came and went like a brown bird. It was exactly as if he were an enchanted brown bird in a fairy tale, one who could turn himself into a man. There was nothing Debbie could find wrong with Stephen, so he came and went, and made himself useful around the house as he did so. In fact Stephen was a good man, an orphan and a person without ego issues or testosterone peaks, and Debbie couldn't have found a better companion. Every one of Debbie's single friends took one look at Stephen and raised her eyebrows both hungrily and warily because though he was beautiful they thought he was living off Debbie's salary as a teacher of Business English to new Canadians. In fact Stephen went away to work at seasonal things and contract jobs. He went to Toronto and worked for five weeks as a properties manager on the set of an Atom Egoyan film, and he picked fruit many times in the Okanagan Valley and the orchard owner had personally phoned to ask him to come back.

Debbie's daughter, Lana, turned five, and at Hallowe'en Debbie made her a rabbit costume which Lana wanted to show to Mrs. Hoddinott across the road who sometimes babysat her and had the year before taken her to Kinderstart on a day when Debbie had to go to the dentist. Debbie wasn't a sewing sort of person but her ex-sister-in-law said she was enchanted, and by that she meant that Debbie could fix or make just about anything.

The rabbit costume was made from a child's white fur coat Debbie found at Frenchy's, and she made the insides of the ears out of luscious pink ribbon in her second-hand trimmings collection which included Indian dancing bells and a string of peacock feathers. The suit was hand sewn in blanket stitch since Debbie did not own a sewing machine and blanket stitch was fast and strong. The rabbit suit was substantial. Lana looked like a small rabbit with personality.

She had just started kindergarten, and Debbie had let her go across the street by herself a few times, looking both ways. Lana was a smart child and she looked both ways this time, with Debbie standing on the curb looking after her, resisting the temptation to go with her and hold her by the shoulder. That was when a white truck came out of Spruce Bud Place. It was full of Florida grapefruit and oranges Frank Vesey was delivering as a fundraiser for the Seventh Day Adventist Church, and for some reason Frank did not see the little rabbit, and he drove right over her. The little rabbit was instantly killed.

I am sorry to tell you that. I was sorry to hear it from Ann, driving us away from the powwow, and I wished she had not begun to tell me the story, but she had. The thing is, I would not tell you this story unless something were going to happen that could somehow relieve its sadness. I would not be able to leave you with one dead child and no source of happiness left. I would keep the story to myself, as I tend to keep all my knowledge of the unredeemed sadness rampant in the world.

    Debbie lost all her interest in living. There was nothing Stephen or any of her friends could do to make her gain it back. Her friends stopped trying after awhile, as friends can do, not meaning to be impatient, or to give up, or to be unfeeling. It was just that they had their lives to live too, and it was easier just to not phone Debbie, as it seemed that was the way she wanted it. She showed no improvement no matter how many times you took her out for lunch, or called her late at night just to ask how she was doing and to genuinely listen. Debbie had nothing you could listen to. She went completely vacant. There was one friend, Joan, who was different, in that she showed no sympathy. Debbie saw her in the grocery store and they would talk, and Joan had this strong look about her with an undercurrent of, "Yes, things can't get any worse, but you have to get on with it," which Debbie didn't mind at all. She felt Joan's attitude was right. It seemed heartless but it was not heartless. It buoyed her up.

    Stephen's poetic quiet also helped her stay afloat. Some men, many men, might have become frustrated that there was nothing they could do. Stephen wasn't like that. He didn't go around trying to solve problems, or to have a big effect on the world. He moved like a river not on the map, not even trying to get on any map. It was a big relief for Debbie to have him around, because he completely understood the situation and he let it be. He might walk to Quidi Vidi Gut and catch two or three trout and come home and cook them in butter and lemon and put them on plates. He always wiped off the counters. Or he might go out to Central Video and rent a couple of Audrey Hepburn movies and watch them at a low volume until three o'clock in the morning, and if Debbie sat up with him, watching or not watching, he did not tell her to go to bed, or to come over here and sit with him, or to try and get over losing Lana. The whole fall and winter went by like this. In February Debbie got rid of Lana's school supplies. Duotang folders, brand new erasers and pencils Lana had sharpened herself in her room using a ridiculous grey electric sharpener Stephen had bought for her at Dicks', the kind of thing a short, bald real estate agent might buy for himself, but Lana had squealed with delight. Debbie read *If You Give A Mouse A Cookie* lying on Lana's bed, then she put the book in a garbage bag with some of her own old clothing and took it to the Salvation Army drop-off. She lay on the bed without a book then, picturing Frank Vesey's orange truck coming around that corner ten thousand times, and herself lunging each of those times and saving her rabbit daughter, and then she forced herself up off the bed and looked for language cartoons on the internet to put on the overhead for her students. Debbie was able to act at her job as if nothing had happened. She even appreciated her students; Heleena with her meticulous attention to detail and Ophelia with her red and gold brocade goddess gowns. Going into the classroom took her mind off what she had lost, although her body remained in a bombed-out state, and there was no sex at home, and no joy in eating anything except red-hot delicacies Stephen would fit, sizzling, on a cake plate.

"He's going to leave her," a mutual friend told Joan in the supermarket, and Joan, loyal out of earshot, replied that he was not, and he didn't. He stayed, and Joan became the only friend who did not avoid Debbie. Twice she saw her on Main Street when Debbie was doing her banking and Joan was getting a prescription for tetracycline filled at Lawton's, and both times Joan made a point of stopping and talking, not inviting Debbie for lunch or asking in a concerned voice if she was doing any better, just joking bitterly about root canals and asking Debbie if she had seen inside the new art gallery. And once every couple of weeks they crossed paths at the supermarket and parked their carts together for five minutes. Joan's cart contained frozen snails in garlic butter and chocolate tart shells. Debbie's contained gourds and purple peppers and sweet Vidalia onions. She was comforted by things that had colour and vitality and held a lot of water, and Joan fit into that category. Joan always wore lipstick and coloured her hair and kept herself propped up in a way that was genuinely cheering for anyone looking at her, because you could see it came out of a desire to be positive in the face of mortality, and was not competitive or desperate. Debbie appreciated that Joan went out of her way to talk to her even though it wasn't much use. The dynamic was always that the energy flow went outward from Joan and into Debbie. It dissipated into the universe immediately Joan's back was turned, but Debbie appreciated it anyway, and she could feel and measure it for those few moments when it buzzed her. So she noticed one day that Joan was tired and preoccupied and did not emit the customary zap. Her cart did not hold its usual contents.

"What's going on?"

Joan looked directly at Debbie, her unmade-up face like damp flowers, and she said, "I guess I'm worried about something."

"What?"

Joan was deciding whether or not to tell.

"You don't need to protect me from anything. If you want to tell me, go ahead. If you don't, don't."

"You remember Barbara from my work."

"Your boss. The one who went on bereavement leave when her budgie died."

"I forgot about that. Yeah. Well something happened to her neighbours. They went out one night last month and they died. They hydroplaned on the parkway and they ploughed into that concrete sound barrier there by Riverview Heights."

"That parkway is nuts."

"I know. But they had a daughter and she was five. Mavis. She was home with the babysitter. Are you sure you want me to tell you this?"

"You think I can't handle five-year-old daughters."

"I don't know if you can or not."

Debbie heaved a sigh that said I don't know if I can handle it or not either but there it is.

Joan said, "So they gave her to this uncle."

"Is he a pedophile?"

"He lives on Holson Place behind Central Pharmacy and the Acropolis." Holson Place is in a part of downtown that is not gentrified. It might be fun to live there but it might not. "Barbara went there to give Mavis some doll clothes and the place was filthy. He sat downstairs watching TV smoking and drinking Dominion and he told Barbara to go on up, so she went upstairs. She couldn't believe he'd let anybody come in and see her living conditions, but she says he's so far gone he doesn't see anything wrong with it. There was a bolt on the outside of Mavis' door. She went in and it looked like Mavis had been there a long time. All the time in fact. He keeps her in that room."

"Did she go to child welfare?"

"I think she phoned somebody to make inquiries. She says it's hard to get anyone to talk to her because she was just the child's neighbour and he's her next of kin."

"I have to go," Debbie said. She left her cart full of toilet paper and wild salmon, things that showed she had begun to think about practicalities again, and about self care through omega three oils, as well as the stout, vital fennel bulbs and snow white turnips. She walked out of the supermarket without her groceries and drove to Holson Place and risked a parking ticket while she knocked on the door of a dark green house to ask where the man lived who had just adopted a little girl.

It was a red house near the end with a station wagon outside. Carson Flynn. Debbie knocked and the uncle came out, and she demanded to see Mavis.

"Hold on there lady. Just hold on. Who the fuck are you anyway?"

"I'm Neighbourhood Watch," she said. "I'm a person who observes what's happening in the community and makes sure no child is held against her will in an upstairs room by a person who has no idea how to care for children."

"Are you now. And are you a person who can mind her own fucking business if she has to? Because that's what I think you need to do right now or I'll have you hauled out of here and committed to the fourth floor of the Civic, would you like that?"

She immediately regretted sounding so ridiculous. Getting on her high horse. She should have sneaked in sweetly but now it was too late. Now it was intimidation and threat or nothing. Complete failure. She had this way of summoning intimidation backed by what she hoped was the direst part of truth. So far it had not failed her with strangers. It failed her only when the victim knew her tricks. She disliked this part of herself because it was a bully, and she had never used it on her daughter or on Stephen. This proved to her that she was capable of softness, and it was one of the reasons she had loved them both so deeply.

"I think you know what I'm talking about. I think you know what will happen if I get on my cell right now and a bright young child protection worker comes and finds soiled bedclothes and dry toast crusts and a little girl with lice bolted into the upstairs bedroom of an abusive criminal who would like to keep spending his childcare money on Dominion and hash oil but who can't because his number is up and he has been dragged to the hole in Her Majesty's that they reserve for skinny child abusers to be buggered fifteen times a day by four hundred pound perverts even more disgusting than themselves." She pressed zero and calmly told the operator to connect her with a child protection officer equipped to handle an emergency situation.

Carson Flynn stood looking at her in his undershirt the whole time, apparently unfazed, and when she was put on hold he said, "You're nuts. Go on up and see for yourself if you want. I don't give a Jesus flying fuck what you do." He moved back into the darkness of old wallpaper and she went upstairs. A toilet was running and the door to the right had an unlocked bolt on it. She swung the door in and the little girl was standing in the middle of the room, looking at her. She had bangs and straight brown hair and she wore a cardigan with a dress under it that did not look too bad. In the room was a piece of foam with an old sheet over it, a pillow and a sleeping bag with a broken zipper. There was no other thing in the room, no furniture, no book or clothing. Two perfect circles were pressed in the skin around her eyes. Debbie stood puzzling over the circles, then she saw the pair of binoculars lying on the windowsill.

* * *

WE'RE HALF WAY to the main highway now, Ann and I, coming from the powwow, when she tells the binocular part of the story. She goes on with the rest, the part about how Debbie goes to court and manages to win custody of Mavis. How she brings Mavis home with her and has a daughter again, and I'm happy to hear that. Really happy. But when she's finished I say, "All I can think about is what she saw through those binoculars."

"I know," Ann says.

And I sit there in the car with this amazing projection of illusory binocular sights, a series of possibilities; wind blowing a lawn chair across grass, a boy in pyjamas, framed by his bedroom window, holding up a paper airplane especially for Mavis, a thin dog sniffing behind porch lattice. Clouds, different one day from the next. Old woman getting the mail in her nightdress. Satellites and the moon. Maybe Mavis saw daddy-long-legs in the clapboard, and carpenter beetles, and dandelion leaves. Drumstick wrappers, man walking to the store for cigarettes, lost pink flea collar. I think of all these things, or things like them, and how they kept Mavis alive, and I weep for the small, moving things of the world, the things that mean something, anything, and how good they are, and how fortunate we are to be able to see them and touch them.

Malcolm in Blue

The first time I remember despairing over Malcolm, loving him, was as I sheltered from rain in the doorway of that store on Water Street that always had weird things in its window; a vacuum cleaner, salvaged office chairs, a pyramid of raisin boxes. It was dark, and all the stores were closed, and I was with Glenn Stonehouse who knew Malcolm, and I confessed to Glenn that I loved Malcolm. Glenn, to whom no one should confess anything, laughed at me, and I wondered if Malcolm was gay. I had only once heard of Malcolm taking a woman out. I had no idea who she was, but imagined her with black fringed hair. I imagined her something like Jann Arden. I knew Malcolm had gone out with her just that once and it had not been a success. All of which encouraged me in a diluted way. Maybe I did have a chance.

What did I love about Malcolm? He was clearly obnoxious. He was involved in the Liberal Party, and I had no connection with that. He argued with men at Globe Bagel. Nothing he shouted meant anything to me, but here is the thing: Picasso had painted around his eyes, nose, mouth, his whole head, the brush dripping with black paint. Malcolm had elegant lines though he was an ordinary street guy. I could look at his cardigan, the bones of his head, and think, there is elegance, and it was an elegance no one discussed. The elegance of Malcolm was like other things about mornings in that street at that time of my life. The railings around the war memorial, the stained glass in apartments over the music shop and the drugstore, how gulls cried through the red maples, the existence of stairs leading from this street to the one farther down. Malcolm's elegance was, in my perception, part of the general elegance of that whole place and time. You could say I made it up.

I am sure, because of the way Malcolm reacted to me years later, that Glenn Stonehouse told Malcolm my confession. Let me just mention about my loneliness that night in the rain, the night I started to tell you about. My body was a bell made not of metal but of something that can't ring; plumbing plastic or Scrabble game board or Masonite – and my loneliness was a big, pounding but impotent clanger that kept beating me from inside. I was hollow otherwise. At times Malcolm's beauty filled the bell, but it was a dream, less substantial than fog. I filled myself with dreams back then. I look back and

I don't understand why I imagine now that those days were happy. Did I love Malcolm for himself, or because he was my youth passing by?

So I got a couple of jobs, and ownership of Globe Bagel changed and things were not as they had been, but that street remained a place where I saw Malcolm. On that street and Water Street below it, down the stairs, I would see him and gradually it got so I did not long over him, though I continued to find him magnetic. As I taught and wrote and found an unsatisfactory lover whom I nevertheless loved with all my heart – loved part of him at least, the unconscious part of him, not the conscious part, which meant of course that I had to leave him – as all of that transpired I continued to catch sight of Malcolm once in awhile, still hanging around coffee bars.

He hung around, and I learned from friends that he did odd jobs on scaffolds, painting high parts of houses or changing window sashes, and the friends who told me this said, "Malcolm doesn't like working when the weather's bad because it's too cold and wet, and he doesn't like working when it's nice out because it's too warm and sunny." I defended Malcolm in my mind, imagining he did not really change window sashes – there was some other thing he did that the disparaging friends did not know about. There was an energy in his eyes that fixed on something important, something connected with the centre of the earth. So whenever I saw Malcolm there was reverence in me that I tried to keep hidden but obviously he knew about it, though he hid any such knowledge behind his voice. Our greetings sounded loud and empty. Still, the fact that I would love him as long as he lived crouched in there somewhere, not because of what Glenn Stonehouse told him about me, and not because I behaved reverently. Just because when you love somebody, that love has some kind of presence.

I love not knowing why I love Malcolm. I love the fact that though I have had lovers, have been married twice, my love for Malcolm is the same. I love that it was never said. I love finding him beautiful though he lost the Picasso lines and became something I was not ready to name. I saw this in Atlantic Place. It's dark in there, but I saw his face had caved in. Losing teeth horrifies me. I was deeply sad about Malcolm's lost beauty. He lost more teeth, so as to become virtually toothless. Why doesn't he get false teeth, I wondered. This was fifteen years after I stood in the rain that night with such longing. I admitted Malcolm had become someone who did change the window sashes of anyone who would trust him to do it. So Malcolm became more and more a street person. He had always been a street person, and so had I, but he was becoming an entrenched and choiceless street person. He sat at the outdoor tables at

Hava Java all day. But by the end of two years something reconfigured in me. His elegance came back. My conviction, that someone with gravity lay beneath his surface, returned. I found pieces of his lost beauty and put them together until it stood before me again. I was glad about this. I had found a lost thing.

Malcolm began, if he saw me walking along Duckworth, to ask if I had time for a coffee. This had not happened in the old days. He took a Sobey's bag out of his pocket. It contained stories he was writing in ballpoint. He offered them to me. I can't bear to say anything here about the stories. Malcolm bought my coffee, which was tea, and all of this was a departure from how things had been. Malcolm began to do kind things. He gave my daughter twenty dollars when she was busking. He came to the house a couple of times with Glenn Stonehouse when Glenn came back from teaching in Korea, and said profound things, not brash or political, as we walked with my daughters and husband under the stars. Glenn Stonehouse invited us to his house for lasagna, my family and Malcolm, and as we left Malcolm hugged me as if he knew I loved him. This was twenty years after the night I stood in the rain, and it is the reason I believe Glenn told him back then what I had said.

My youngest child grew older so I could go out more and I went to a book signing by an author I like. I sat after the reading, not eating from the buffet because I know more about germs than I did and because I am not as hungry as I was, and Malcolm asked if he could sit down. He wore a beautiful periwinkle sweater and looked as elegant as he had ever done, and I felt a tidal pull back into a good world in which love and elegance are not lost. Someone saves the love and elegance in their hands to surprise you. Malcolm had bought a copy of the book, which cost over fifty dollars and which I could not afford. It was the kind of thing I could mention to him after all these years but I resisted for the moment. I sat the way I always do near Malcolm, secretly thrilled to feel him near me, and after awhile I said, stupidly, inexplicably, "Are you still living downtown?" I guess I said this because we weren't downtown now and Malcolm seemed out of context.

"No."

"Where are you living?" I could not imagine Malcolm living anywhere but downtown. He was the definition of downtown, like Harmonica Guy and Halliday's Butcher and sunflowers and tulips crammed in boxes in front of people's clapboard.

"Out there," he nodded through the Arts Cafeteria windows to the grey roofs of the east end.

"Out by the airport?"

"My father died and left me his condominium."

All I could think about was how far it was from his haunts. "Do you like it?"

"It's alright."

"But how do you get downtown? Do you walk?"

"He left me his car."

"Is that why you can afford to buy the book?"

"I could buy enough of those books to supply the third world."

I didn't ask him if his father had left him the blue sweater. I wanted the sweater, which made him look so beautiful, to be his own. Part of me got excited for him. But there was a worried part as well.

"So what are you doing all the time? Do you still go downtown? I mean you like it there, right? You don't sit all day in your father's condominium?"

"I like it downtown. But he had another condo in Florida. I have to go down and see it."

"You have two condos, one here and one in Florida, and a car?"

"Yeah."

We talked about the other people at the launch; old academics. I keep going to cultural events where everyone is older or younger than I am. What has happened to everyone my age? Are they at work? Making tuna sandwiches? Or chauffeuring teenagers, or slung on their couches reading the paper?

"These people are ancient," I said. "Especially the men. They're creaking. Look at that one in the red velvet blazer and green trousers. He can hardly walk. The men look as though as soon as they go home their wives take their blazers and pants off and fold them up and put them away for the next book launch."

"They don't just fold the clothes," Malcolm said. He ate a mushroom in phyllo and drank wine out of a Dixie Cup with orange stripes. "They fold their husbands up. They fold the whole guy and put him away till next time. That guy in the red blazer, you don't know who he is do you?"

"No." To me he was an ancient English professor. I hoped for the sake of his students that he had retired.

"You have heard of the Taylor railway?"

"Yeah." Everyone sort of knew someone called Taylor had built the railway.

"Have you heard of Aloysius Taylor?"

"Mm." The founders of this whole civilization had preposterous names and I felt I couldn't be expected to remember them all, since they were dead anyway and here were their descendants, thoroughly decrepit.

"You don't do you? Well Aloysius Taylor built the railway. Then he sold it to the government in 1932 for three million dollars. And that guy in the red blazer inherited it all. That's his grandson. Aloysius the third. And that guy over there? That's Donald Rennie. You don't know who he is either do you?" And so Malcolm went on, not only telling me the names of every decrepit old person in the room, but showing me how the whole academic hierarchy had at its apex the senile heirs of the railroad men and mine owners and lumber barons in my grade five history book, and Malcolm knew them all. He had not told me who his father was.

"Did you have some sort of a feud with your father when he was alive?"

"No."

"You never mentioned him."

"Probably not."

"Did he leave everything to you?"

"I only had one sister and she died."

For months I did not see Malcolm. I never saw him downtown and I never saw him at another launch or gallery opening. I never saw him in the paper, and I never heard anyone talk about him. I figured he must be in Florida checking out what the hurricanes might have done to the condo there. I imagined him treading hall carpet past closed doors to a vanishing point.

MY FRIEND ANNA SAUNDERS once told me she hired the old Malcolm to change her window sashes and after three days she fired him because he didn't know what he was doing and made tea for himself and painted a door she didn't want painted. I imagined him ineffectually checking out the Florida condo and it taking forever for the tenants to figure out he would never fix anything. Then one day I was reading *In Cuba I Was A German Shepherd* at a window stool in Hava Java where you can see the whole street. But this time I couldn't see because a window washer was washing the window in front of me and I was thinking how weird it was that his body, armpits exposed and neck muscles ropey as he rinsed and squeegeed, was only six inches away from mine. It was a strange dance, me drinking Sicilian cappuccino and chewing an oatmeal raisin cookie and reading about old men playing dominoes, and the window washer's spreadeagled body nearly touching mine. So I didn't see Malcolm come in, but when I got up to leave I did see him at the cash, and he didn't turn or speak, which had happened before through the years, so I couldn't tell if he was pretending not to see me. He was with a woman, and she looked like a woman who had sense. Her hair was tied in a way that was possibly businesslike, but with curls that were possibly drenched with bed sweat escaping their tie, and she had an athletic waist and was smaller than Malcolm, but stood straight and confident in charcoal and blue. She was not a street person, or psychotic, or anyone I had seen downtown before. Malcolm may have found her at the university. Maybe she was someone he used to play with when he was a kid and his father took him to houses of his friends. Maybe she knew Aloysius Taylor personally and had seen him in the housecoats he wore long before he owned his red velvet blazer, before I ever knew Malcolm or saw him at Globe Bagel for the first time.

Everything in the Bag Changed

Nell flicked the earrings between her cup and spoon in the diner booth. The brass chains were tiny, the pendants intricately carved. If I lose one, she thought, I'll kill myself. Wearing them would start the last enchantment but not wearing them was driving her crazy. She wanted to wait and wear them to something special, but somehow nothing special enough came up. What would happen if this wasn't the right time? If she wasted the earrings?

The earrings had not been ordinary since Nell's last airline trip. Looking back she was sure it had to do with her special ticket. She phoned her regular travel agent but the young man normally at the desk wasn't there. A woman sold her the ticket by credit card and asked her if she wanted regular or exotic fare.

"What's the difference?" Nell asked.

The woman laughed. "You sound like someone who can tell between something ordinary and something exotic." Nell did have a small tattoo but there was no way the travel agent could know this. Maybe her voice revealed the yoga breathing she'd stopped doing, or the times she'd tried to yodel. "The difference is fifty dollars and it's worth it. For another seventy-five on top of that you get exotic plus, but you might not want it to go on forever."

Nell decided to go with just plain exotic. This trip wasn't a real holiday. Nell was visiting her brother to cheer him up after he lost his job. Still, she packed her bag the way she always did when going away by herself. Part of her knew she wouldn't be spending the whole week with her brother. The skirt with gold threads, her Costa Rica sarong, her red underwire push-up bra from *Barely A Catalog*. Her tiny opera binoculars with red lenses. Vintage gold brocade clutch bag with inner coin purse containing the Indian earrings wrapped in an emergency hundred dollar bill. The gold voile with net underlay Saks dress she bought off the Salvation Army Hallowe'en rack for two dollars. One black silk T-shirt that crumpled into a ball you could hide in your hand. Thongs. Jeans. Her men's leather belt with a big turquoise buckle.

You can't cheer anyone who has decided to be miserable, so after three afternoons eating seafood baskets in a sports bar listening to her brother's woes she had booked into a brownstone hotel and treated herself to a week of late breakfasts and fascinating streetcar rides while her friend Deb looked after Johnny. It was pretty good but she kept thinking the travel agent hadn't provided anything for that extra fifty that Nell hadn't provided all by herself.

Her black Coors bag went missing at the airport and when she got it home a day later it wasn't quite the same. She noticed one small thing as she took it from the courier; the silver rings holding the strap seemed bigger than she remembered, but only slightly. She did undo five inches of zipper and when she saw her own skirt and roll of duct tape she took the bag home where it stayed on the landing for three weeks in the manner of many holiday bags that don't get fully unpacked until someone else needs them.

Johnny was the first to notice the second strange thing about her bag.

"Mom." Nell was trying to play the piano.

"You know I don't want you to shout from one room to another."

"I'm not in a room I'm on the landing." No answer. "Landings are between rooms." He knew Nell was chewing her top lip first, then dangerously the bottom one. He walked halfway down the stairs and quietly told her thread was moving in her skirt.

"Are you looking in my bag?"

"I needed the duct tape. Mom your skirt has live threads. Could silkworms still be in something after the store sells it? Are silkworms gold? Are they long?"

"I wish you'd stay out of my stuff." Nell put Rimsky-Korsakov's *Song of India* back in her piano bench. It was a beautiful piece but she'd have to find some time when the world would leave her alone or she'd never learn it. Luckily piano fragments she had learned always came back to her even with Splenda Dinners and action packed kids' videos between one practice session and the next. She should know by now not to expect to get far when her youngster was on his summer holidays.

As soon as she stopped playing Johnny left to go to the swimming hole on his bike with Bryan and Scott. She heated a stuffed green pepper and for dessert had a mug of tea and some frozen Easter bunny shavings. As she licked the chocolate dust off her hands she decided to look in her Coors bag. She spread everything on her futon. It all winked and sparkled, like blue-eyed grass after rain. The threads in her skirt did seem to move, but she thought it could have been the light. The earrings felt as if they had been in the fridge. The black silk shirt fell on the bed in the shape of a breathtaking rose.

This stuff is the real exotic me, she thought, not my deadbeat brother or my nose-picking son. And she put everything away among her everyday sweatshirts and work socks. But one by one, every time she used one of the things that had been in that bag, something happened.

She wore the skirt right away, to a chamber music concert in the university's Oratory Hall. Just before the performance began, the woman sitting next to her got up and left, and a petite man scented like vanilla and cloves sat there instead and took Nell's hand. He gave her such a kind and reassuring smile as he did so, that she left her hand in his through the first string rhapsody, after which he released her hand into her lap, leaned over and whispered, "You are the only woman in the room wearing Quantum Physics. These threads are waves, then particles, then waves again. You are an illustration of what I have been hoping to see all my life. Not that I mean to be forward." There was no denying her skirt's gold threads were doing just as he said, wiggling in waves, then breaking into glittering particles, then melting back into waves again. "Would you do me the honour of pouring them in my samovar?" he asked.

He rested his samovar on a small flame in his bedsitting room. He had a neat closet from which Nell could see peeping sage and dun suits and several pairs of shoes with pointed toes and exquisite eyelet leather. He had put a clove in her teacup and while they waited for the tea to brew he gave her a spoon. "Even just a spoonful," he told her, and gave her a spoon to hold near her hem where gold threads wiggled. She caught a couple of drops like mercury. He lifted the samovar lid and she slipped them in. They drank the tea and everything in the room became as intricate as an old fashioned frosted window, the kind that made fairylands happen before double paned glass put an end to fairylands. Her own hair turned into black Spanish lace, and the man put on a pair of black Spanish leather shoes and they danced the whole night. The main thing she remembers about the night, even more than its lacy beauty, is that her heart felt like a baked potato. It was so full of plain well-being she thought forever after that he had somehow warmed it for her in the samovar along with the tea. He lived in the kind of little street you can never find twice, and she had nothing to remember him by except that he said, "Youth isn't everything," as she was going out his door. Now how did he know she'd been worried about that?

The duct tape was the second thing she used from the Coors bag, and she used it to tape a couple of boxes of books her friend Mona was moving out of the apartment she'd shared with Greg. Nell accidentally taped a Mona box to a Greg box. Within two weeks Mona married Greg, and by then Nell knew that whatever she taped with that roll of duct tape would never come apart again. Before Greg and Mona's wedding Nell squandered half the roll on things as unimportant as taping up cereal boxes she'd opened at the wrong end. When she realized what was going on she put the roll in her underwear drawer for special use only.

Everything else that had been in the Coors bag had its story. The red underwire bra turned into a snake when she tried to put it on. It was a talking snake, and it said to her, "I need to go back to Venezuela. Remember the coin in the fish's mouth in the Bible? Well if you dig down in my mouth you'll find our plane tickets for November the seventh." They had the time of their lives in Venezuela. The snake didn't talk much; just enough to let her know a hotel room had been paid for and where it was, and where the best cantinas were, and that octopus is very good when fried in the best olive oil. When it thought the wrong people might see it, it slipped down her neck and turned back into the red bra until the coast was clear. It told her to rent a scooter and gave her directions to the grove where it wanted to be let off, and they parted amiably with stomachs full of good wine.

Nell was having such a great time working her way through the things from the bag that she started dreading what life would be like after the fun was over. She was like someone who's won money who stops having fun when she notices she'll have to win more or face going back to the same old life that existed before. Wearing her black shirt she sang perfect operatic soprano in a street festival. But when the shirt turned to the fabric of hollyhock petals and she walked home in a cloud of Patagonian butterflies, she hardly noticed. With waning joy she used up everything from the bag except her Indian earrings. She kept thinking once I wear them it'll all be over.

And so she waited. Months went by and she remembered how the travel agent had said for a further seventy-five dollars she could have the exotic plus fare. Maybe you could get an extension on the first fare if you went back before everything was used up. As soon as she went through the door she saw the regular young man was back.

"I was wondering if I could get an extension on the exotic fare I bought last time. Make it exotic plus before it runs out."

The young man stared then pointed to a tea crate hand-labelled *Tryphenia*. "Mrs. Steppings isn't here any more, but she did say she might check that for messages once in awhile." He went back to sorting files in his computer. Nell thought about going out without leaving a message, but wrote a cheque for seventy-five dollars, and a note on a ragged bit of paper from the bottom of her bag. Two more months went by and nothing happened except that Nell waited. She waited through dates with a dentist and an accountant who tried to give her a year's worth of his old *Forbes* magazines. She kept thinking about the man she'd met at the chamber music concert. Now there was someone she'd like to find again. She put the skirt on one more time even though the threads had not wiggled since that night, and went out to the all-night diner near the Castlemount Hotel. She thought she remembered seeing the top of the hotel from his street. Maybe he'd come in here.

Nell loved the neon diner sign, the old vinyl seats. She'd brought Johnny here before for the king burger platter, but coming alone was more fun. You couldn't tell who was a genius or a bag lady. There was an air of magnificent desperation. The liver and onions had crispy edges. Nell tasted her coffee, sharp and dangerous, not mellow like in an expensive coffee place where everyone pretended to be content, and thought maybe this was where she should wear the earrings. It was the kind of place that made you say to hell with it. So she put them on.

An old woman opposite her dipped bread in soup. She had on a seafoam green hat someone born in 1900 would have worn in church. Maybe the earrings had transported Nell to another time, even another city. I'll go over to that old woman, she thought, and ask her where we are. But if she says I'm still in such and such a town, what will that do? Only confirm the sort of disappointing fact that doesn't help anyone.

So Nell sat for the longest time, wondering if the woman was even real. She imagined she smelled mothballs and cologne, the kind of cologne whose story you read through the bottle, on the inside of the label; Napoleon himself wore this cologne while charging his horse into battle.

Then she imagined the woman was herself, aged eighty-eight. Twice her age exactly, sent by the enchanted earrings to warn her how lonely life can get if you don't look after your son properly and be content with your colleagues at work. The woman's solitude looked so wonderful Nell tried to inhale it.

Nell watched the old woman as she'd watch a fish in a tank. The hat made her aquamarine, beautiful, separate. Maybe the woman was dead. Maybe she had skin that crumbled if you touched it. Maybe she was dust held together by memories and old taffeta.

Nell whispered to a waiter, "Who's that woman?" and he whispered over a hot dish of rice pudding, "She lived here before this was the Golden Dragon."

"But it's Kenny's Diner." She noticed he held a pitcher of ice water that looked delicious. She meant to ask him for some of it.

"I know but before that it was the Golden Dragon. She's been around forever."

The old woman smiled at Nell with gracious brown teeth like the Queen Mother's, then bit bread and rummaged in her purse. The smile lit up the idea of courage in Nell. I'll go out, she thought, face this and every moment for as long as the earrings last. Then when it's over I'll take them off and make my own fun.

Kenny's Diner had two turnstiles, one in and one out. When she'd come in here with Johnny he made a game of chasing her through one and then the other so the arms confused you, made you feel like you'd been caught by a silver spider. The spider caught her again this time. For a few seconds she jiggled the silver V that held her. The waiter smiled from across the room, pointed down. "Have a seat," he called. "You'll be there awhile." She could hear the ice crash around in his pitcher of water. She noticed a green chair under her as the whole turnstile moved up and she fell into the seat, which was comfortably curved. Someone opened the diner door and the whole seat, turnstile and all, swung out into the night, then up. Lights under her, moon and stars above. Little, scurrying clouds. The air cold but not too cold. Exhilarating. A little crowd of people looked up beneath her and she realized one of them was the woman in the seafoam hat, waving. She noticed the Paris skyline. She knew it was Paris the way anyone would, even if they had never been there. Nell had been to Paris and knew its smell; coffee and tobacco and carnations, so even if she had not believed the Eiffel Tower and Notre Dame de Paris were real, she'd have known the fragrance. As the seat rose she made sense out of the fact that she was on a giant Ferris wheel; wheel and spokes lit with her favourite yellow and red neon. All she could assume was that Kenny's Diner had melted into this, and all the people who had been sitting eating there were now part of the little crowd milling around down there, so tiny.

It's the earrings, she thought. I might as well enjoy it.

So the wheel went up and slowly swooped down again, and as it did so she saw the woman in the seafoam hat was still waving, the old brown tooth smile giving off courage, one glove clutching something, the other pointing to it; a ragged bit of paper. Mouthing words, nodding eagerly. "I got your message." There was the waiter behind her, his pitcher of ice water glittering and crashing.

Before Nell could answer she was on her way up again, this time above Tahiti. She knew it not from experience this time, but from reading about Gauguin and his paintings. Thatched huts. Women who lay on fronds day and night, naked and bright yellow. Gauguin had a door, on which he painted trees and fruit, and then he painted the walls, and the window sills. Gauguin was crazy, that's what Gauguin was, working in a bank all those years, then escaping, only to wall himself off in a poverty-stricken little hut that the rest of the world thought was oh, so exotic, but they didn't have to live in it, did they? Nell looked up and down at the other chairs on this flying turnstile, to see if there was some ticket-master, a person with a uniform on, of whom she could ask what to expect, or if there was a station stop, and what it was, exactly, that she had got herself into. That was the trouble with these fly-by-night travel agencies. They contracted a person like Queen Mother Tryphenia, but where was she when you wanted to ask her a specific question? Down in Kenny's Diner, drinking Tetley and eating nutmeg with a teaspoon, that's where. The people in the other chairs were passengers like herself, and in this light she could not see them plainly, except for the anonymous glow of their faces and the odd night-coloured scarf that blew around dangerously and could easily get caught in the mechanism. I do not have a night-coloured scarf, Nell calculated, but I do have a long sleeved leotard and this extra chemise, and, thank god, these leggings. If I discreetly disrobe, and tie all my sleeve and leg ends together with reef knots, and secure an end to the bar of this seat with a half hitch, I will be able to lower myself strategically out of this predicament onto a suitable height of land. Onto some minaret. Onto any one of the world's countless fingers that point to heaven.

Acknowledgments

I thank family and friends for their support, especially Jean Dandenault, who built me a studio with Mexican tiles and a door I can lock.

I thank Elizabeth Dillon for giving me permission to use some of her own profoundly personal images in the story *Eating the Bones,* and Anita Best for permission to use the floating dumplings and silk parachute images in the same story, images I first heard on interviews with Mrs. Mary Margaret Pittman in Anita's radio series "A Little Ball of Yarns."

I also thank the Canada Council and the Newfoundland and Labrador Arts Council for their financial support, and The Gibraltar Point Artists Residency Program in Toronto for the space in which some of this work was composed. Thanks as well to the editors of *Geist, PRISM international, The Malahat Review, grain, The New Quarterly, Crumbs, The Antigonish Review, the Fiddlehead,* and *Zeugma,* in which some of these stories first appeared. Special thanks to Jacob Siskind and Joan Clark for their earlier encouragement, and to John and Myrna Metcalf and Dan Wells for their kindness and editorial support.

KATHLEEN WINTER is the author of the novella *Where is Mario* (Xx press, 1987), and two books of creative non-fiction entitled *The Road Along the Shore* (Killick, 1991) and *The Necklace of Occasional Dreams* (Killick, 1996). She has written dramatic and documentary scripts for Sesame Street and CBC Television and writes a weekly Saturday column for the *St. John's Telegram*. Her short fiction has appeared in leading Canadian literary journals.